To Jeannette Larson
and Reka Simonsen

LONDON, ENGLAND, C. 1870

𝒰NDERGROUND

Newgate Market was an empty, echoing shell. Doors hung crookedly. Windows were smashed. Iron hooks were rusting away. The market clock was no longer ticking, and the stalls were silting up with rubbish.

All the butchers had long ago moved to Smithfield, taking their sides of beef and saddles of mutton with them.

"I don't know why this place ain't bin torn down long since," Alfred Bunce remarked. He stood hunched in the rain with his bag on his back, gazing across an expanse of muddy cobbles, toward the central pavilion. Water dripped off his wide-brimmed hat and trickled down his long, beaky nose. Even his drooping mustache was sodden. "Ruined buildings breed every kind o' strife, from coining to murder," he added. "Bogles would be the least o' yer problems round here."

Beside him a brown-eyed boy was scanning the shops that fronted the square. Some of them were boarded up, and those that remained in business were for the most part seedy-looking taverns or coffeehouses.

"I don't see Mr. Wardle," said the boy, whose name was Ned Roach. He was dressed in a navy-blue coat with brass buttons, very worn at the elbows, and a pair of buff-colored trousers, damp and soiled. A flat cap sat on his springy brown hair. Despite his missing tooth and scarred hands, he looked respectable enough. "Which o' these here establishments would be Mother Okey's?"

"Ask Jem," Alfred replied. "He knows the neighborhood better'n I do."

"Jem!" Ned turned to address another boy lagging behind them. "You bin here once. Which pub is Mother Okey's?"

Jem Barbary didn't answer. He was too busy peering at the dark silhouette of someone who was skulking on a nearby doorstep. Ned didn't blame Jem for being nervous. This was John Gammon's territory, and Gammon—also known as Salty Jack—was a dangerous man.

"What's that feller doing there, lurking like a cracksman's crow?" Jem hissed. He was smaller and thinner than Ned, with so much thick black hair that his head looked too big for his body. He wore a bedraggled suit of speckled brown tweed. "D'you think he works for Salty Jack?"

"Mebbe he's sheltering from the rain," Ned offered.

But Jem scowled. "I don't trust him. I don't trust *no one* hereabouts."

"Which is why we should pick up our pace." Alfred spoke in a gruff, impatient voice. "Wardle said to meet at Mother Okey's. Any notion where that might be?"

Jem considered the half-dozen public houses scattered around the market square. "'Tain't that'un," he announced, pointing. "That there is the Old Coffeepot. I spoke to the barmaid last time I passed through."

"And that?" Alfred nodded at the nearest tavern. Although it had a sign suspended above its front door, none of them could read the lettering.

"There's a cat on that sign," Ned observed, "so it's more likely to be the Cat and Fiddle. Or the Cat and Salutation . . ."

"Here!" Jem suddenly clutched Alfred's sleeve. "Ain't that Mr. Wardle?"

It was. Ned recognized the man who had emerged from the alehouse to their right. He was large and middle-aged, with fuzzy side-whiskers and a slight paunch. Though

respectably dressed, he had an untidy look about him—
almost as if his clothes were buttoned askew. Wisps of wiry
gray hair escaped from beneath his bowler hat. His necktie
was crooked. There was a crusty stain on his waistcoat lapel
and an unshaven patch on his chin.

Even when he spotted Alfred, his worried expression
didn't change. The anxious lines seemed permanently en-
graved across his brow.

"Mr. Bunce!" he exclaimed. "You found me!"

"Aye," said Alfred, touching his hat.

"I was afeared you might have taken a wrong turn." Mr.
Wardle's small blue eyes swung toward the boys. "I see you
brought your apprentices with you."

Alfred gave a brusque nod. "Can't kill a bogle without
bait," he growled.

"Yes, of course." Mr. Wardle blinked uneasily at Ned,
who wondered if the Inspector of Sewers could even remember his name. They had been introduced to each other only
a week before, at the Metropolitan Board of Works, where
they had all sat down at a very large round table to launch the
Committee for the Regulation of Subterranean Anomalies.

But more than a half-dozen people had been present
at that meeting, and a lot of business had been discussed.
And since neither Ned nor Jem had made much of a contribution, it seemed likely that Mr. Wardle had forgotten who
they were.

"This neighborhood ain't safe for Jem," Alfred continued. "There's a butcher as runs all the rackets hereabouts, and he's got a grudge against the lad. We ain't bin troubled thus far, since the butcher don't know where I live. But the longer we stay, the more likely it is we'll be spotted by one of his cronies. And I don't want that."

Mr. Wardle looked alarmed. "No, indeed."

"So you'd best tell me about this here job, and then we can set to it," Alfred finished. "Back at the Board o' Works you mentioned there's three young'uns vanished, and one sighting in a sewer. Which sewer, and where was the kids last seen?"

Mr. Wardle hesitated. "Perhaps it's best I show you what was shown to me," he finally suggested, then began heading for the central pavilion. Alfred hurried after him with the boys in tow.

As they approached the dilapidated structure that had once sheltered row upon row of hanging carcasses, Ned felt uneasy. There was no telling what might lurk in that labyrinth of dark, rotting wood. As Alfred had said, bogles might be the least of their problems.

"You don't think this is an ambush, do you?" Jem whispered, as if he were reading Ned's mind. "You don't think Mr. Wardle is in John Gammon's pocket?"

"No." Ned was sure of that. John Gammon was a "punisher" who liked to threaten local shopkeepers with bodily harm if they didn't hand over a portion of their earnings to him. But Eugene Wardle wasn't a local shopkeeper; he was a municipal officer who hailed from Holloway. "Ain't no reason why Mr. Wardle should know Salty Jack Gammon. *I'm* just concerned them missing boys is all a hum. Mebbe Jack's bin spreading tales, to lure us into a dark, quiet corner—"

Jem cut him off. "It ain't no tale. There's at least one kid gone, for I heard it from the barmaid at the Old Coffeepot when I were here last." After a moment's pause he added, "She said the lad passed a bad coin at the inn, then legged it into the market cellars. No one's seen him since."

" . . . chased a printer's devil into the cellars, after he passed a counterfeit coin," Mr. Wardle was saying as he led Alfred through the gloomy depths of the central pavilion. There was a rank smell of old blood and manure. Water was pooling under leaks in the roof. Here and there a rat would skitter out of the way, frightened by the crunch of broken glass underfoot. "The second child was a young thief who went down to look for scrap metal," Mr. Wardle continued, "and never returned to the sister he'd left waiting above. The third was a coal merchant's son who used to play in these stalls, though no one can be certain if he found his way beneath them."

"And the sighting?" asked Alfred.

"Ah," said Mr. Wardle. "Well, that didn't happen up here." He stopped suddenly, having reached a kind of booth, behind which lay the entrance to a wide room with an opening in its stone floor. "You see, the heads of four sewers meet under Newgate Market. They used to be flushed out regular from a big cistern fitted with iron doors, though it's not much used these days. I had a team of flushers down there last week, oiling the screws and checking the penstocks. They caught a glimpse of something that scared the life out of 'em. And when they alerted me, Mr. Bunce, I thought about you." The Inspector stamped his foot, as if marking a spot. "That cistern's close by, and one of the sewers runs beneath the cellar—which used to be a slaughterhouse, or so I'm told. They had to wash down the floors—"

"And the dirty water had to go somewhere," Alfred concluded with a nod. "There'll be drains, then."

"I believe so."

Alfred dropped his sack and began to rifle through it, pulling out a box of matches, a small leather bag, and a dark lantern with a hinged metal cover. "You boys stay up here till I call you," he told Jem and Ned as he struck a match to light his lantern. "I need to look downstairs and don't want no bogles lured out ahead o' time."

Jem grimaced. Ned couldn't help asking, "You think there's more'n one of 'em, Mr. Bunce?"

Alfred shrugged and said, "Ain't no telling in this part o' the world. That's why I had to risk bringing Jem." He appealed to the Inspector. "I'd be obliged if you'd mind the lads for me, Mr. Wardle. I don't favor leaving 'em up here by themselves."

"Yes, of course, Mr. Bunce." Mr. Wardle sounded more anxious than ever. "If that's what you'd prefer . . ."

"I'll not be gone long," Alfred assured him before disappearing down the cellar stairs.

For a minute or so the others stood mute, listening to his footsteps recede underground. Then Mr. Wardle said, "You boys can't be very old, I'm persuaded. Are you?"

Ned and Jem exchanged a sideways glance.

"I'm eleven," Jem volunteered. "And Ned here—he's just gone twelve."

To Ned's surprise, Mr. Wardle shook his head in bewilderment. "Why would any man of sound mind be nursing a fatal grudge against an eleven-year-old boy?" the Inspector wanted to know. "What kind of offense could you possibly have committed to merit such bad feelings?"

"It weren't *me* as committed the offense!" Jem spluttered. He went on to explain that John Gammon, the butcher, had tried to feed him to a bogle only a couple of weeks before—and was therefore afraid of what Jem might tell the police. "Which I ain't about to tell 'em *nothing*, since they'll not believe me in any case," Jem finished. "But Gammon don't know that and is likely not to care."

"Villains like him don't never take no risks," Ned murmured in agreement.

"But why *wouldn't* the police believe you?" asked Mr. Wardle. "I don't understand."

Again the boys exchanged a quick look. Jem flushed. It was Ned who finally answered. "It's on account o' Jem used to steal for a living and wouldn't make a good witness in a court o' law."

"Though I ain't prigged *nothing* since last summer," Jem blurted out, "and won't never hoist so much as a twist o' tobacco ever again! I'm done with all that now—ain't I, Ned?"

"You are," Ned confirmed. Though he'd seen Jem's eyes latch onto many a passing watch chain and snuffbox, the former pickpocket had never once given into temptation—not while Ned was around. "Besides," Ned added, "most beaks don't believe in bogles and wouldn't credit any claims to the contrary, no matter *who* made 'em."

"I see," said Mr. Wardle. He studied Jem for a moment, as if wondering how they'd ended up on the same committee. Then he turned to Ned. "And you? Are you a reformed thief?"

"No, sir," Ned replied stiffly. For six years he had been supporting himself, and not once had he stolen so much as a dirty handkerchief. "I were a mudlark until Mr. Bunce took me in. I used to scavenge along the riverbank."

All at once Alfred's voice hailed them, echoing up from the chamber beneath their feet. "Are you there, Mr. Wardle?"

"I am, Mr. Bunce."

"Could you send them lads down? And I'll have me sack along with 'em."

"Yes, of course." As Ned picked up Alfred's sack, Mr. Wardle cleared his throat and added, "I take it you've found something of interest?"

"Oh, aye. This here is a bogle's lair, make no mistake." Alfred appeared suddenly at the foot of the stairs, his lantern raised, his long face grim. "What I *don't* know is how many of 'em might be a-lurking down here. For I ain't never seen no den more suited to a bogle's taste, nor better laid out for the trapping o' children. If you ask me, Mr. Wardle, there's more'n three kids has met their doom in this rat's nest."

And he motioned to Ned, who reluctantly clumped downstairs with Alfred's sack on his shoulder.

2

THE SLAUGHTERHOUSE

N ed had explored a few sewers in his time. He'd spent years digging through river mud and had more than once been forced to sleep in a coal hole. But when he arrived at the bottom of the cellar stairs, he felt his heart sink.

It was the most unpleasant spot he'd ever seen.

The ceiling was low and slimy, the floor caked with filth. Iron hooks, stained with old blood, hung from the ribbed vaults overhead. A great wooden tank, topped with a grill of metal bars, was slowly disintegrating in one corner. The whole place stank of corruption.

"Where would you like me to stand, Mr. Bunce?" called Mr. Wardle from the top of the stairs. Alfred shushed him.

"The fewer folk is on hand, the better," Alfred softly replied. "One thing you *could* do is keep others from coming down here."

"By all means," said Mr. Wardle in a much quieter voice. "I'd prefer to stay up here. For this stench is worse than any sewer I've ever flushed."

His silhouette vanished as he withdrew. Alfred, meanwhile, was gesturing at the ring of salt he'd laid down near a large open drain in the middle of the cellar floor. There was a gap in the salt circle directly opposite the drain. But when Ned glanced from the salt to Alfred, the bogler shook his head.

"Not you. You're over there." Alfred jerked his chin at a smaller ring of salt across the room. Ned realized that Alfred had appointed him as decoy, in case more than one bogle should appear. While Alfred polished off the first monster, Ned was supposed to distract any others that might show up unexpectedly.

It was a technique that Alfred had used only once before, as far as Ned knew, because normally bogles were solitary creatures. For most of his bogling career, Alfred hadn't needed more than one apprentice. But a recent plague of bogles around Newgate had prompted him to change his methods. Though the reason behind the plague had been dealt with, no one yet knew whether the bogles attracted to the neighborhood had begun to drift away.

Jem's former employer, Sarah Pickles, had caused the plague by feeding babies to bogles. Ned thought about her as he stepped into the smaller ring of salt. He'd met her just once, having helped capture her while she was trying to escape from the police. Now awaiting trial for the murder of sixteen infants, she was sitting in Newgate Prison, no more than a few hundred yards from where Ned stood.

Her good friend John Gammon was surely close by—but *he* wasn't in gaol. Ned wondered if he might be circling Newgate Market at that very moment, making plans to stop Jem from testifying against him. It was a chilling thought. Gammon, after all, had been involved in Sarah's baby scheme.

Ned felt certain that, given a choice, Alfred would have turned down the Newgate job because it was just too dangerous to work in Salty Jack's territory. But because Alfred was now on the municipal payroll, he'd had no choice. He couldn't pick and choose his bogling jobs anymore—not when they came from a municipal officer such as Eugene Wardle.

"Ssst!" Alfred had stationed himself against one side of the wooden tank. In his right hand he carried a short spear; in his left, the leather bag. He nodded at Jem, who was already waiting inside the larger ring of salt with a small mirror in his hand and his back to the bogler. Between them, the drain yawned like a mouth; it was the size of a manhole,

but any cover that might once have rested on top of it was gone.

Ned decided that Alfred had chosen his hiding place well. The tank provided excellent cover and also gave Alfred a clear view of the drain—and of Jem, too. Ned found himself wondering what the tank had been used for. To hold blood, perhaps? Had freshly slaughtered sheep been laid across its metal grill?

Suddenly Jem began to sing.

"Ten or a dozen cocks o' the game
On the prigging lay to the flash house came,
Lushing blue ruin and heavy wet,
Till the darkey, when the downy set.
All toddled and began to hunt
For readers, tattlers, fogles, or blunt."

Jem's husky voice sounded like a cricket's chirp in that big, hollow space. Would the bogle hear it? Ned was glad that *he* didn't have to sing. It was hard enough simply breathing the foul air, let alone shaping it into a tune. Besides, Ned wasn't much of a singer. During his six months as a coster's boy—before Alfred had hired him for bogling work—Ned had strained his vocal cords touting his wares on busy street corners. "Ripe damsons!" "Potatoes, full weight!" "American apples, round and sound!" Ned knew all the cries but couldn't hold a tune.

Jem could. He piped away gamely, his gaze riveted to the mirror in his hand, which framed a small, murky image of Alfred's shadowy form.

> *"As I were crossing Saint James's Park,*
> *I met a swell, a well-togg'd spark.*
> *I stopped a bit: then toddled quicker,*
> *For I'd prigged his reader, drawn his ticker;*
> *Then he calls, 'Stop, thief!' Thinks I, my master,*
> *That's a hint to me to toddle faster."*

Ned understood that he was quite safe inside his small ring of salt. There wasn't a bogle on earth that could break through the magic circle protecting him. Yet he felt weighed down by a peculiar sense of dread, which grew stronger as he thought about John Gammon and Sarah Pickles and the hole in the floor. What if *two* bogles emerged from that hole? Or three?

What if a whole pack of them appeared? What was he supposed to do then?

In his entire life he'd only ever laid eyes on three bogles, and although he had personally killed one of them, he still wasn't properly trained. Compared with Jem, he was a raw recruit. Suppose he made a mistake? Suppose something went wrong?

Suddenly Ned gasped. This black despair wasn't natural. He recognized it from previous bogling jobs. And Jem must have recognized the feeling too, because his voice began to shake as he launched into another verse.

"Whatever swag we chance for to get,
All is fish as comes to net:
Mind yer eye, and draw the yokel,
Don't disturb or use the folk ill.
Keep a lookout, if the beaks is nigh,
And cut yer stick afore they're fly."

When Ned first heard the underlying noise, it was so faint that he couldn't quite make out what it was. A draft? A sigh? Gradually he identified it as a kind of whispering gurgle, and he licked his lips nervously as he peered at the drain.

But he couldn't see any movement in its depths. Though the air seemed to thicken, no bogle emerged from the sewer. It wasn't until Ned glanced toward Alfred to seek guidance that he spotted something black and shiny spilling over the rim of the tank.

At least a dozen long, boneless arms were unrolling like wet streamers, clinging to whatever surface they touched.

The pliable bulk of the creature soon followed, hauled out of the tank by its own straining arms like cargo winched from a ship's hold. The bogle was covered in jagged spines that waved about as it inched its way toward the floor, dragging itself along as silently as a snail.

Horrified, Ned opened his mouth, then shut it again. Alfred had told him over and over again not to speak while bogle hunting, except in an emergency. But surely this *was* an emergency? Alfred hadn't yet noticed the bogle; he was staring at the drain. When Ned shot a quick glance at Jem, he saw the mirror shaking. Clearly *Jem* could see what was happening.

In fact, it might have been the sudden catch in Jem's singing voice that caused Alfred to look up. For an instant he froze, wide-eyed, as the bogle slid down the front of the tank, barely a foot away from him. Luckily its wet, slithering shape passed him by.

It seemed anxious to reach Jem, who was still bravely singing.

> "B-but now the beaks is on the scene,
> And watched by moonlight where we went—
> Stagged us a-toddling into the ken
> And was down upon us all, and then
> Who should I spy but the slap-up spark
> What I eased of the swag in Saint James's P-Park?"

Slowly the creature advanced. It had a gaping maw lined with spinelike teeth, and glowing yellow eyes with no pupils. Alfred was edging forward behind it, adjusting his grip on the spear. Ned could hardly breathe. Jem was faltering; his voice was now just a hoarse squeak, and it nearly failed altogether when the bogle's reaching arms slipped through the gap in the ring of salt. They fastened themselves to the floor like suckers, then tightened until the rest of the bogle surged forward, leaving a slimy trail in its wake.

> *"There's a time, says King Sol, to dance and sing;*
> *I know there's a time for another thing:*
> *There's a time to pipe, and a time to snivel —*
> *I wish all Charlies and beaks to the —"*

"Go!" Alfred yelled, and jumped out of the shadows. There was a white flash as he tossed a handful of salt. Jem threw himself into a forward roll, bowling along like a hoop. Alfred raised his spear. The bogle reared up, frothing and hissing, its tentacles writhing, caught in the glittering trap —

Bang! It exploded like a giant grape, releasing a geyser of black liquid.

There was a long, shocked silence. Then Mr. Wardle reappeared at the top of the stairs.

"Mr. Bunce?" he murmured. "Are you all right?"

"Aye," Alfred said hoarsely. He shuffled forward and

stooped to retrieve his spear, which was lying in a sticky black puddle. His green coat was dripping with goo. Even his shaggy salt-and-pepper hair was splattered with the stuff.

"That weren't so big," Jem croaked, climbing stiffly to his feet. He, too, had been sprayed with slime.

"Nay," Alfred agreed. "I've seen bigger." He took a handkerchief from his pocket and began to mop his face. "You'd best get that off you," he told Jem. "Though it don't burn none, I doubt it's summat you'd want on yer skin."

Mr. Wardle was advancing down the stairs. "Uh—Mr. Bunce?" he asked. "Was there a bogle?"

"Aye," said Alfred.

"And you killed it?"

"I did."

"Um . . ." Mr. Wardle hesitated. His gaze drifted toward the puddle on the floor. "I should tell you that there may be another close by," he said at last.

Alfred frowned. "What do you mean?"

"Well . . ." Again the Inspector seemed lost for words. Finally he cleared his throat. "I just had a young lad wander up to me, saying there was a bogle in his father's house. Somehow he knew that I was with a bogler—perhaps he'd heard me speaking to the barmaid at Mother Okey's. But when I asked him for an address, he grew very anxious. He asked why you couldn't come directly. And as soon as I pressed him, he ran off." Seeing Alfred wince, Mr. Wardle blurted out, "He was in such a state that he made *me* nervous!"

Ned swallowed. He caught Alfred's eye, then looked away. Jem was grimacing as if he'd just caught his hand in a door.

"We need to get out of here," Alfred declared. He thrust his spear toward Ned, who took it obediently, since it was his job to clean it. "There ain't no saying who sent that boy. Or who might decide to follow him here."

"D'you think—?" Jem began, but Alfred cut him off.

"I don't know what to think. All I know is, I ain't taking no risks." Alfred went to pick up his sack, which lay under his hat near the dark lantern. "Come on," he told the boys. "We'll go straight home and clean up there. I'd sooner take me chances with a crusting o' bogle innards than I would with John Gammon."

By the time he'd finished speaking, Jem and Ned were already on their way upstairs.

3

Theater Folk

Alfred Bunce lived with his two apprentices in a garret off Drury Lane. The crowded room was six floors up—a very long climb with a bucket of water. So when they finally arrived home, Ned wasn't surprised to discover that the jug on the washstand was empty.

"I'll fetch another pail," he offered, since he was the only one not covered in smears of dried bogle. Orange Court didn't have its own water supply; it was just a narrow alley full of costers' carts, cabbage leaves, and grubby children. To reach the nearest pump, Ned had to head down Drury Lane toward Covent Garden Market. But this didn't worry him, as he regarded Orange Court as the height of luxury. After years spent sharing beds in cheap boarding houses, Ned felt very, very fortunate to have a paillasse all to himself. And he was profoundly grateful to Alfred Bunce, whose generosity had transformed his life.

Baiting bogles was a small price to pay for a roof, a fire, and a full belly.

Ned was on his way back from the pump when he spotted a knife grinder parked outside a coal merchant's shop. Ned loved to watch knife grinders at work. This one was bent over his machine, sharpening a pair of scissors. As he pedaled away furiously, a wooden wheel on his cart turned the circular whetstone by means of a leather belt.

Ned couldn't help admiring the smooth, efficient way the mechanical parts interacted. For a moment he stood entranced, forgetting that he had to hurry home.

"There he is! The barrow boy!" a loud voice suddenly exclaimed. "Hi! Ned Roach! We've been looking for you *everywhere!*"

Startled, Ned spun around. He saw a knot of people surging toward him, all young and handsome and well groomed. The oldest was a man of perhaps twenty-five, with a thick mustache and curly hair parted in the middle. He wore striped trousers, a silk cravat, and a coat with a velvet collar. Accompanying him were three girls who looked very much alike. They had huge, pale eyes under finely arched brows. Their heads were crowned with masses of brown ringlets, which tumbled out from beneath frivolous little hats. The youngest, who was about sixteen, wore violet taffeta. The other two were dressed in gold-braided, brass-buttoned Garibaldi coats.

"Hold up there!" cried the young man. "Do you know me? Frederick Vokes? My sisters and I have bought fruit from your master's barrow."

"Y-yes, of course," Ned stammered. He knew the Vokes family very well — at least by sight. They were actors from the Theatre Royal just down the road, and they had always been highly visible. What surprised Ned was that they recognized *him*. Although he had worked as a coster's boy, he hadn't exchanged a single word with the Vokes siblings. "But I ain't on a fruit barrow no more."

"We know *that!*" said the youngest girl, who had a very loud voice for such a little person. Ned recognized her as Rosina, the most famous of the Vokes sisters. "We were at Covent Garden Market, searching high and low, until we discovered that you were no longer to be found there!"

"That's right." Ned found himself edging backwards as the family closed in on him. "I'm a bogler's boy now."

The Vokes sisters gasped, then burst into squeals of excitement. By this time they were all gathered around Ned, striking poses and waving their hands about, while rougher, dirtier, busier people swerved to avoid them. Some passersby briefly slowed down, because the girls were worth a look. But none of the Vokes siblings seemed conscious of these curious stares. They fixed their attention wholly on Ned—who felt dazzled, like a mouse caught in the glare of a miner's lamp.

"Why, what a fortunate thing!" Rosina trilled. "We were told that you lodged with a Go-Devil Man, but not that you *worked* for him!"

"We wish to engage him, you see," Frederick explained.

"And here you are, placed in our path, just when we'd given up hope!" said the eldest sister, whose name Ned struggled to recall. The middle one was Victoria; he remembered that. He also knew that the siblings were renowned for their dancing and that after every show they would eat a late supper (or early breakfast) at the Tavistock Hotel, near Covent Garden Market, before picking up a handful of fresh plums or grapes on their way home.

But they weren't on their way home now; they were heading in the opposite direction, *toward* the theater.

"Who told you I lodged with a Go-Devil Man?" Ned asked, unable to imagine why the Vokes family would be discussing him with anyone. But then Frederick briskly related how he and his sisters had been lamenting the loss of "poor Noah" while they passed through Covent Garden Market that morning and had been overheard by a fat, bald coster with a reddish mustache. "He said that if we wanted to hire a bogler, you were the person to find," Frederick concluded with a very theatrical flourish. "And now—*voilà!* We've found you!"

Ned still didn't understand. "Who's Noah?"

"He is a boy from the ballet," the eldest sister replied. "He's missing."

"And he was last seen near the entrance to an underground tunnel," Rosina said eagerly, "so he *might* have been taken by a bogle—don't you think?"

"Unless, he's tucked away in the Nell Gwynne public house, drinking himself witless," Victoria suggested. "That tunnel leads straight from the theater to Mr. Cooper's tavern, does it not?"

"Oh, *Vic!*" Rosina shot her sister a reproachful glance. "How can you be so heartless? The poor boy's only nine years old!"

"Besides, the passage to Mr. Cooper's has been bricked up for years, if it ever existed," Frederick pointed out. But Victoria didn't seem convinced.

"Has it? Truly?" Her tone was skeptical. "I've been hearing about some very odd smells down there. And you know what the cooking is like at the Nell Gwynne."

The eldest sister laughed. "That smell isn't cooking, dear, it's *drains.* I heard Mr. Todd say so himself."

Ned stiffened. A missing child was one thing. But when

a child vanished near a tunnel, directly over a sewer pipe, in the presence of a mysterious stench . . .

He didn't like the sound of it.

"Of course, that smell *could* be a rotting carcass," Frederick remarked with a wicked glint in his eye. "Mr. Chatterton has been threatening to kill any number of theater critics. Perhaps he's been hiding the corpses backstage."

"Oh, do stop joking!" Rosina bristled at him. "I *like* Noah! And he isn't the first—why, what about that poor little lost girl?"

"What poor little lost girl?" asked her eldest sister.

"Oh, *you* know, Jessie!" Rosina cried. "The little girl who came to watch *Tom Thumb*! She wandered off into the crowd, and her mother made *such* a fuss."

"But she was found again, surely?" Frederick objected.

"I don't think she was." Rosina glanced at Victoria, who shrugged.

By this time Ned was thoroughly confused. Listening to the Vokes family was like watching a team of jugglers tossing balls. "So there's two missing kids?" He was trying to get things straight. "A boy and a girl?"

"Yes, indeed. And a lot of talk about something in the tunnel beneath the theater," Frederick replied. "That's why we need your bogler, Ned."

"At *once*," Rosina added. "Or what will befall all the other poor children?"

"Like our darling Rosie." Jessie flung her arms around her youngest sister. "How can we risk losing our dearest and daintiest?"

Ned doubted very much that Rosina was young enough to tempt a bogle, since she was in her teens. But instead of pointing this out he said, "Mr. Bunce can't do nothing for you now, miss. He's due at the Board o' Works in an hour."

"The Board of Works?" Rosina echoed. "Goodness me!"

"Are there bogles at the Board of Works?" Frederick asked, with real interest.

"No, sir, but Mr. Bunce is hired by the Sewers Office now. On a regular wage, like." Seeing the three sisters blink in astonishment, Ned suddenly remembered that he wasn't supposed to be telling people that the Sewers Office had hired a Go-Devil Man. So he quickly did his best to change the subject. "That's why I don't know as how Mr. Bunce can help you. He ain't taking on private jobs no more, see."

"Oh, but he'll help *us,* I'm sure," Frederick declared in ringing tones. "You could hardly describe us as *private* people. We're very, very public."

"You must persuade him. For our sake." Jessie leaned toward Ned, twining her arm through his. "You must tell him we're in dire need, and so very frightened."

"Ladies in distress," Victoria confirmed stoutly.

"And think of the poor little children, Ned!" Glittering tears had welled up in Rosina's expressive eyes. "Why, there are twelve in the ballet, as well as all the backstage boys! What will happen to them if Mr. Bunce refuses to help? Surely he couldn't be so *wicked* . . . ?"

Ned didn't know what to say.

Or was it all just an act?

"M-mebbe you should talk to Mr. Bunce," he stammered. "Mr. Bunce'd listen to you."

"Is that so?" When Ned began to nod enthusiastically, Rosina continued, "Then tell him to come to the theater. Tonight. Once he's finished at the Board of Works."

"Oh, but—"

"*Please*, Ned. *Dear* Ned. You know how wretched you'll feel if you fail us!" Rosina cried as Jessie patted Ned's cheek and Frederick clapped him on the shoulder.

"I defy you to refuse my sisters, my lad, for they're not the least accustomed to disappointment," Frederick warned. Then he drew his watch from his pocket and spluttered, "Dash it, is that the time? We have lingered too long, my beauties! Come along, now. Hop to it."

"Ask for Mr. Todd at the stage door," Jessie advised Ned as her brother hustled her away. Rosina blew a kiss, and Victoria lifted a graceful hand in farewell.

"We'll be expecting you!" Rosina said. "Tell Mr. Bunce how keen we are to meet him!"

Soon they were gone, though they left a drifting cloud of perfume in their wake. And the crowded street suddenly seemed empty without them.

Ned was still reeling when he arrived back at Alfred's lodgings.

"You took yer time," the bogler growled.

"I couldn't help it." Ned set down his bucket of water. "Someone stopped me."

Over by the fireplace, Jem was poking at embers. He stiffened and looked up. "Not Salty Jack?"

"No." As Ned explained, Alfred's long face settled into creases that were gloomier than usual. "I told 'em you don't take private jobs no more," Ned finished. "But they wouldn't listen."

Alfred gave a grunt. Jem looked surprised and said, "No private jobs? Who told you that?"

Ned hesitated. He shot a glance at Alfred before mumbling, "Mr. Bunce said as how we're all living on public money now, so we should allus put official business first."

"Truly?" Jem turned to Alfred, eyebrows raised. "*I* never heard no one warn you off yer own work."

"Not yet, no," said Alfred, pouring water from the bucket into the chipped white basin on the washstand. "But I'll not take on no extra jobs till they're cleared with the committee. For if there's rules to follow, I'd not want to break 'em."

"Rules?" Jem echoed. "I didn't hear no mention o' rules at the last meeting."

Alfred shrugged. "We'll find out soon enough if I can still take private jobs. If I can, we'll go straight to the theater from the Board o' Works. But I ain't so sure it'll be worth our while." Having splashed his face with water, he wiped his eyes and peered at Ned. "Them Vokes young'uns," he continued, "would they be the kind to let their fancies run away with 'em?"

Ned frowned. Then he sighed and reluctantly admitted, "I think their fancies would have a hard time *keeping up* with 'em."

"I thought as much," said Alfred. "Actors is all the same. Wherever there's a choice, they'll favor a tale above the truth."

And he started scraping bits of bogle out of his hair with a gap-toothed comb.

4

PLANS

Mark Harewood was an engineer, employed as a Clerk of Works at the Sewers Office. He was tall and young and vigorous, with flashing blue eyes and a broad, clean-shaven face. Everything about him was sunny: his gleaming smile, his thick blond hair—even his yellow waistcoat.

Ned had met him only once before but had quickly decided that he was an excellent fellow. Now, seeing him on the third floor of the Board of Works building, Ned was relieved to know that they were in the right place at the right time.

"Why, here you are!" Mr. Harewood exclaimed upon

catching sight of Alfred and his apprentices hovering at the door. "Come in! Take a seat! I've something to show you."

Obediently Alfred led the way into a room lined with oak paneling. Red velvet curtains were draped across two lofty windows, and the walls were hung with oil paintings so dark that Ned couldn't tell if they were portraits or landscapes. In the center of the room stood a large circular table surrounded by hard chairs.

Mr. Harewood and Erasmus Gilfoyle, the naturalist, were leaning over this table, studying what appeared to be a map. Though they were about the same age, they looked very different. Mr. Gilfoyle was shorter and slimmer than his friend. His wispy fair hair was plastered down with oil, whereas Mr. Harewood's golden fleece fell into his eyes. Mr. Gilfoyle was as neat as a pin in his dove-gray suit, while Mr. Harewood was wearing ink-stained shirtsleeves and an un-knotted ribbon necktie.

"Look at this," Mr. Harewood urged Alfred. "D'you see what I've done here? Thanks to what you told me last week, Mr. Bunce, I was able to mark up the exact location of every bogle you've killed in London during the past five years." He began to jab at the map with one finger. "See those red dots? Each represents a dead bogle. And this is the river, of course, with all its bridges. And this is Saint Paul's." As Ned edged closer, Mr. Harewood retrieved another roll of paper from one of the chairs, began to unroll it, and said, "Now, *this* is a plan of the city's sewer system, traced onto wax paper. If I position it over the top of the map, you will see how our underground waterways intersect with London's bogle sightings."

Ned stared in amazement. Before him lay an intricate network of pipes and channels and gates, superimposed upon an even *more* complex tangle of streets and squares and canals. The effect was like a three-dimensional model. He had never seen anything so exquisite—or so fascinating.

He only wished he could read the street names.

"It's evident that there is a connection between subterranean water and the incidence of bogles," Mr. Harewood went on. "Consider the clusters of red dots here . . . and here . . . and here, of course, near the Fleet Sewer—"

"Is that the Fleet?" asked Ned. He was so excited that he forgot about keeping his mouth shut. Alfred had told him many times to hold his tongue while a gentleman was talking. But the sight of London's innards, spread out before him like something dissected, had pushed everything else out of Ned's mind.

"That *is* the Fleet," Mr. Harewood confirmed. He didn't seem offended. In fact, he smiled at Ned. "And that is the viaduct, and that is Newgate Street—"

"So *that* must be the flushing tank!" Ned exclaimed, pointing. "The one beneath Newgate Market!"

"Perhaps." Mr. Harewood lifted his head. "Mr. Wardle — *you* would know, I'm sure."

"Know what?" the Inspector of Sewers said. Despite his bulk, he had slipped into the room without attracting much attention. "Good evening, Mr. Bunce. Mr. Gilfoyle. Good evening, boys," he went on, mopping his red, sweaty face with a crumpled handkerchief. Seeing Mr. Harewood beckon to him, he moved across to the table. "Ah!" he exclaimed. "So my plans arrived."

"They did indeed." Mr. Harewood tapped the wax paper. "This symbol here — does it represent a flushing tank?"

Mr. Wardle squinted at a tiny black star that looked like an inkblot. "Why, yes," he replied. "That's one of 'em. We have ten altogether — at Newgate, and Leadenhall —"

"If the bogles live in the sewers," Ned interrupted, "mebbe they could all be *flushed* out." The idea had struck him as he traced the course of a sewer line from one end of London to the other. "If you was to flush the bogles from pipe to pipe, until most o' the sewers was closed off, would you be able to herd 'em all together like goats?"

Mr. Harewood grinned his approval. "An interesting notion, young Ned. I must admit, the same thought crossed my mind when I saw this pattern of red dots. But it would be a difficult task, I fear, what with the variable water pressure and the restricted number of flushing gates and the unknown degrees of resistance we'd be facing from the creatures themselves ..." Mr. Harewood trailed off, his brow furrowed in concentration, before he turned to the Inspector. "What do you think, old boy? Could we blow 'em all into the Thames?"

"What for?" asked Mr. Wardle. It was a good question. How were the bogles to be disposed of once they'd been expelled from their lairs? Ned was wondering if Alfred could be positioned over a sewage outfall, where he might spear each bogle as it emerged from the pipe, when all at once every man in the room snapped to attention.

"Good evening," a familiar voice remarked. "Forgive us for being so late. Saint Martin's Lane was at a standstill, and the porter seemed reluctant to admit us."

Ned saw that Miss Edith Eames had appeared at the door. She was wearing a mustard-colored mantle, a matching skirt without frills or flounces, and a slightly peevish expression. Her black brows were knitted together beneath the tip-tilted brim of her modest felt hat. Her face was even paler than usual, and she pursed her lips as she impatiently peeled off her beige kid gloves.

Clearly she was annoyed about something.

But Ned was far more interested in the girl beside Miss Eames. She seemed to glitter like cut glass. Her golden curls were even brighter than Mr. Harewood's. Her blue eyes gleamed like stars, and her fair skin glowed beneath a light dusting of freckles. From the ribbons on her hat to the buttons on her boots, she was dressed all in white.

Ned smiled at the girl, hoping to receive a smile in return. But she had already flung herself at Alfred.

"Mr. Bunce!" she exclaimed. "Did you go to Newgate Market?"

"We did," he replied, holding her off. "Mind yer pretty clothes, Birdie—I've mud on me trousers."

"Was there a bogle?" she demanded. "Did you kill it?"

"Aye." Alfred turned to the Clerk of Works. "You should make a note o' that, Mr. Harewood."

"I shall." As Mr. Harewood produced a pot of red ink, Birdie McAdam continued to question Alfred about the Newgate bogle. She was particularly curious about its size, its exact location, and the traces that it had left behind. Mr. Gilfoyle was also interested; in fact, he began to take notes in a little black book. But Ned knew that Birdie's interest was more than academic. Having once been a bogler's girl, she still felt personally involved in every job that Alfred agreed to do.

"Samples of the residue would be useful," Mr. Gilfoyle remarked when Birdie had finished. "Perhaps I should be present at your next encounter, Mr. Bunce."

"Perhaps," Alfred responded, though he didn't sound very enthusiastic. Meanwhile, Mr. Harewood was carefully drying the new red dot on his map with a piece of blotting paper.

"Now that we're all here," he said, "I think we should commence formal proceedings. We'll start with last week's minutes, perhaps—unless anyone has any questions?"

No one did. So all found chairs and sat down facing each other across the table. Then Mr. Gilfoyle cleared his throat, donned a pair of spectacles, and began to read from a stack of loose papers.

First he reminded everyone that committee elections had been held the previous week. As a result, he said, Mr. Harewood was now Chairman, Mr. Wardle was Treasurer, and he was Secretary. He went on to relate that the committee had agreed to meet every Monday afternoon—at which time a sum of fifteen shillings would be paid to Mr. Alfred Bunce, by way of a salary.

"Miss Eames then moved that our mission as a committee should be to rid London of its bogles," Mr. Gilfoyle continued in his gentle, precise voice, "and this motion was carried without dissent. The next item on the agenda was a discussion regarding the typical characteristics of a bogle. Mr. Bunce, Miss McAdam, and Miss Eames all contributed to the discussion, after which the Secretary suggested that he and Miss Eames form a subcommittee entrusted with the task of studying bogles as a species. Mr. Gilfoyle will undertake to write a report on any information gleaned, in order to classify the creatures in accordance with the standard bio-logical taxonomy of Linnaeus . . ."

Ned strained to remember what the "biological taxon-omy of Linnaeus" meant. Mr. Gilfoyle had explained the pre-vious week that it had something to do with the way plants and animals were divided into different classes and families. But the families didn't have mothers and fathers, and the classes didn't have anything to do with school. According to Mr. Gilfoyle, these were simply scientific terms that gave people a better understanding of the world.

Ned wished that *he* had a better understanding of the world. Sometimes, when Mr. Gilfoyle was speaking, he felt as if he were trying to catch soap bubbles; the meaning of each word either drifted out of Ned's reach or vanished completely just when he thought he had a grip on it. *If only I had some schooling,* he thought, shooting a glance at Birdie. Thanks to Miss Eames, Birdie was becoming educated. She had learned to read and write. And for that reason, perhaps, she was staring at Mr. Gilfoyle with an expression that wasn't blank, bored, or bewildered, but intent and absorbed. She looked as if she were really *listening* to what he said.

Jem, on the other hand, was twisting restlessly in his seat, his gaze flitting around the room.

"Mr. Harewood then proposed that he and Mr. Bunce form another subcommittee," Mr. Gilfoyle continued. "He further suggested that this subcommittee's first task would be to circulate a memorandum amongst all the municipal offices, asking that they notify Mr. Harewood of any unusual subterranean activity that may pertain to bogles. The motion was carried without dissent. Mr. Harewood promised to alert the committee if his memorandum uncovered any evidence of bogle activity. He also asked Mr. Wardle to provide him with a map of London's sewage system . . ."

Jem caught Ned's eye and grimaced. Ned immediately looked away. He sympathized with Jem, but he didn't want to be caught yawning or wriggling. He knew that of all the committee members, he was probably the least qualified. Birdie had been a bogler's girl for nearly eight years—since she was just three years old. Her voice was so fine that she could sing *any* bogle out of its den. Jem was as nimble as a monkey; he had once climbed a six-story chimney to escape a bogle's clutches. Mr. Bunce was a bogler; Mr. Wardle knew the sewer system; Miss Eames was a folklorist.

Ned, on the other hand, had no skills to speak of. He couldn't even read. He had nothing to offer but sturdy good health, a willingness to work, and an ability to concentrate. He felt dispensable, and so he always took great care not to offend, intrude, or disappoint.

Since the age of six, when his mother's death had cast him onto the street, Ned had struggled to find a place in the world. He had worked for a rag-and-bone man, who had beaten him, and for a beggar, who had starved him. He'd spent a very short time in the Whitechapel workhouse before running away to become a mudlark. And in all that time, no one had cared whether he lived or died.

But things had changed, thanks to Alfred. And Ned wasn't about to jeopardize his new life by making silly faces.

" . . . and the meeting closed at six o'clock." Mr. Gilfoyle raised his eyes and glanced around the table. "Are there any objections to the contents of these minutes? Does anyone wish to amend them?" No one spoke. "Very well," the naturalist murmured. "Then we'll proceed to the next item on the agenda, which is, I believe . . . um . . ."

"The report of the Chairman's subcommittee," said Mr. Harewood. And he reached for the rolled-up map nearby.

5

ALL IN FAVOR?

Birdie and Miss Eames leaned over the map, their noses almost brushing against it, and marveled at its complexity as Mr. Harewood explained what the red dots meant.

"As you can see, there appears to be a link between bogles and underground water," he said. "In fact, it's been suggested that we try to *flush* the bogles out of our drains." He winked at Ned, then turned to Mr. Gilfoyle. "Make a note of that, Razzy, will you? *Mr. Harewood to consult the Chief Engineer about flushing the sewers.*"

Mr. Gilfoyle began to scribble on the paper in front

of him as Ned pondered the surprising nickname. Razzy seemed much too undignified for someone so gentlemanly.

Meanwhile, Miss Eames was frowning at Mr. Harewood. "Do you propose to exterminate all of London's bogles by pushing them into the river, and thence to the sea?" she asked him. "Will that have the desired effect?"

Every eye swiveled toward Mr. Harewood, who shrugged. "I've no idea," he admitted. "What's your opinion, Mr. Bunce? Would saltwater kill bogles?"

Alfred scratched his scrubby cheek but said nothing.

"Salt keeps 'em at bay," Birdie pointed out. "*And* cures their bites."

"Aye. It does that," Alfred agreed—at which point Ned raised his hand.

"Thames water is fresh as far as London Bridge," he piped up, just in case no one else knew the Thames as well as he did. After five years scouring the river's muddy banks, he was only too familiar with its habits. "Beyond that, 'tis brackish until Southend."

"Brackish?" Miss Eames echoed thoughtfully. And Jem, who was finally paying attention, said, "What's 'brackish'?"

"Brackish is half salt, half fresh," Mr. Wardle kindly informed him.

"But would brackish water kill bogles?" Mr. Harewood appealed to Alfred. "What do *you* think, Mr. Bunce?"

"I don't know as how it would," Alfred replied. "Fact

is, I don't know as how *salt* would. For I ain't never seen it done — nor heard of it, neither."

"Perhaps if a bogle was *completely immersed* in salt?" This suggestion came from Miss Eames. "Or even a very highly concentrated solution?"

"Mebbe we should flush out the sewers with saltwater," Birdie added.

"I doubt we'd get leave to do that," the Inspector remarked. "Salt in our sewers? It would rust all the sluice gates *and* kill half the trees in London."

"Ahem." Mr. Gilfoyle, who had been busy taking notes, lifted his head. "We should not be employing salt as a weapon until we determine what it would do. Mr. Bunce uses salt to deter bogles. Is that correct, sir?"

"Aye," Alfred conceded.

"But when you kill them, you employ your spear, which once belonged to Finn MacCool. Is *that* correct?"

"Aye."

"How do you know?" Seeing Alfred blink, Mr. Gilfoyle rephrased his question. "That is to say, who told you about the origins of the spear?"

"Daniel Piggin. Me old master." Alfred was looking more and more uncomfortable, Ned thought. But that wasn't surprising. The bogler had always hated discussing his past. "Mr. Piggin's bin dead these twenty years, though. And he weren't talkative at the best o' times."

"Did he happen to tell you what your spear is *made* of, Mr. Bunce?" Mr. Harewood broke in. "Or if it has been treated with any kind of unusual substance?"

As Alfred shook his head, Ned gasped. *The spear! Of course!* If Alfred's spear could be copied, somehow . . .

"According to Irish legend, Finn MacCool's spear *was* poisoned," Miss Eames volunteered. "But I'm afraid nothing else was said on the subject."

"Which doesn't mean that we couldn't find out more," the naturalist observed. "It so happens I know a Chemical Operator who works at Apothecaries' Hall, on Water Lane. I shall ask him if he would examine Mr. Bunce's spear, with a view to identifying any toxins adhering to it." He abruptly dropped his chin and began to scratch away so energetically that his pen sputtered. "*Mr. Gilfoyle to make inquiries at the Great Laboratory on Water Lane,*" he muttered to himself.

Jem was bouncing up and down in his chair. "If Mr. Bunce's spear is poisoned and we find out what the poison is, then we can make a thousand spears!" he cried. "And we can send a whole *army* down the sewers, to kill every one o' them bogles!"

"We wouldn't need no army, Jem." Birdie seemed unaware of the horrified looks that were being exchanged around her. "Not if we put the poison in the flushing tanks—"

"Whoa! Hold up, there!" Mr. Harewood raised both hands. "We will *not* be flooding the drains with poison! *Or* armed men!" As Birdie opened her mouth to protest, he added, "The river water is bad enough. We don't want to make it worse."

"Oh." Birdie stared at him for a moment, then blushed. "No. Of course not," she mumbled. Ned wanted to reassure her that the same thought had crossed *his* mind — at least for an instant. But Mr. Harewood had something else to say.

"Was Finn MacCool a real person?" he asked Miss Eames, with a crooked smile. "I thought him a myth."

Miss Eames hesitated. It was Mr. Gilfoyle who answered.

"When the mists of time descend, history can sometimes become confused with mythology," he informed Mr. Harewood. "A rhinoceros might turn into a unicorn, and an ancient king might be given a magic sword. It's my belief that by studying fantastical beasts through the lens of scientific method, we may be able to assign them a place in the natural hierarchy. A sea monster may actually be a sea creature, misidentified. And perhaps Finn MacCool suffered a similar fate . . ."

As he trailed off, there was a brief silence. Glancing around the table, Ned saw that Mr. Wardle looked impressed, Mr. Harewood was nodding, and Miss Eames wore an approving smile. Even Mr. Bunce seemed resigned.

Only Birdie and Jem hadn't been won over. Jem's attention had wandered again, and Birdie was frowning at Mr. Gilfoyle.

"But bogles *are* magic," she protested.

"Perhaps," said Mr. Gilfoyle. "Or perhaps not. Once upon a time, people used to believe that the pelican fed its young with blood from its own breast. Now we know better, thanks to scientific observation."

Ned didn't know what a pelican was. He wasn't sure that Birdie did either. It hardly mattered, though, because she wasn't really listening.

"But big bogles can squeeze through the tiniest holes!" she argued. "And they vanish like soap bubbles when you kill 'em! No *ordinary* creature does that!"

"Not all bogles do that either," Mr. Gilfoyle gently pointed out. "Mr. Bunce just told us that the bogle under Newgate Market left a great deal of itself behind."

"But—"

"There are certain jellyfish that disintegrate when touched," the naturalist went on. "And even the humble rat can fit through a hole no bigger than a five-shilling piece." As Birdie scowled and folded her arms, Mr. Gilfoyle concluded, "We don't know enough about bogles to classify them as magical creatures. Not yet."

"Then what *do* we know about 'em?" asked Mr. Harewood. Ned wondered if he was trying to change the subject for Birdie's sake. She looked so flustered that Ned felt sorry for her.

He also agreed with her. How could a normal, everyday creature make you feel miserable before you even laid eyes on it?

"So far we don't know much about bogles," Mr. Gilfoyle admitted, "and what we *do* know will be covered in my report. But before we hear that, we need to make sure that the Chairman's subcommittee has nothing else to contribute." He cocked his head, eyebrows raised. "Did you circulate your memorandum to the municipal offices, Mark?"

"I did," Mr. Harewood replied. "But so far I've received only one response." Reaching across the table, he picked up a sheet of paper. "This letter was sent to me by the office of the Postmaster General. It concerns the mysterious disappearance of three telegraph boys. I wrote back suggesting that Mr. Bunce pay a visit as soon as possible, but I've yet to receive an answer." To Alfred he said, "Naturally I shall inform you the very *instant* I have a date and a time."

The bogler nodded. Then, to Ned's surprise, he asked Mr. Gilfoyle, "May I say summat?"

"Why, of course, Mr. Bunce."

"It so happens I've another job on. At the Theatre Royal, in Drury Lane." He shifted uneasily. "But I'll not do it if you'd prefer I didn't."

Mr. Gilfoyle blinked. "Why on earth would we want to stop you?"

"On account of it's private work, and I'm on the city payroll. I thought as how there might be rules."

"Oh, I shouldn't worry about *that*," said Mr. Harewood. "Every time you exterminate a bogle, Mr. Bunce, the city benefits greatly. In my opinion, you have *always* been working for the common good."

"Hear, hear!" Miss Eames exclaimed. Ned half expected Birdie to say something similar—until he caught sight of her expression. She was gazing at Alfred the way a dog might gaze at a butcher's shop.

"Please, Mr. Bunce," she begged, "may I go with you to the Theatre Royal?"

"Well . . ." Alfred glanced uneasily at Miss Eames, whose dark eyebrows had already snapped together.

"Oh, *please*, Mr. Bunce!" Birdie's voice cracked as she wrung her hands. "Let me do a job at Drury Lane! For if the folk there hear me sing, they might put me in a show!"

"Aye, but . . ." Alfred was no match for Birdie's pleading. Ned felt sure that he would have buckled already if not for Miss Eames. "I thought you wasn't keen to go bogling no more," he said.

"Just this once!" cried Birdie.

Miss Eames was shaking her head. "Birdie, you can do better than a Drury Lane pantomime," she objected. "Why,

Signora Paolini has high hopes for you. If you apply yourself, you could be a lyric soprano at the Royal Opera House."

"But I don't want to be a lyric soprano! I want to be in a pantomime!"

"It's too dangerous." Conscious of all the reproachful looks being leveled at her, Miss Eames said crisply, "She wouldn't be singing — she would be bogling. And you know what my position is on *that*."

"But when it comes to bogles, it ain't down to you no more," Ned blurted out. The pitiable look on Birdie's face had compelled him to speak. Why *shouldn't* she sing in a pantomime? He knew that she was bound to light up the stage. "Birdie's on the committee now, same as the rest of us," he continued. "So we all get to vote on what she does."

Seeing Miss Eames's indignant expression, he subsided abruptly, cursing himself for being too bold. But Jem was already raising his hand.

"I move Birdie should go bogling at Drury Lane!" Jem declared.

Mr. Harewood winked at Mr. Gilfoyle. Mr. Gilfoyle shrugged. Then he said, "All in favor?"

Ned's hand shot up. Alfred raised his more slowly, keeping his eyes lowered. When Birdie's hand joined Alfred's, and Mr. Wardle's joined Birdie's, Mr. Harewood offered the girl a lopsided grin and said, "The Chairman has the deciding vote. I suppose you'd hate me forever if I ruled against you?"

"No," Birdie replied stiffly. "Of course not."

"I'd rather not risk it, all the same." Mr. Harewood put his hand in the air. "The *aye*s have it. Miss Birdie McAdam may go bogling at the Theatre Royal." To Miss Eames he said reassuringly, "I'm sure she will be safe enough in Mr. Bunce's hands. He's never let her come to any harm before."

As Birdie caught Ned's eye, the gratitude in her gaze sent the blood rushing to his cheeks.

6

BACKSTAGE

Though he lived very close to the Drury Lane theater, Ned had never gone inside. He couldn't afford even the cheapest seat, which cost nearly two shillings. He was also intimidated by the grandeur of the building's fine stone portico. And he had seen stagehands cuff and curse boys his age as they lined up beneath the colonnade on Russell Street, hoping to be engaged for the Christmas pantomime. This, more than anything else, had put him off the place.

But he had formed an idea of what the interior was probably like. He assumed that it was full of gilt and plush and marble — not to mention haughty ushers in spotless evening dress. So he was surprised by the cluttered, dirty warren that greeted him when he stepped through the stage door, which was tucked down the side of the building.

"We're looking for Mr. Todd," Alfred informed the doorkeeper. "I am Alfred Bunce, and this is Miss Edith Eames and Miss Birdie McAdam—"

"Mr. Todd is with Mr. Chatterton," the doorkeeper interrupted without glancing up from his newspaper. He was a glowering, unshaven, middle-aged man perched on a high stool; it was obvious from his manner that if Queen Victoria herself had appeared on the threshold, he wouldn't have been impressed.

Alfred glanced at Ned, who cleared his throat and squeaked, "Miss Rosina Vokes sent for us. Mr. Bunce is a Go-Devil Man."

The doorkeeper heaved a long-suffering sigh. "Mr. Spong!" he barked. "Are you off to the painting room?"

A very young man in a dirty smock had been trying to slip past. Now he paused and said, "I'm finished for the day, Mr. Jorkins."

"Not yet you ain't. You can take this here crew to see Miss Rosina Vokes. She'll be getting dressed, I daresay."

"But—"

"And if you run across Mr. Beverly, you can tell 'im his parcel's arrived," the doorkeeper concluded, rattling his newspaper as he shielded his face with it.

Mr. Spong didn't look happy, but he jerked his chin at

Alfred and headed back into the bowels of the theater. Ned couldn't believe how busy the place was. At times the narrow, gas-lit corridors were so crowded that Mr. Spong was unable to push his way through the costumed performers. Instead, with Alfred and the others close at his heels, he had to take long detours through rooms full of laboring seamstresses, racks of clothes, or gigantic pieces of painted scenery. At one point he was buttonholed by a bearded gentleman who smelled of turpentine. "I cannot stop," Mr. Spong told him. "I've an errand to run."

And run he did. Ned and Jem and Birdie soon fell behind as they stopped to gawk at passing knights and princesses. Miss Eames had to keep rounding them up like stray chickens. "Hurry, please, or we'll lose our way!" she chided.

Sure enough, it wasn't long before her party found itself adrift in the property room, with Mr. Spong nowhere in sight. All around them were shelves laden with masks, trumpets, swords, bellows, plaster fish, and wooden fruit. Silver wings dangled from the rafters. Bits of tinsel were scattered across the floor. A woman scurried past with an armful of fake pewter as a man in an apron boiled something gluey over an open fire near a stone sink.

"I can't see Mr. Spong," said Alfred, who by this time was pouring sweat and red in the face. "Where did he go?"

Ned shook his head. He glanced at Jem, who shrugged.

"Perhaps we should return," Miss Eames suggested. But

before she could move, a loud voice cried, "What ho! Is that Ned Roach, the bogler's boy?"

It was Frederick Vokes, all dressed up in a gold crown and a velvet doublet. He had been rushing down the corridor outside the prop room. One glimpse of Ned's worried expression caused him to stop short, swing around, and bellow, "Rosie! He's here!"

"Who is?" came the high-pitched reply.

"That bogler!" Mr. Vokes dodged two men in a horse suit as they shuffled past, then took a step into the room. "Are you Mr. Bunce? I'm Frederick Vokes. You'd best come with me, for you'll do no good here." Mr. Vokes caught sight of Miss Eames. "Hello. Would you be *Mrs.* Bunce?"

"Certainly not!" Miss Eames snapped. "My name is Edith Eames. I came with Birdie."

"And who is Birdie?"

"I am." Birdie thrust herself toward the actor, eagerly extending her hand. She was dressed in her bogling outfit: a plain, dark dress and matching bowler hat. "I'm a bogler's girl," she announced with a dazzling smile. Mr. Vokes looked startled. He was about to take Birdie's hand when his youngest sister burst into the room, almost knocking him sideways.

"A bogler's girl! How *very* brave!" cried Rosina, who wore a great deal of fluttering gauze. Her arms were bare, and her hair tumbled down her back. "Goodness, aren't you a pretty thing!" she exclaimed, upon catching sight of Birdie. "Isn't she pretty, Fred?"

"Shocking waste," Mr. Vokes agreed as he motioned to Alfred. Then Birdie, who had been staring at Rosina in mute admiration, said, "I ain't as pretty as you."

Ned didn't agree. Neither did Rosina. "It's all slap, my dear. Makeup," she confided. "I only wish my cheeks *were* this pink." Then she tucked her arm through Birdie's. "Come along and I'll show you where the tunnel is. Come along, Ned! Come along—what's your name?"

"Jem Barbary."

"Hello, Jem Barbary. I'm Rosina Vokes." The actress began to follow Alfred, who was already following her brother. She hardly paused for breath as she bustled along. "Bogling must be just like the theater these days," she babbled. "There are so many children involved! D'you know that our Tom Thumb is only six? Or so he says. I'm beginning to wonder if he's as young as he claims, but there can be no doubt that he *is* a prodigy . . ."

Trailing after the two girls, Ned marveled at how silent Birdie was. He had never seen her quite so subdued. Even Jem was speechless, though he gave Ned a nudge when they passed a gaggle of fairies in short skirts.

Miss Eames was looking cross. She trudged along in the rear, eyeing everything suspiciously. "Should not we speak to the manager?" she asked Rosina, who replied, "Oh, Mr. Chatterton doesn't believe in bogles. His secretary, Mr. Todd, agreed to engage Mr. Bunce. But poor Mr. Todd is so busy at the moment—"

"Our Merlin has fallen ill," Mr. Vokes cut in, clattering down a set of stairs. "And it's less than an hour until the curtain rises."

"But never fear," Rosina finished. "*We* shall take care of you, Miss . . . er . . ."

"Miss Eames. Edith Eames. I'm a folklorist."

"Oh, yes? How lovely for you." Rosina's attention had shifted to Mr. Vokes, who was banging through a door at the foot of the staircase. "I'm very fond of floral arrangements."

Miss Eames frowned. "I am a folklorist, Miss Vokes, not a *florist*," she said sharply.

The actress, however, had already surged forward, dragging Birdie with her. "Wait, Freddie! Slow down! Anyone would think you were running away from us!"

By this time Ned was completely lost. He thought they were probably underground, but he couldn't be sure. Then he found himself in a large space full of pipes and pulleys, and he stopped worrying about everything else.

"Do you have a hydraulic lift ram?" he asked Rosina, halting in front of a pressure gauge mounted at eye level. He had last seen a hydraulic lift ram beneath Smithfield

Market—at Birdie's last bogling job—and he had never forgotten it.

"What? Oh. I'm not sure." Rosina didn't even pause to look. "I think this may be part of the substage machinery. Isn't it, Fred?"

Mr. Vokes had already disappeared into a forest of shafts and gears and weights on chains. "Not far now!" he yelled over his shoulder as his sister blew a kiss at a grimy, pallid little man tightening a bolt on a piston. The man's jaw dropped when he caught sight of the mismatched group scurrying past.

But his astonishment was nothing compared with Ned's.

"Why, what kind of a wrench is that?" Ned demanded. "I ain't never seen one like it!"

The man blinked. "This? It's brand new, from America. They call it a ratcheting socket wrench."

"And you don't have to move it off the bolt?" asked Ned.

"Clever, ain't it?" The man proudly demonstrated. "Them two pawls have springs inside, which work to hold the ratchet wheel—"

"Ned!" Miss Eames exclaimed. "Don't dawdle!"

Reluctantly Ned dragged himself away from the remarkable socket wrench. He followed Miss Eames through the maze of machinery under the stage, past the orchestra pit, and into a narrow cellar room with a vaulted ceiling. One side of the room was lined with low, blind arches that had been turned into storage bays for bags of coal and planks of wood. Utility pipes ran along the walls.

Ned identified two water pipes, a possible boiler pipe, and a gas pipe that fed the lamp that hung from the ceiling.

"What an unpleasant smell." Miss Eames pressed a handkerchief to her nose. "Is it sewage?"

"Seems to be," said Alfred.

Ned remembered what Mr. Wardle had told them earlier that afternoon. "The Norfolk Sewer lies below," he remarked, sniffing.

"If we're smelling sewer gas, there must be a hole somewhere." Alfred dropped his sack on the floor and proceeded to rummage through it. "And if there's a hole, it may be big enough for a bogle."

"I can *show* you the hole!" cried Rosina. "It's behind those crates!" She pointed at one of the blind arches, then turned to her brother. "Help him to move them, Freddie, so we can see!"

"My dear girl, are you joking?" Mr. Vokes spread his arms. "I can't afford to tear this costume—it'll be overture and beginners soon!"

"I'll do it," said Alfred. As he lifted the topmost crate, Ned rushed to help him. Together they worked to clear the storage bay while Rosina explained that the missing boy had last been seen practicing his steps in this very room, well away from the scorn of his fellow dancers.

"He was last seen *dancing?*" Birdie interrupted, just as Jem blurted out, "Could he have bin singing as well?"

"Perhaps."

Jem looked at Birdie, who looked at Ned. They all grimaced. Then Alfred dragged another crate from the pile and said, "Here it is."

He had uncovered a deep, ragged hole in the brick wall.

"Oh dear!" Miss Eames's voice was muffled by her handkerchief. "You seem to have found the source of that smell, Mr. Bunce."

Jem began to cough. Rosina clapped a hand across her face. Holding her nose, Birdie turned to Mr. Vokes and asked, "What *is* that?"

"I've been told it's the tunnel that once led to the Nell Gwynne tavern," he replied from behind his sleeve. "It was bricked up long ago, and then later this hole was made — I'm not sure why. Perhaps someone was hoping to find another corpse." He started to explain that some thirty years earlier a skeleton had been discovered behind a wall upstairs. But the bogler wouldn't let him finish.

"Shh!" Alfred flapped them all away from the hole before thrusting his own head into it. Rosina gave a shriek. Ned glanced at her in alarm — but realized that she was simply overexcited.

"Don't worry, miss," Jem assured her. "Mr. Bunce knows what he's doing."

"Shut yer mouth!" Alfred suddenly rounded on him, startling everyone with his ferocity. "D'you want to lure the bogle out ahead o' time?"

Rosina gasped. Her brother struck a dramatic pose. Miss Eames whispered, "You think there's a bogle, Mr. Bunce?"

"I know there is," Alfred replied. And he began to make his preparations.

7

THE TUNNEL

According to Alfred, the hole *did* seem to be a tunnel, though it was badly choked with rubble and other debris. "Only a bogle could get through there," he muttered as he began to lay a ring of salt on the floor. He placed it at one end of the long, narrow room while everyone else hovered at the other end, watching him.

The ring looked very small to Ned, though it was as wide as the available space. He wondered if there would be a second circle. Alfred had often said that most bogles were solitary creatures, but it seemed a little risky to assume that they shared their dens only in the neighborhood of Newgate

Market. What if Drury Lane had become overcrowded as well?

"This is as good as a play," Mr. Vokes said in a low voice as his sister tried to smother her excited giggles. "I'd wager people would pay a shilling a head for this."

"Aye, but we don't want no audience down here, getting in the way," Alfred rejoined. "That's why you'll have to leave, Mr. Vokes."

The actor's face fell. "Am I not to witness the proceedings?" he lamented.

"The proceedings, Mr. Vokes, might take some time," Miss Eames weighed in. "And you yourself are due on stage very soon, are you not?"

Before Mr. Vokes could answer, Alfred looked up from his work and said, "They both are. That's why neither of 'em can stay in this room."

Rosina caught her breath.

"I'm sorry, miss," Alfred continued. "I'll not have you slipping out suddenly when you're called, or you'll disturb the bogle."

"Oh, but Mr. *Bunce*—"

Alfred stood firm. "I ain't about to argue. If you'll promise not to move or speak for the next few hours, then you can join us. Otherwise you'd best leave."

Rosina's eyes brimmed with tears and her bottom lip quivered. Mr. Vokes, however, wasn't impressed by this display. He flicked her cheek with two careless fingers as he began to hustle her upstairs. "Turn off the plumbing, Sarah Bernhardt," he said breezily. "Mr. Bunce knows what he's about." On the landing he paused to say, "If we're gone when you finish, Mr. Bunce, you must report to Mr. Todd. But do try not to wander onstage while you're at it."

He then turned a corner and vanished up the second flight of stairs — though not before throwing a sly wink at his unhappy sister, who was following him reluctantly. Ned caught the wink and was puzzled, but he didn't say anything. He knew that Alfred wouldn't want to hear a child's voice.

Not while a bogle was listening.

"There's a deal too many ways into this cellar," Alfred remarked. He was already laying down a second ring of salt near the foot of the staircase, where a door stood opposite the first blind arch. Made of scarred oak, this door was shut, though not locked. The door on the landing was also shut.

A third door, at the other end of the room, was ajar. It led to a dingy space full of old furniture.

"You're to go in there," Alfred told Miss Eames, nodding toward the storeroom. "The fewer adults are in here, the better."

"But *you'll* be in here," Miss Eames pointed out.

"The bogle won't see me. Not where I'll be waiting," said Alfred. He moved to stand flat against the wall beside the tunnel, then jerked his chin at the door near the foot of the stairs. "Jem, you're to guard that door. I doubt as how any bogle would try to use it, but there ain't no telling. So if a strange noise should trouble you, throw me a signal. And Ned . . ." His gaze shifted away from Jem, who was already on the move. "I'll want you on the landing, for I ain't easy in me mind regarding that other door up there."

Surprised, Ned glanced at the door in question. He couldn't imagine why a sewer bogle would use such a round-about route. But then again, the door might lead to a closet, and Ned had often heard Birdie talk about closet bogles.

"That door's locked," Jem informed Alfred. "I tried it on me way downstairs."

"It's still worth watching." The bogler's dark gaze skipped from one boy to the other as he lectured them. "You must yell if you see owt as seems untoward. And if yer way upstairs is blocked, just remember—you'll be safe inside this circle. Ain't no bogle on earth could pierce it."

He stamped his foot, drawing Ned's attention back to the second ring of salt. It was a closed circle and looked smaller than the other. But as Alfred explained, it was just a precaution.

"I'm expecting the bogle to come through that tunnel and head straight for Birdie," he assured the two boys. "It shouldn't trouble you—not while Birdie's singing. Just be sure to keep mum and stay still."

He waited for a moment. When no one said anything,

he went to stand beside the gaping hole, armed with his spear and his bag of salt. The others then took up their positions. Birdie stepped into the larger magic ring. Miss Eames hurried into the neighboring room — where she had to hide herself away, since Alfred didn't want her hovering on the threshold, scaring off the bogle.

Ned trudged up to the landing. He didn't have much of a view from there. Even when he squatted down, he couldn't see Birdie in her ring of salt. But he *could* see Jem and Alfred, as well as a tiny sliver of the hole in the wall.

He could also see Rosina Vokes sitting on the upper flight of stairs. When Ned caught her eye, she put a finger to her lips — and flashed him such a soft, pleading look that he couldn't bring himself to alert Alfred.

Then Birdie began to sing.

"I've traveled about a bit in me time
And of troubles I've seen a few
But found it better in every clime
To paddle me own canoe."

Birdie's voice was as clear and sweet as a cascade of silver bells. In that confined space it was also very loud, cutting through the air like a razor. Ned found himself marveling all over again at its strength and purity.

He saw Rosina's jaw drop and her pale eyes widen. But

he knew that he shouldn't be watching the actress. His job was to monitor every visible approach.

So he flicked a look at the door behind him as Birdie continued.

"Me wants are few. I care not at all
If me debts are paid when due.
I drive away strife in the ocean of life
When I paddle me own canoe."

A slight scuffling sound reached Ned's ears. Glancing sideways, he spotted Mr. Vokes creeping toward Rosina, one step at a time. Birdie's song appeared to be drawing him back downstairs.

Ned frowned at the actor before shifting his attention to Alfred, who stood quite still, poised to pounce. Ned couldn't decide if the sewery smell was getting worse, though he *did* feel a creeping sense of unease. Did it stem from his own anxiety, or was it evidence of an approaching bogle?

Suddenly he realized that Rosina was sitting very close to him now, on the bottom step of the second flight, trying to poke her head around the corner for a better view. And Ned couldn't stop her, because he wasn't allowed to move or speak.

Then Birdie launched into her next verse.

"Love yer neighbor as yerself
As the world you go traveling through.
And never sit down with a tear and a frown
But paddle yer own —"

A shriek from Jem cut her off. Something had shot out of the tunnel, slammed into the wall opposite, then bounced off and hit the floor. It looked like a giant flea, except that it was jet black, with a rubbery hide, huge fangs, and four pink eyes as big as salad plates. It landed by Jem, blocking his route to the ring of salt. He instinctively sprang straight up in the air, grabbed one of the water pipes, and swung himself *over* the bogle.

By the time the bogle rose to its feet, Jem had turned a midair somersault and landed inside the magic circle.

Water was now gushing from the pipe; he'd wrenched it apart at the joint. Horrified, Ned saw that the water was rapidly dissolving the salt, so he lunged toward a likely-looking shutoff valve he'd spotted earlier.

"Jem! Duck!" Alfred roared as the bogle reared up, hissing. Jem obeyed, and Alfred's spear flew over his head.

Foomp!

Suddenly there was no bogle. Nothing remained except a rapidly deflating, crusty black thing that looked like an oversize boil. Alfred's spear was sticking out of it.

"Are you hurt, lad?" The bogler dropped down beside Jem, who was curled up into a ball. As he slowly uncoiled himself, shaking his head, Birdie descended on him in a flutter of petticoats, with Miss Eames close at her heels.

Rosina, meanwhile, was staggering downstairs. "Oh my! Oh dear! I never did!" she croaked. Even her heavy makeup couldn't conceal her pallor; she was as white as the salt that had begun to liquefy at her feet.

Luckily Ned had been right about the shutoff valve. Water wasn't gushing from the pipe anymore.

"That pipe needs to be soldered," Ned observed hoarsely. He was still hanging off the valve, trying to stop his hands from shaking. But Rosina didn't seem to hear. She had reached the little group clustered around Jem, who was on his feet again, looking stunned.

"Are you a *circus performer?*" she squeaked. "Why, Freddie has the liveliest legs in the business, and *he* couldn't have done that!"

"Not to save my life," Mr. Vokes agreed, from the bottom of the stairs. He had taken off his crown to mop his damp forehead. "You ought to be on the stage, boy."

"And Birdie, too!" Rosina cried. "Have you ever *heard* such a voice, Fred?"

"Never."

"We must arrange an audition for you." By now the

color was returning to Rosina's face, though she still sounded very shrill. She reached out to grasp Birdie's arm. "My dear, you'll be the next Jenny Lind! And Jem might be the next Joseph Grimaldi!"

"Who's Joseph Grimaldi?" asked Jem.

"Oh, he was a *famous* dancing clown," Rosina replied. "They say he haunts this very theater. Don't they, Fred?"

As Mr. Vokes nodded, Alfred glanced at him and growled, "How do *you* know Jem's so fast on his feet? You was told to leave."

The actor made a sheepish face. Then he quickly produced some coins from the purse at his belt, by way of a distraction. "For your trouble, Mr. Bunce. Six shillings and sixpence was it not?" As he surrendered the money, the sound of a distant bell made him wince. "That's our call," he told his sister. "We must go."

Rosina grabbed both of Birdie's hands. "Come tomorrow morning. Come for an audition. I'll arrange one for you. *Promise* me."

Birdie nodded, her expression radiant. Ned had never seen her look so happy. When Rosina finally released her grip and retreated toward the staircase, Birdie rounded on Miss Eames and stammered, "I *must* go. You—you see that, don't you? I *must!*"

"Bring Jem with you!" Rosina cried from the landing.

Then she disappeared in a flurry of white gauze. Her brother followed more slowly, executing an elaborate farewell bow.

There was a brief silence. Finally Ned, whose gaze had drifted toward the bogle's remains, observed diffidently, "We should keep a bit o' that for Mr. Gilfoyle. Don't you think?"

8

OFFICIAL BUSINESS

Alfred Bunce received an unusual number of visitors the next morning.

The first arrived at around eight o'clock. He was an errand boy from the Theatre Royal, and he carried a message from Mr. Todd, the manager's secretary—who had scribbled down Alfred's address the night before. "Mr. Todd says as how Jem Barbary is to report to Mr. Chatterton's office at eleven o'clock, for an audition," the errand boy announced, lisping slightly. He then turned and ran back downstairs, leaving Ned open-mouthed on the threshold.

Alfred's next two visitors turned up at ten, while Ned was darning one of Jem's socks. Jem was darning the other.

Alfred didn't seem very surprised to see Birdie and Miss Eames at the door, though Birdie's glossy appearance made him blink.

"You look a picture today, lass," he said, ushering them into his stuffy garret. "You're off to the theater as well, I daresay?"

"Mr. Todd sent us a telegram," Birdie replied. She wore a dress of pale blue satin trimmed with silk braid and seemed to glow like a gas lamp.

Ned was dazzled.

"The gentleman declares himself very anxious to see Birdie—and I've no wish to disoblige Mr. Vokes, who seems respectable enough," Miss Eames explained in a sniffish tone that hinted at many hours of debate between herself and Birdie. "We thought we would take Jem along with us, if he's also been summoned."

"I have," Jem proudly confirmed.

"And you're going?" asked Birdie.

"Of course!" Jem stared at her as if she were mad. "Why not?"

Birdie raised her eyebrows but said nothing. Ned could imagine how she felt. Unlike Birdie, Jem had never expressed any interest in performing. He'd always talked as if bogling was his dream job. So Ned had been very surprised to hear him babble on about a stage career as they followed Alfred home from the theater the previous evening.

"Frederick Vokes is a dancer, and *he* has a watch worth at least thirty shillings!" Jem had confided to Ned, behind Alfred's back. "I saw him pull it out!"

"But what about Mr. Bunce? You *begged* him to take you on. Don't you want to be a bogler's boy no more?"

Jem had shrugged. "Bogling's better'n prigging, or sweeping out a grocer's shop. There ain't no future in it, though. Soon as I'm too big for a bogle's stomach, I'll be out o' work. 'Tain't the same for theater folk. Them Vokes sisters — why, they bin onstage since they was babies! And can expect to earn their keep as long as they're limber." Seeing Ned frown, Jem had quickly added, "Besides, I don't see as how there'll be much call for boglers now we got a committee doing the same job. Once the committee knows how to kill bogles in a scientific way, Mr. Bunce'll find hisself catching rats for a living. And *you'll* be selling fruit out of a coster's cart."

Ned now wondered if this was true — and if Alfred himself might be thinking the same thing. Certainly the bogler had raised no fuss about Jem's audition. Even when Mark Harewood suddenly appeared, with the news that Alfred was urgently needed at the General Post Office, Alfred didn't change his mind about Jem. "I'll have Ned to help me," the bogler said. "Besides, that post office is on a street off Newgate. So it's probably safer if Jem don't come."

Watching everyone exchange courtesies, Ned decided

that Mr. Harewood was much happier to see Miss Eames than she was to see him. The engineer even asked her to join the trip to the post office. "I couldn't persuade Razzy to come, because he had a previous engagement," Mr. Harewood remarked. "But if you were to replace him, Miss Eames, you could take notes and write the report yourself. As a representative of our research subcommittee."

Miss Eames, however, refused his invitation. Her first duty was to the child in her care, she said. Birdie's future was of great importance, and Miss Eames wanted to ensure that the Theatre Royal's management wouldn't exploit or misuse the girl.

"As if I'd let *that* happen," Birdie muttered, rolling her eyes. But she didn't say anything else. Instead she waved at Alfred, smiled at Ned, and disappeared downstairs before Ned had a chance to wish her good luck.

The whole room seemed dingier without her.

"Ah, well," said Mr. Harewood as Miss Eames hurried after Birdie, "it seems that *I* must do the note taking this time. I cannot endure the shame of being the only member of our committee not to have laid eyes on a bogle, Mr. Bunce. Even old Gilfoyle has the better of me there. But I'm about to remedy the situation and will be chaffed no longer for my failings."

"Mr. Wardle ain't never seen no bogle neither," Ned interrupted. "He weren't in the Newgate cellar yesterday."

"Was he not? In that case, I shall be able to chaff *him.*"
Mr. Harewood was looking tidier than he had at their last
meeting. He wore a soft felt hat, a pair of gray kid gloves, and
a silk-lined frock coat. Nevertheless, there was something
wild about his appearance. His hair was too long, perhaps,
or his manner too energetic. Was that why Miss Eames had
been slightly cool with him?

"I walked here from Trafalgar Square," Mr. Harewood
went on, "but we must take a cab to the post office. If you're
ready, Mr. Bunce?"

"Aye." Alfred reached for his sack.

"I shall want a full report on your job at the theater last
night. Was there a bogle? Yes? I thought as much." Mr. Harewood held the door open for Alfred and Ned, just as if they
were gentlemen. Ned could only assume he had done it in a
fit of absent-mindedness. "I've been studying our maps and
have established that Mr. Wardle was correct: A sewer *does*
pass beneath the Theatre Royal. It commences at the junction of Drury Lane and Long Acre, runs along the Strand,
then enters the Thames via Norfolk Street."

Ned thought about this as he made his way downstairs.
It was only after a hansom cab had been hailed and they had
all piled into it that he finally ventured to ask Mr. Harewood
if there was a gate on the Norfolk Street sewer outfall.

"I never bin that far west—not along the riverbank,"
Ned admitted. "It's the eastern mudflats I know."

"Alas, I fear I'm no better acquainted with the outfalls than you are," said Mr. Harewood, "though I'm sure Mr. Wardle can help us. Why?"

"Well ..." Ned took a deep breath. He always felt slightly tongue-tied in the presence of well-educated people and couldn't help stammering as he answered Mr. Harewood's question. "I—I were puzzling as to how we might flush them bogles into the river, and then I thought to meself: What if they already live there?" When the engineer didn't scoff at this notion, Ned found the courage to suggest, "Mebbe we should check the tide tables. If there's kids being taken when the tide is high—"

"Then we might have ourselves a crop of river monsters coming up the sewers!" Mr. Harewood finished. He beamed at Ned, who was wedged into the seat beside him. "My word, but you're a sharp lad! I like the way you think— indeed I do!"

Ned flushed with pleasure.

"Tide tables are easy enough to procure," the engineer went on. "As for river monsters, Gilfoyle is the one to ask about *them*. He's made a study of the subject." Mr. Harewood suddenly shifted his gaze to Alfred, who was sitting on Ned's right. "I should tell you, by the by, that Gilfoyle intends to consult his friend at Apothecaries' Hall today, concerning any toxins that might have been applied to your spear, Mr. Bunce. If the news is good, he'll inform us directly."

"I bin thinking about that" was Alfred's unexpected response. "And I've a better idea."

Ned stared at him in surprise. Even Mr. Harewood was taken aback. "You do?" he asked.

"Aye." Alfred's voice quavered as their cab bounced over a rut in the road. "Me old master, Daniel Piggin, were a Derbyshire man. His sister still lives near Derby. She's a 'cunning woman,' trained in herbs and old lore." He glanced inquiringly at Mr. Harewood, who gave an encouraging nod.

"Folk medicine," the engineer said. "I understand."

"If anyone knows owt about that spear, it's Mother May," Alfred continued. "She and her brother was very close at one time."

"I see." Mr. Harewood was still nodding. "Then perhaps you should write to her, Mr. Bunce?"

A rare smile cracked across Alfred's dour face. "I never learned to write, Mr. Harewood," he pointed out, "and I doubt Mother May ever learned to read. But I thought as how I might take a train to the Peak District, if you've no objection."

"None at all, Mr. Bunce!" Mr. Harewood sounded very keen. "I think it an excellent notion! And I shall ask Mr. Wardle to reimburse you for any expenses you might incur, since the committee has a fund to cover such costs. When were you planning to go?"

Alfred shrugged. "Just as soon as I ain't needed here. Which may be a good while."

The engineer turned his head to peer out the window. "Personally I'd encourage you to take your trip before our next meeting, since Mother May's contribution could be vital. Aha! We've arrived! Good. I told Mr. Clegg we'd be here by eleven."

"Who is Mr. Clegg, sir?" Ned asked as the cab lurched to a standstill.

"He is Chief Clerk to the Secretary of the Postmaster General."

Ned didn't find this answer very illuminating. But he climbed out of the cab without saying another word and was soon standing in the street with Alfred while Mr. Harewood paid their driver.

Ned had never seen the General Post Office up close before. Its immensity awed him, for the building occupied an entire city block. Each column on its façade was at least six feet wide. Each window was nearly as big as Alfred's whole garret room. The entrance was thronged with people, who poured in and out with more parcels and letters and sacks than Ned had ever seen in his life.

There was construction going on across the street, and the noise was deafening.

"Come along!" Mr. Harewood said loudly as their cabman cracked his whip. "We'll ask for Mr. Clegg in the main office." He began to climb the front steps, with Ned and Alfred close behind. Though pushing through the crowds wasn't easy, they at last found themselves in a grand public hall. The hall was perhaps fifty feet high and at least five times as long, and so crammed with people that Ned had to grab Alfred's sleeve for fear of losing him.

"Stay with me!" Mr. Harewood bellowed over the roar of voices. Then, instead of joining a line, he went straight to the nearest counter and interrupted a transaction involving a parcel bound for Walthamstow.

"Pardon me," he said to the bemused mail clerk, "but I've an appointment with Mr. Clegg. Could you direct me to the Secretary's office, please?"

"You'll have to wait your turn, sir," the clerk replied, causing Mr. Harewood to throw out his chest, square his broad shoulders, and scowl impatiently.

"Indeed I shall not!" the engineer snapped. "I'm here at the request of Mr. John Tilly, Secretary to the Postmaster General! He has engaged my friend, Mr. Alfred Bunce, on an urgent matter! Now kindly tell me where I may find Mr. Clegg."

Ned was glancing around the room when Mr. Harewood uttered Alfred's name. So when a nearby newsboy started at the sound and fixed his penetrating gaze on Alfred,

Ned observed that fleeting look. For an instant the newsboy stood frozen. Then he bolted toward the front door before Ned could do more than open his mouth.

"*Thank* you!" Mr. Harewood spat. He was still addressing the mail clerk, who must have grudgingly passed him a scrap of information, because he suddenly whirled around and said to Alfred, "This way! Follow me!"

Ned was given no choice. If he didn't set off with them immediately, he would be left behind. But he kept looking back, trying not to lose sight of the newsboy, until a heavy door suddenly cut off his view of the hall.

After that there was nothing for him to do but go forward into the mysterious depths of the post office.

The Lowest Level

"Mr. Harewood. How do you do, sir?"

"Mr. Clegg."

The two men bowed. Mr. Clegg was a plump, elegant, gray-haired gentleman with a discreet mustache and a bland expression. His boots shone like polished jet.

"I take it this is Mr. Bunce?" he asked, peering at Alfred through a gold-rimmed monocle.

"Mr. Alfred Bunce. The bogler," Mr. Harewood confirmed.

Mr. Clegg nodded. "Good morning, Mr. Bunce," he said smoothly. Then he gestured at the policeman beside him. "May I introduce Constable Juddick? We have an

Internal Police Office here, and Emmet Juddick is one of our four constables. I have asked him to help you, since I am unfortunately pressed for time."

Constable Juddick was large and burly, with a crooked nose, a freckled face, and bushy red side-whiskers. His voice sounded like gravel crunching underfoot.

"Good morning, Mr. Bunce. Mr. Harewood, sir," he growled. When his gaze fell on Ned, he didn't say a word, but his brisk nod was comforting. Unlike Mr. Clegg, the policeman actually seemed aware of Ned's existence.

"Constable Juddick is far better informed than I am on the subject of disappearing boys," Mr. Clegg went on. "Is that not so, Constable?"

"Yes, sir."

"I am merely a humble conduit, transmitting his concerns." The Chief Clerk smirked a little, as if he'd just told a joke. Then he excused himself. "Do tell me how you fared," he politely requested, bowing again to Mr. Harewood. "I shall be most interested in your findings. And I'll be expecting a full report from *you*, Constable."

"Yes, sir."

"Good day, gentlemen. Please forgive me. I really must go . . ."

Within seconds he'd vanished, leaving his visitors marooned with Constable Juddick in a small, wood-paneled office. Mr. Harewood didn't look terribly impressed, Ned thought. And Alfred was becoming impatient.

"Where was them kids last seen?" he asked the policeman.

"Downstairs." Constable Juddick spoke flatly, in clipped sentences. "Three of 'em went missing. All telegraph boys. The new Telegraph Office ain't open yet, so the boys still congregate in our basement before and after their shifts."

"In that case, you'd best show us the basement," said Alfred, hoisting his sack up onto his shoulder. With a nod, Constable Juddick turned on his heel and marched into the corridor outside, setting a course for the nearest staircase.

As they made their way down to the lowest level, past a room full of stamping machines, another full of weighing equipment, and a third lined with pigeonholes, Alfred continued to ask questions. How old were the missing boys? Were they small for their age? Had anyone seen or heard anything peculiar before they vanished? To all these inquiries Constable Juddick gave only one answer, in a grinding monotone.

"Corporal Catty will know, for he's the head delivery boy."

Ned was surprised to hear that telegraph boys had military ranks. Despite their blue serge uniforms, they'd never impressed him as being very disciplined. He was just wondering if they saluted each other, like real soldiers, when he found himself in a room full of pipes and valves and pressure gauges — and he immediately lost interest in the telegraph boys.

"This ain't no hydraulic lift!" he exclaimed before he could stop himself.

Ahead of him, Mr. Harewood paused and said, "No. It's a warm-air apparatus, for heating the gasometer. See that device? It regulates the supply of gas to all the burners in this building — including that one over there."

"I seen dry meters on occasion, but nothing like this." Ned spoke absent-mindedly as he gazed at something that looked like a cross between a tank and a steam engine. He knew that he shouldn't linger, because Alfred and the policeman were already out of sight. But he couldn't tear himself away. "It's a wonder, ain't it?"

Mr. Harewood sniffed. "It does its job, I daresay, but not with any degree of elegance. A *perfect* piece of engineering combines several functions in an aesthetically pleasing manner." He took Ned's arm and began to lecture him as they slowly made their way out of the room. "Take Christopher Wren, for instance. Although his Monument was designed to commemorate the Great Fire of London, it is also a giant zenith telescope. By opening a trapdoor in the gilded orb at the top of the tower, you can watch the night sky from a laboratory in the basement."

"You mean a thing's much better if it does twice the work?" Ned asked. "Like the street lamps on Holborn Viaduct? *They* got vents in 'em as lets out sewer gas . . ."

"Exactly! That is exactly what I mean!" Mr. Harewood's grip on Ned's arm tightened. "Only consider, for example, how ingenious it would be to combine the regulation of the gas supply in this building with the regulation of its pneumatic dispatches! They both rely on a careful manipulation of pressure—"

"Excuse me, sir, but what is a pneumatic dispatch?"

Mr. Harewood stopped abruptly. "Oh, my dear fellow, a pneumatic dispatch is the very *latest* engineering marvel!" He began to describe how mail was now being carried all the way from Euston Station to the General Post Office inside capsules that traveled along an underground tube. Powered by compressed air in one direction and atmospheric pressure in the other, each capsule acted as a kind of piston, moved by a steam-powered reversible fan that created a vacuum.

Mr. Harewood's vivid description filled Ned with excitement.

"Can we see it?" he demanded. "Is it down here, Mr. Harewood?"

"I believe there *is* a terminus," the engineer replied, then glanced around and winced. "Oh dear," he said, dropping Ned's arm. "We seem to have lost the others."

It was true. They had taken a wrong turn and were now

standing in a long, empty hallway lined with doors and utility pipes. Two of the doors were sheathed in iron. Another was studded with locks.

"Hello?" Ned's raised voice echoed off the vaulted ceiling. *"Mr. Bunce?"*

"Oi!" came a sharp rejoinder. "What're *you* doing down 'ere?"

Ned and Mr. Harewood spun around to find themselves face to face with two telegraph boys: one sandy haired and bandy legged, the other tall, swarthy, and chinless. Ned judged them to be between thirteen and sixteen years old.

"We're looking for Corporal Catty," Mr. Harewood informed them.

"Catty? He's in the kitchen." The taller boy jerked his thumb at an adjoining corridor. "Did you come with them others? Old Judd and that Go-Devil Man?"

"We did," said Mr. Harewood.

The smaller boy, who appeared to be chewing tobacco, spat on the floor. "Then I wish you the best o' luck," he said. "I'm right sick o' pairing off. Why, we can't go to the privy alone now! And must report every other step we take . . ."

He was still grumbling as he and his friend squeezed past Mr. Harewood, on their way to something they called the dispatch room. "Tell Catty you saw us," the taller boy added, "else he'll send out a search party, the silly old hen."

"Tell him Joe's too big for a bogle's stomach, and I'm

too stringy," his friend joked before vanishing around a corner.

Watching them go, Mr. Harewood murmured, "Safety in numbers, eh? I'm not surprised they're pairing off, though I have to say, they don't *seem* very worried."

"Uh—Mr. Harewood, sir?" Ned wasn't much interested in the telegraph boys. "I bin thinking . . ."

"Again?" The engineer flashed Ned an amused look before starting down the kitchen passage. "Perhaps we'd better find the others before we distract ourselves with more scientific speculation. We don't want to get lost a second time, do we?"

"No, sir, but—well, there's summat I need to know." Scampering to catch up, Ned breathlessly inquired, "If we can't flush them bogles out o' the sewers with water, can we do it with air?"

"Like the pneumatic tube, you mean? I doubt it. London's sewer system is so riddled with leaks that the amount of pressure required would be beyond our capacity to generate."

"Oh."

"It's a cunning thought, though." Mr. Harewood stopped in front of a closed door at the end of the passage, his hand on the knob and his eyes on Ned's face. "You're a clever lad. Can you read, by any chance?"

Ned shook his head.

"What a pity," said Mr. Harewood. "Still, that's not an insurmountable problem. Not at your age." Then he pushed open the door, revealing a stone-floored kitchen warmed by a grate full of glowing embers. Alfred and the policeman were standing in front of the grate with a skinny youth in a blue-serge uniform. Their heads snapped around when they heard the hinges creak.

"Ah!" The skinny youth's worried expression was transformed into one of intense relief. "We was wondering where you'd got to!"

"Would you be Corporal Catty?" asked Mr. Harewood.

"I am, sir. How did you know?" Without waiting for an answer, the youth glanced nervously at Alfred. "I sent all them other lads away. I thought it best."

"They spend too much time down here in any case, drinking tea and making mischief," the policeman remarked. He glared at the skinny youth, who stammered, "I—I do what I can, sir! They're right downy, some of 'em!"

Constable Juddick sniffed as Ned studied Corporal Catty. Several years older than the other two boys, the corporal was all skin and bone, with a long neck, stooped shoulders, and anxious, blinking, bloodshot eyes. He had no beard to speak of, and his prominent Adam's apple slid up and down like a piston when he swallowed.

Ned suspected that he'd been promoted to his present

rank because he obeyed the rules, not because he was confi-
dent enough to enforce them.

"This is a curious space." Mr. Harewood was peering at
one of the brick walls, which had three stone pillars embed-
ded in it. Even Ned could see that these massive, rounded
pillars were at odds with the rest of the kitchen, which was
small and mean. The fireplace was skimpy; the ceiling was
low; there was only one gas jet, and no scullery to speak of.
"I've heard that a crypt was laid open here, when the site
was being cleared for construction," Mr. Harewood continued. "It contained a stone coffin, with a skeleton inside." As
Corporal Catty blanched, the engineer cheerfully concluded,
"Perhaps Saint Martin's crypt has been incorporated into
this basement! It certainly looks older than the building
above."

"If that's true, then mebbe it *weren't* the bogle as took
them lads," said Corporal Catty. "Mebbe a ghost done it."

"Nonsense." The policeman snorted. "Ghosts don't ab-
duct people."

"What makes you think they was abducted?" Alfred
broke in. "Boys have bin known to run away on occasion."

"Not these boys, sir. They never had cause to complain,
for all they was the youngest." Corporal Catty turned to
Constable Juddick for support. "Ain't no bullying here. And
the money's good too. Five shillings a week they start on."

Ned blinked. Although five shillings a week sounded a little meager, he himself had lived on much less. He decided that if Alfred was ever to dismiss him, he'd be glad enough to work as a telegraph boy.

But he didn't like to think about being on his own again.

"Was them boys the smallest as well as the youngest?" Alfred queried. On receiving a nod from the corporal, he went on to ask, "Where did you last see 'em?"

"The boys, sir? Why—they was last seen in this room." As Alfred's gaze flickered toward the fireplace, Corporal Catty added, "But that don't signify, since we know this ain't where they perished."

Alfred frowned. "You do?"

"Of course. Didn't Mr. Clegg tell you?"

"Tell me what?"

"We seen the bogle, Mr. Bunce. Me and two of the other boys, Davy and little Dan. All three of us."

Ned blinked. Alfred said, "Where?"

"In there." Corporal Catty pointed at a door to his left. "It lives in the lavatory. Didn't you know? Them poor lads never stood a chance, what with their kicksies being down around their ankles . . ."

10

THE PRIVY BOGLE

Ned was growing hoarse.

He had been standing in the lavatory for a couple of hours, tonelessly chanting nursery rhymes — which were the only songs he really knew. To his left was a row of urinals. To his right, six wooden cubicles each contained a porcelain toilet bowl and a suspended cistern. In front of him was an open door leading to a short, narrow passage. Behind him were two basins, complete with cold-water taps, and a covered drain in the floor.

Alfred had identified this drain as the most likely source of bogle activity. So he had traced out his circle of salt just a few feet away from it, then positioned himself in the cubicle closest to the basins.

Half of Alfred's shadowy figure was reflected in the mirror that Ned was holding.

"Who killed cock robin?
I, said the sparrow,
With me bow and arrow
I killed cock robin."

As Ned droned on, he could see Alfred shifting his weight—but he couldn't see Mr. Harewood. The engineer was hiding in the cubicle next to Alfred's, having been warned to keep well back, out of sight. Corporal Catty and Constable Juddick had been told to stay in the kitchen.

Yet still the bogle didn't come. Ned wondered if it could somehow sense that there were adults in the room. This seemed unlikely, since Alfred had never encountered any problems before. By keeping still and silent, the bogler had fooled every bogle he'd ever been hired to kill.

Ned coughed and cleared his throat before launching into the next verse.

"Who saw him die?
I, said the fly.

With me little eye
I saw him die."

"Mr. Bunce?" Constable Juddick's voice echoed down the passage to the kitchen. Lifting his gaze, Ned saw the policeman's head appear around a distant corner, backlit by a wall-mounted gas jet. "We've a lot o' people out here waiting to use the water closet, sir. Will you be much longer?"

Alfred didn't reply, but his furious scowl was captured in Ned's looking glass.

"Mebbe there *ain't* no bogle," the policeman continued. "If there was, surely it would have showed itself by now?"

Still Alfred didn't answer. Perhaps he was hoping that Constable Juddick would take the hint and withdraw. Ned knew that it sometimes wasn't easy to lure a bogle out of its lair. Birdie had once told Ned about a three-hour ordeal in an empty tanner's vat.

Ned gnawed at his bottom lip, feeling useless. Could his singing be the problem? Would Birdie have succeeded where he had failed?

He was sure that Alfred must be asking himself the same question.

"Mr. Bunce?" Suddenly Mr. Harewood spoke from his hiding place, in a rough whisper. "Should we come back this evening? It will be less busy by then I daresay."

Ned winced, expecting Alfred to explode. But instead of snarling at Mr. Harewood, the bogler simply remarked through clenched teeth, "This place don't close at night."

"Oh, yes. Of course. How silly of me." Mr. Harewood sounded embarrassed.

"And Catty said them kids disappeared during the day," Alfred continued as a series of gears turned in Ned's brain.

With a gasp, Ned swung around. "Mr. Bunce?"

"Shh!"

"I'm sorry, Mr. Bunce, but what if it's waiting for a signal?" Before Alfred could do more than glare at him, Ned quickly added, "Mebbe the bogle comes whenever it hears a cistern flush. Mebbe *that's* what it's bin listening for."

There was a brief silence. The only sound was a tap dripping. *Plink. Plink. Plink.* Then Mr. Harewood murmured, "I say! What a clever notion!"

"It is." Alfred stepped into the light, his spear in one hand, his bag of salt in the other. His gaze traveled around the room, darting from the drain to the door to the basins and back to the cubicle. Then he said, "This here is a trap. You pull the chain, go to wash yer hands—"

"—and the bogle pops up between you and the door!" Ned finished.

"If you're young enough." Alfred was nodding, his expression grim. "I mislike this arrangement. It don't give you nowhere to run, Ned."

Ned saw that instantly. "Mebbe if we was to put a ring o' salt in there, I could use it to shield meself," he suggested, pointing at the booth that Alfred had just left. "A *closed* ring o' salt. All around the bowl."

By this time Mr. Harewood had emerged from his cubicle. "Are you certain that our bogle is going to come through the grate in the floor?" he asked. "What if Ned pulls the chain and it comes shooting straight out of the water closet?"

"'Tain't likely," said Alfred. "But if I lay a circle around the bowl, Ned'll be safe enough." Retreating into the nearest booth, he proceeded to surround the toilet with a ring of salt as Mr. Harewood went to the exit and loudly declared, "We shan't be much longer, Constable! Have a little more patience, if you please!"

"What about *this* circle, Mr. Bunce?" Ned indicated the ring that lay near the drain. "Should it be left?"

"Aye. It won't do no harm." Alfred held the cubicle door open as he told Ned to head straight for the nearest basin after he'd flushed the toilet. "Keep yer eyes on yer looking glass. I'll be in the farthest booth but one. It's the closest I can get without alerting the bogle." His dark, solemn gaze was fixed on Ned. "I ain't easy in me mind about this, lad. Are you? For if you'd rather not do it, I can allus come back with Jem. He's quicker'n you, though not so canny."

Ned colored. He didn't resent the comparison—which was a fair one—but he had no intention of admitting that he wasn't up to the job.

"I can do it," he croaked, wondering if this was actually true.

"A glass hung up here might have saved three lives," the bogler went on, his gaze shifting to the blank tiled wall above the basins. "Or at least given the poor lads a warning." Then he sighed and turned to Mr. Harewood, who was still hovering on the threshold. "You'd best get in there," he instructed, jerking his chin at one of the more distant cubicles. "But don't so much as blink, if you please, and stay quiet."

Mr. Harewood nodded. He moved into position as Ned asked in a nervous undertone, "Am I to sing, Mr. Bunce?"

"Aye, lad. Keep at it. You might as well."

So when Ned finally found himself alone in a cramped little cedar booth, staring down at a white porcelain toilet, he cleared his throat, took a deep, calming breath, and started singing again.

"Who caught his blood?
I, said the fish.
In me little dish
I caught his blood."

He stood with his toes almost touching the ring of salt. There was writing on the toilet, which Ned couldn't read. But that didn't matter. He knew how flush toilets worked, though he'd seen very few of them. He tried to comfort himself with thoughts of the cistern's ingenious ball cock as he croaked out yet another verse, his pulse racing and his knees trembling.

> *"Who'll make his shroud?*
> *I, said the beetle.*
> *With a thread and needle*
> *I'll make his shroud."*

Ned found it hard to sing because his mouth was so dry. He couldn't seem to breathe properly either. And he *certainly* didn't feel ready to confront the bogle. But at last he braced himself, lifted his hand mirror until his own face was reflected in it, and made a grab for the chain dangling above his head.

Who-o-osh!

Water was still sloshing down the pipe when Ned reached the basins. Groping for a tap with one hand, he kept his eyes fixed on the little scene captured in the other. He could see the drain. He could see the exit. He could see Mr. Bunce peering out from behind a cedar wall . . .

He could see the bogle, silently appearing.

"Who'll dig his grave?
I, said the owl.
With me pick and shovel
I'll dig his grave."

Ned's voice cracked as he watched thick, black, bubbling goo dislodge the drain's metal grate and carry it sideways. Then came something long and sticky and featureless, like a giant slug, which reared up and suddenly expanded—*Pop!* Four long, spiky arms erupted, each topped with a bouquet of blood-red talons. A lashing tail was crowned with spikes. There were two clawed feet and three forked tongues and a gargoyle's head and two rows of barbed teeth . . .

Ned kept singing while Alfred stealthily raised his spear.

"Who'll toll the bell?
I, said the bull.
Because I can pull—"

The spear flashed past. Ned ducked and leaped sideways into the nearest cubicle as a deafening screech filled the air. The smell that followed was even worse than the noise.

Coughing and gagging, Ned jumped into the ring of salt and scrambled up onto the wooden toilet seat.

He was still perched there when Alfred rasped, "Ned? Are you all right, lad?"

Ned couldn't speak. He was still retching when Alfred appeared at the cubicle door, holding his nose.

"Are you hurt?" the bogler demanded.

Ned's response was a shake of the head.

"We'd best hook it. This stench may be poisonous." Alfred ushered Ned out of the cubicle and toward the exit. The bogle's formless remains were so bulky that Ned stopped in his tracks, astonished.

"Why ain't it gone?" he asked hoarsely, aware that most bogles either popped, melted, or evaporated when they were killed. They usually left a smear or a scorch mark, not a heap of singed jelly the size of a small cow. "I don't understand."

"Neither do I," Alfred said grimly. He yanked at Ned's arm, pulling him away from the fumes that were making their eyes water. "I ain't never seen so much gristle left behind, nor heard such a noise, nor smelt such a reek. 'Tain't customary. Summat's wrong."

"Wrong?" Ned echoed in alarm. But Alfred had already turned to Mr. Harewood, who was emerging from his hidey-hole white-faced and gasping.

"Out," snapped Alfred. "Now."

"But I must collect a sample," Mr. Harewood wheezed. "I promised Gilfoyle—"

"We'll come back when the air's clear." As Alfred crossed the threshold, he glanced back over his shoulder. "And we must clean up that bogle, if it's still there—though I'm puzzled as to how we'd go about it."

"Wash it down the drain?" Ned suggested.

"Aye, if it don't poison the sewers." Alfred hawked and spat, then looked up and grimaced as he saw Constable Juddick advancing down the passage toward them. "Yer friends'll have to wait a little longer, Constable," he announced. "The bogle's gone, but I wouldn't go in there just yet. The stench is enough to turn yer stomach."

11

Hunted

There was a message waiting for them when they emerged from the lavatory. It was a note from Erasmus Gilfoyle, hand delivered by an errand boy. Mr. Gilfoyle was requesting that Alfred come directly to Apothecaries' Hall on Water Lane as soon as he'd finished at the General Post Office.

"Two laboratory boys have vanished under mysterious circumstances," Mr. Harewood explained as he studied the note. "Apparently the Superintending Chemical Operator is willing to concede that a 'creature of indeterminate origin' may be responsible for their disappearance." The engineer raised his eyebrows. "What do you think, Mr. Bunce? We could walk to the hall from here. We might walk straight up

Newgate Street, then left at the prison and across Ludgate Hill."

Ned and Alfred exchanged a wary glance. The bogler looked as tired as Ned felt.

"I daresay we *could* do it," Alfred rumbled at last, "if Ned's fit enough."

"I am," Ned replied stoutly. Though he was still shaking from his encounter with the bogle, he didn't want to disappoint Alfred—or Mr. Harewood. "When I were a mudlark, there was rats as big as bogles on the riverbank, and cutthroats more dangerous still," he went on, hoping to convince himself as much as Alfred. "Ain't no need to fret about me, Mr. Bunce. I'm game, sir."

Alfred eyed Ned skeptically but refrained from voicing his doubts to Mr. Harewood. So when the three of them finally emerged from the post office, they walked south toward Newgate Street, turning right when they reached the first corner. Mr. Harewood took the lead. He marched along energetically, flushed and talkative, carrying a chunk of dead bogle in a china jar obtained from one of the telegraph boys. "That creature was so *big!*" he gabbled. "I had no idea! And so difficult to classify. Was it a reptile? A mammal? A curious conflation, like the Australian platypus? Poor Razzy will have a hard time of it!"

Alfred responded with the occasional grunt. As he shuffled along, bent beneath the weight of his sack, he kept glancing around suspiciously, his dark gaze flitting from face to face. Ned didn't blame him, for they were back in Jack Gammon's territory. Every step took them closer to Cock Lane, where the butcher's modest little shop front, festooned with sausages, cleverly concealed the extent of Salty Jack's criminal empire.

Walking down Newgate Street, Ned felt as if he were entering a bogle's lair. There was an ominous quality to the whole scene. Perhaps it had something to do with the wintry light or the looming bulk of Newgate Prison. Perhaps it was because Alfred had killed a bogle in almost every building scattered along their route: Newgate Market, Christ's Hospital School, the Viaduct Tavern, Saint Sepulchre's Church . . .

"I must mark it on our map," Mr. Harewood was saying. "It's a pity I cannot recall which sewer passes under the post office."

They were approaching Giltspur Street, where Ned had once tackled the fugitive Sarah Pickles and brought her to the ground. Although she was now in Newgate Prison, awaiting trial, her accomplice Salty Jack was lurking far too close for comfort, in Ned's opinion. As he passed Giltspur Street, Ned caught a fleeting glimpse of Cock Lane and quickly turned his head away.

At the same instant, he spotted a familiar face across the road.

Why, he thought, *it's that newsboy from the post office!*

" ... and the Chemical Operator might undertake to analyze this sample, if we make it worth his while ..." Mr. Harewood continued, oblivious to Ned's sudden intake of breath. There was no mistaking the newsboy's tartan tweed cap or bright blue eyes. Though he couldn't have been more than eight or nine years old, he already had the kind of pinched, cagey, watchful expression that marked him as a thief or a lookout. Jem Barbary had worn the same expression when he was working for Sarah Pickles.

"Mr. Bunce?" Ned grabbed Alfred's sleeve. "We're being followed."

"What?" Alfred stopped short.

"I didn't tell you earlier ..." As Ned hurriedly explained, Alfred began to frown, but he was smart enough not to glance in the newsboy's direction.

Mr. Harewood wasn't quite so quick on the uptake, though he soon turned back when he realized that his friends had fallen behind. He joined them eagerly, his eyes sparkling and his cheeks flushed. On hearing Ned's report, however, his sunny face darkened.

"Why, what a damnable cheek!" he growled—and then looked at the newsboy.

"*Sst!* No!" Ned hissed, but it was too late. The newsboy caught Mr. Harewood's eye. There was a heartbeat's pause. Then the boy ducked, swiveled, and darted into the nearest cross street.

"I'll catch the rascal!" Mr. Harewood exclaimed. He thrust his china pot into Ned's hands before bolting across the road like a foxhound.

"Wait!" Ned cried. "Mr. Harewood!"

"He'll get hisself killed," Alfred muttered, setting off in pursuit. With Ned at his heels he dodged a hackney cab, jumped over a puddle, and headed after Mr. Harewood, who was struggling to keep up with the newsboy. After dashing past the Newgate pump, Mr. Harewood elbowed his way through the crowds spilling out of a tavern door, then plunged into a narrow lane opposite the prison.

Alfred swore under his breath. His pace slowed as he eyed the mouth of the lane, which looked dark and seedy. "I don't like this," he said. "This here is a trap, like as not."

Ned shivered. "Mr. Harewood!" he yelled. "Come back!"

"Mr. Harewood! Come back!" mimicked a youth lounging against the tavern wall. His friends all laughed. Ned blushed.

"You stay close to me, d'you hear?" Alfred told him, ignoring the jeers of their drunken audience. As he slowly advanced, he pulled his sack off his shoulder and tucked it under his arm. Ned couldn't help wondering if Alfred planned to use his spear.

Beyond the tavern a cobbled passage ran between two rows of sooty, blank-faced shops. The passage was cluttered with carts and barrows. About halfway down its crooked length another alley opened onto it — and Ned spied Mr. Harewood vanishing around a corner, pursued by the shrill curses of a woman who'd just been knocked sideways. "Watch where ye're going!" she squawked, stooping to pick up her basket. One glance told Ned that she probably wasn't a threat, even though she looked a bit like Sarah Pickles. The man near her also seemed harmless; he was small and thin and wore an ink-spattered apron. But what about the heavily pockmarked porter hovering behind him? Or the man in the blue butcher's smock crossing the street up ahead? Were *they* dangerous?

Ned couldn't tell. He'd never laid eyes on Jack Gammon — or on any of his associates. Except, of course, for Sarah Pickles.

All at once a volley of furious shouts was cut short, as if a door had slammed shut on the sound. By the time Alfred and Ned rounded the next corner, Mr. Harewood was already on his back in the middle of the alley, with both hands clamped over his nose. There was no sign of the newsboy. But through a screen of startled bystanders — all of whom were converging on Mr. Harewood, offering their assistance — Ned saw a man running away.

"There!" Ned shouted, nearly dropping the china pot. "Stop! Thief!" As he took a step forward, however, Alfred dragged him back. "That man!" cried Ned, pointing. "He'll escape!"

Alfred wouldn't let go of Ned's arm. "Leave it. We shouldn't linger. Though Jack Gammon knows what Jem looks like, that don't mean his cronies do. For all we know, there's folk in this neighborhood as think *you're* Jem, on account o' you're with me."

Ned felt a chill run down his spine. Mr. Harewood scrambled to his feet, pushing away every helping hand extended toward him. He was fumbling in his pockets—for a handkerchief, perhaps. His nose was bleeding, and his voice sounded odd.

"Thad scoundrel strugg me!" he barked. "I shall inform the police *ad once.*"

"Mr. Harewood? We cannot stay," Alfred began. Then he frowned on seeing the engineer rifle through his pockets more and more frantically.

"My poggedbook!" Mr. Harewood rounded on Alfred, wide-eyed and gasping. "Id's been stolen!"

There was a murmur of shocked sympathy from his audience. "Aye, no one's safe in these parts," said a stonemason who was powdered with white dust. And a watchmaker wearing a bulky eyeglass on a chain murmured, "Are you sure it is nowhere about?"

Ned scanned the surrounding cobbles but saw no sign

of any pocketbook. Alfred, meanwhile, was drawing Mr. Harewood aside, away from the curious crowd. "Did you see where the boy went?" Alfred asked in an undertone.

"The boy?" Mr. Harewood seemed confused.

"The boy you was chasing," said Alfred. "I'm persuaded he had a protector. One o' the butcher's men, I daresay."

"You thing so?" Mr. Harewood accepted the rag Alfred had produced from his sack, pressing it to his bloody nose. "*I'm* inclined to believe a gang of pigpoggeds lured me here. Thad wretched fellow toog me by surprise." Before Alfred could object, Mr. Harewood turned to Ned and murmured, "I didden catch more than a glimpse of the boy. Can you describe him to me?"

"Yes, sir," Ned replied. "He were eight or nine years old, smaller'n I am, with blue eyes and light hair, wearing a tartan tweed cap—"

"Good." Mr. Harewood cut him off. "And I saw the *other* blaggard well enough—he was a big fellow with no hair and a scar on his lefd eyebrow. So you musd come with me to the nearesd station house, Ned. I believe id's in Smithfield. Or perhaps there's a constable ad the Old Bailey?"

"Ned cannot stay, sir. Not in this quarter." Seeing the engineer blink, Alfred quickly explained, "I'm a marked man hereabouts, and Ned is likely to be mistook for Jem. He ain't safe here."

"Oh." Mr. Harewood glanced at Ned, then at the small crowd now dispersing nearby. "I see . . ."

"And Mr. Gilfoyle is expecting me at Apothecaries' Hall, besides," Alfred continued. "I should take Ned straight to Water Lane while you go to the police." Eyeing Mr. Harewood's stained rag, the bogler finished, "I'd have that nose seen to, in addition."

Mr. Harewood suddenly capitulated. "Yes, you should go. Id would be wrong to delay poor Razzy. I shall repord to the police, and perhaps join you in an hour or so." He nodded at Alfred but paused for a moment in front of Ned. "You musd give thad sample to Mr. Gilfoyle. He'll know whad to do with id. Can I trusd you with such a commission, my boy?"

"Yes, sir," Ned answered.

"I hope id's nod been too knogged aboud," Mr. Harewood went on, lifting the lid of the china jar. Then he yelped in dismay and spluttered, "Why, whad's this? Whad happened? I cannod understand . . ."

For inside the jar was nothing more than a brown smear, where once there had been a great dollop of black jelly.

12

A Very Strange Place

Apothecaries' Hall was a fine old building wrapped around a central courtyard. It was several stories high, constructed of brick and stucco, with a carved coat of arms set over its main entrance. To the left of this entrance was a shop that sold medicine, herbs, and chemicals. The building also contained a packing room, a warehouse, a mill house, a factory, an accountants' office, a series of examination rooms, and all the various chambers required by any guild or society: a great hall, a courtroom, a library, a kitchen—even a beadle's office.

Not that Ned saw any of these. When he and Alfred

arrived at Water Lane, asking to see the Superintending Chemical Operator, they were directed straight to "the laboratory." A porter conducted them across the courtyard, past a gas lamp on a plinth, and through a set of swinging doors into a narrow but well-lit passage. As he walked, he listed the building's many features, pointing some of them out along the way.

"The Great Hall is up the stairs to our right . . . The library above us contains many rare botanical works . . . This colonnade is sometimes used as an extension of the packing room . . . There is an old friary well under the gas lamp—"

"A *well?*" Alfred interrupted sharply, glancing at Ned. But before the porter could reply, they pushed through another set of doors and into the laboratory, and Alfred forgot to press for an answer.

Like Ned, he froze in his tracks, drop jawed and blinking at the sight.

"Ah! Mr. Bunce!" a familiar voice exclaimed. "Thank you so *very* much for answering my summons."

Mr. Gilfoyle was standing with another man in the middle of a sweltering room full of huge copper tanks. Ned instantly realized that these tanks were stills, like those he'd sometimes seen in dank cellar kitchens around Wapping, back when he was a scavenger. Such equipment had been used to distill alcohol from old vegetable peelings, though on a very small scale. Ned couldn't understand how these larger versions could possibly work without a fire burning beneath them.

"Mr. Warington, let me present Mr. Alfred Bunce, our committee's bogler," Mr. Gilfoyle continued. Though rather damp and flushed from the heat, he still looked beautifully groomed in his glossy top hat, gleaming shoes, and spotless white linen. "Mr. Bunce, this is Mr. Warington, who has kindly offered to assist our committee in its endeavors."

Mr. Warington bowed slightly. He was a short, wiry man with sallow skin, a brisk manner, and pale, piercing eyes. Though quite young, he had flecks of gray in his dark hair, which was also dusted with some kind of yellowish powder. He wore his shirtsleeves rolled to the elbow, and an apron that reached his knees. Every inch of his clothing was stained, splotched, scorched, smeared, or splattered.

"How d'you do?" he said drily. Then his searching gaze settled on Ned.

"This is Ned Roach, Mr. Bunce's apprentice," Mr. Gilfoyle explained before turning back to Alfred. "According to Mr. Warington, it *should* be possible to isolate some of the substances on your spear, Mr. Bunce. To do so, however, he would probably have to destroy a good portion of it."

"To break down the constituents," Mr. Warington added.

"But you can't do that!" Horrified, Ned spoke without thinking—then flushed as everyone stared at him.

"He won't have to," Alfred said, then went on to describe his planned trip to Derbyshire. Meanwhile, Ned's attention shifted to a nearby set of hanging scales and to the brick oven that stood beyond it. The scales were big enough to sit in, and the oven was fitted with two iron doors. There were also half a dozen boilers, a complex tangle of pipes, a collection of oddly shaped beakers, and two sweating men in dust coats.

"Well, that does sound like a sensible thing to do," Mr. Gilfoyle observed when Alfred had finished. "I've always believed that village healers, with their old tales and traditions, can sometimes be quite helpful." Hearing Mr. Warington snort, he said quickly, "At the very least, we should leave no stone unturned."

"Aye. I thought that as well," agreed Alfred, then addressed Mr. Warington. "I'm told you had two boys go missing. Can you tell me where they was last seen?"

"Downstairs," Mr. Warington replied. "They were collecting fuel for the steam engine."

Ned was thrilled. "You have a *steam engine?*"

"We do. It runs the forcing pump that feeds hot water to the steam boiler heating our distilleries. We distill nitric acid, muriatic acid, hartshorn, sulphuric ether—although that, of course, is distilled in an *earthenware* vessel." Mr. Warington cocked his head. "Are you interested in steam, Master Roach?"

"Yes, sir. Oh, *yes.*"

"Then it may amuse you to know that you are standing on a steam pipe." As Ned instinctively jumped sideways, the toe of Mr. Warington's boot prodded a line of steel plates underfoot. "The main pipe from the underground boiler branches off into smaller pipes, which run beneath the still-house floor and intersect with each still. The pipes running *out* of each still carry condensed water to a cistern, which in turn supplies the boiler—"

"Ahem." Alfred cleared his throat, and Mr. Gilfoyle remarked, "Forgive us, but we're a little pressed for time."

"I need to know if anything else were seen." Alfred fixed his somber gaze on Mr. Warington. "Around the time them lads disappeared. Anything . . . strange."

"Anything like this," Ned interjected, taking the lid off his china pot.

Mr. Warington and Mr. Gilfoyle both peered into the pot. Mr. Warington even sniffed at it. Then Mr. Gilfoyle asked, "What on earth is this, Mr. Bunce?"

"It's dead bogle," Alfred said flatly.

"Ah." Mr. Gilfoyle straightened. "I see."

Mr. Warington tapped on the side of the pot, which he had taken from Ned. "In truth, Mr. Bunce, there is such an endless supply of smears and smells in this laboratory that no one working here would be likely to notice anything of this sort. But if you've no objection, I shall attempt to analyze these remains, it being easier to kill a thing if you know what it's made of."

"Why, what an excellent idea!" Mr. Gilfoyle began to thank Mr. Warington profusely before Alfred could even open his mouth. "That is *most* kind, sir. Our committee would be *extremely* grateful."

"As to unusual signs in the basement . . . well, it's a very peculiar place down there." Tucking the pot under his arm, Mr. Warington regarded his visitors with a keen, measuring look. "I'll show you, shall I? Follow me. And mind what you touch."

He led them across the still-house, through a pair of large iron doors, and into another, even hotter room full of open fires and furnaces. "This is our chemical laboratory," he explained. "And this is our calcining furnace, and our wind furnace, and our furnace for sulphate of quicksilver . . ."

It wasn't until they entered something he called a mortar room that they finally reached the stairs to the basement, which were tucked away in a corner near a drying stove. According to Mr. Warington, the missing boys had marched down these steps, carrying their empty coal buckets, and were never seen again—though their discarded buckets were later found.

"Where?" asked Alfred.

"Let me show you," Mr. Warington said, and plunged into the basement ahead of his visitors. When Ned arrived at the bottom of the stairs, he found himself in a large, dark, vaulted space, with the biggest chimney he'd ever seen standing squarely in its center. The chimney was so massive that four other flues fed into it, one on each side.

"Where exactly was them buckets found?" Alfred wanted to know.

Mr. Warington moved past the chimney toward a towering heap of coal and stopped at a point midway between the coal and the chimney. "Both buckets were discovered in this area," he said as Ned scanned the floor.

No drains or steel plates were visible.

"What's that?" Alfred demanded, pointing to a small hatch set into the flue that faced the coal heap.

"A chimney will not perform its proper function if it can't be cleaned or repaired," Mr. Warington replied, then went on to describe how smoke from every upstairs furnace was directed underground and into the main chimney through a number of flues. Access to the chimney's interior was through the hatch in the flue. "Now that I think about it," he murmured, "a sweep's boy *was* reported missing hereabouts. That is to say, some sort of complaint was made to the Warden, though I wasn't informed of the particulars . . ."

"A *sweep's boy?*" Alfred cut in. "There's *boys* sent up this chimney?"

"Of course," said Mr. Warington. "But only when the fires are out. And the fires were unquestionably lit when our laboratory boys vanished."

Alfred looked at Ned. Then they both looked at the hatch in the flue. It was perfectly placed, Ned realized. You had to turn your back on it if you wanted to shovel coal into a bucket . . .

"I think you got a chimney bogle," Alfred announced grimly.

Mr. Warington stared at him. "A what?" he said as Mr. Gilfoyle hurriedly produced a little black book from his pocket.

"It's a bogle as lurks in chimneys," Alfred explained. "I've killed a good few."

Mr. Warington's stare didn't waver, though his mouth twitched. "Mr. Bunce, the temperature in our furnaces can reach six hundred degrees Fahrenheit. No creature could survive such conditions."

"Can we be sure of that, Mr. Warington?" Mr. Gilfoyle suddenly came to Alfred's defense, scribbling away in his little black book as he spoke. "After all, our understanding of bogles is in its infancy."

"Yes, but—"

"Is that hatch ever left open when there's fires burn-ing?" Alfred interrupted.

Mr. Warington's thoughtful gaze moved from Alfred to the hatch and back again before he replied, "Occasionally. If more air is called for."

"In that case, we'll open it now," said Alfred. When he turned to Ned, his expression was grave. "It'll feel hot on yer back," he rumbled, "and there ain't no telling what might come out o' that door. But I'll be close to you, lad. I can hide behind the chimney."

Ned swallowed. Then he glanced at the huge pile of coal.

"You don't think it's hiding in that coal heap?" he qua-vered.

"Mebbe," Alfred had to admit—at which point Mr. Warington said, "You don't mean to tell me this boy is here as *bait?*"

"He'll be safe enough," Alfred said. "I'll make sure of it." As Mr. Warington raised a skeptical eyebrow, the bogler scowled and added, "You'd best warn all o' them folk up there to stay well away till we're finished."

"If you'd be so good," Mr. Gilfoyle inserted quickly, with a placating smile.

"Of course." Upon reaching the bottom of the staircase, Mr. Warington paused and studied Ned for a moment. "It's my belief, Master Roach, that you should consider a different job—especially given your interest in steam. Despite the extreme temperature and caustic chemicals involved in laboratory work, you'd probably be safer here than you are in your present position."

"Except when there's bogles about!" snapped Alfred. And Mr. Warington's mouth twitched again.

"True," he conceded. "You have a point." Then he briskly made his way upstairs.

13

THE SNARE

A drift of smoke curled out of the open hatch. Ned could see it reflected in his mirror. He was standing inside an open ring of salt, with his back to the chimney and his face to the coal heap. Alfred had given him some extra salt, just in case a bogle happened to emerge from the coal heap instead of the hatch. "You'll be safe as long as you close that circle," Alfred had insisted. "If anything attacks you from the front, you can allus drop yer salt and stand fast. But I ain't persuaded it'll happen."

The bogler was now lurking by the chimney, ready to leap forward at the first sign of trouble. Mr. Gilfoyle was hiding behind the nearest coke bin. But Ned couldn't help feeling very lonely as he waited, bleating away like a tethered lamb, his mouth dry and his skin clammy.

> *"Oranges and lemons,*
> *Say the bells o' Saint Clement's.*
> *You owe me five farthings,*
> *Say the bells o' Saint Martin's."*

Mr. Warington was nowhere to be seen. He hadn't returned from his trip upstairs, and Ned wondered what he was doing. Standing guard on the top step? Toiling in the still-house? Either way, he was luckier than Ned—who couldn't help comparing his own job with Mr. Warington's.

Given the choice, Ned would have preferred to be doing almost anything else: shoveling coke into a furnace, say, or grinding up toxic powders. Mr. Warington had been right. Laboratory work was *much* less dangerous than bogling. If it hadn't been for Alfred, Ned might have considered applying for a position as laboratory boy. (There were at least two vacancies now.)

But he couldn't desert Alfred. It was Alfred who had rescued him from a life of mud and misery. It was Alfred who had given him a home. So when he had needed another bogler's boy, Ned had willingly volunteered, even though he couldn't leap like Jem or sing like Birdie.

In fact, he was surprised that his cracked voice didn't frighten bogles away.

"When will you pay me?
Say the bells of Old Bailey.
When I grow rich,
Say the bells o' Shoreditch."

Smoke was still curling from the hatch—and it was getting thicker. There was a faint haze in the air now. Ned smelled sulphur. Was tainted smoke coming from an upstairs furnace? Or was that sulphurous stench a sign that the bogle was nearby?

Peering into his mirror, Ned could see only smoke emerging from the hatch behind him. But as his eyes began to sting and his throat became scratchy, something clicked inside his head.

Of course.

There was no *need* for the bogle to emerge. Not if Ned went to shut the hatch.

"Mr. Bunce . . ." Ned turned and beckoned to Alfred, who had become harder to see through the haze. When the bogler scowled, Ned motioned even more urgently, knowing that it would be dangerous to close the gap between himself and the chimney hatch by even one step.

At last Alfred moved toward Ned, still scowling. When

the bogler finally reached him, Ned put his mouth to Alfred's ear and whispered, "That creature's not about to show itself. Not till I go to shut the hatch."

Alfred hissed as his bushy brows knitted together. He glanced back at the chimney.

"That there is a smart bogle," Ned added under his breath. Then he coughed, swallowed, and licked his dry lips before quavering, "If . . . if you was to give me yer spear, Mr. Bunce—"

"Oh no. Not that."

"Ain't nothing else'll work," Ned pointed out. He actually preferred the idea of confronting the bogle face to face, with a spear in his hand. And he felt sure that Alfred's reputation would suffer badly if they just walked away without even *trying* to kill the bogle. "Please, Mr. Bunce. If you go back to where you was, you'll be close enough to grab me. *Or* throw salt. You'll be there if summat goes wrong."

"Which it's bound to," Alfred muttered.

"No, sir. It ain't." Ned spoke staunchly, striving to ignore the sense of black despair that was creeping over him. He recognized it, of course. It was the gloom that every bogle used to protect itself—and Ned knew by now that it had no basis in reality. "I already killed a bogle with yer spear, remember? At Smithfield Market. I can allus do it again." Seeing that he'd made an impression, Ned concluded, "I can't jump like Jem nor sing like Birdie, but I'm stronger'n both of 'em. You know that."

"Aye . . ." Alfred's long face was growing longer by the second. "All the same, it don't sit well with me."

"It sits well with me. For I'd rather walk up to that bogle and look it in the eye than wait for it with me back turned." Ned had to smother a cough; by this time the smoke was so thick that he could barely see the chimney. "We got to do it now, Mr. Bunce."

"Aye," Alfred said again. Then he surrendered his spear and moved his hand to Ned's shoulder. "Don't aim twice," he warned in an undertone, his dark gaze boring into Ned's. "If you miss yer target, run. You've only one chance, lad. *Drop* that spear if you have to."

"Yes, sir."

"It's you I want to keep, not the weapon." Alfred's hand fell away as he swung around, heading back to his post by the chimney.

By now Ned's eyes were streaming. He was afraid that the smoke must be leaking into the laboratory above. And when he heard Mr. Gilfoyle smother a cough, he realized that he didn't have much time.

So he took a cautious step toward the chimney, raising his voice to drown the choked splutters coming from behind the coke bin.

"When will that be?
Say the bells o' Stepney.
I do not know,
Says the great bell o' Bow."

Ned quickly cast aside the salt he'd been clutching and fastened both hands firmly around the shaft of Alfred's spear. A cloud of black smoke billowed toward him. He advanced one step. Then another. Then another. The smoke blocked out the light as he carefully adjusted his grip.

Suddenly he couldn't see Alfred. He couldn't see the chimney. But despite the darkness and the tears in his eyes, he could just make out that there was a dense, black heart in the cloud of smoke—a heart that seemed to be growing bigger.

And though he was gasping for breath, he doggedly kept croaking out another verse.

"Here comes a candle
To light you to bed!"

Coughing, Ned raised his spear and aimed it. Then he waited, poised on the balls of his feet, as the black shadow grew . . . and grew . . .

"Here comes a chopper
To chop off yer head!"

And he rammed the spear home.

There was a jolt—then nothing. Darkness.

He couldn't breathe.

Had he failed?

"Ned?" Someone was slapping his cheeks. *"Ned!"*

He opened his eyes. Alfred's face was hanging over him, drawn and anxious. What had happened to the smoke? When Ned's gaze shifted, he saw a whitewashed ceiling behind a ring of heads and realized he wasn't in the basement anymore.

"Ned? Can you hear me?" Alfred was speaking again. "Can you move? Can you talk, lad?"

"Wha—what happened?" Ned croaked. He had spotted Mr. Harewood standing between Mr. Gilfoyle and Mr. Warington. Mr. Harewood's nose was swollen. One of his eyes was purple and puffy.

"You killed the bogle," said Alfred. "Don't you remember?"

"There was an explosion," Mr. Gilfoyle added. He was as white as chalk. "You were thrown clear across the room."

"I killed it?"

"You did." Alfred dangled a dirty rag in front of him. "We bin cleaning it off you ever since."

Ned raised his hand and saw that it was smeared with gray soot and covered in small reddish spots that stung when he touched them.

"It burned you," Alfred explained gruffly. "Just a little. Nowt to speak of. You was lucky."

"*Lucky?*" Mr. Gilfoyle echoed in disbelief as Ned struggled up onto his elbows. "You call that *lucky?* He might have been killed!"

"We're in the mortar room," Ned suddenly declared. He had recognized the drying oven.

"Aye." Alfred flashed a quick look at Mr. Gilfoyle, whose clenched features relaxed. Even Mr. Warington heaved a sigh of relief.

"He musd be well enough," said Mr. Harewood, "if he knows where he is."

"Of course I do!" Ned sat up. His head was rapidly clearing. "When did *you* arrive, sir?"

"Afder you were knogged out," Mr. Harewood replied. His voice still sounded very odd. "I hear you were as brave as a lion, young Ned."

"Yes, indeed." Mr. Gilfoyle spoke before Ned could. "Though I must confess I'm still unclear as to why he should have been exposed to such danger. I thought the usual technique was to lure the bogle *out* of its lair?"

Alfred gave a grunt. He didn't seem inclined to defend himself. Ned murmured, "This'un wouldn't never have showed itself. It stayed in the flue, blowing smoke and waiting for me to come to it."

"You mean you didn't *see* the bogle? *Any* of you?" Mr. Warington's tone was drily incredulous. When Ned and Alfred and Mr. Gilfoyle shook their heads, he asked, "Then how can you be sure there was one? That noise sounded just like a gas explosion to me. It's quite possible that you accidentally ignited a combination of volatile chemicals—"

"We didn't." Ned tried not to sound as resentful as he felt. "It were a bogle. I could feel it."

"So could I," said Alfred. He was glaring at Mr. Warington. "This boy killed a bogle. Don't you take that away from him, sir. He's a brave lad."

Mr. Gilfoyle nodded furiously. Beside him, Mr. Warington raised his hands in a halfhearted gesture of submission. Then Mr. Harewood remarked, "I'm persuaded thad there musd be someone with medical training on these premises. Am I ride, Mr. Warington?"

"Of course." Mr. Warington flashed him a quizzical look. "This is Apothecaries' Hall."

"Then perhaps you could arrange a brief consultation for me? *And* for poor Ned here, who musd have a lump on his head as big as a crab apple." Mr. Harewood smiled crookedly as he addressed Alfred. "Before I hail a cab for us, Mr. Bunce, we should probably arm ourselves with a few salves and plasders. Do you nod agree? For I'd argue thad some of us have done enough for one day and should be off to bed as soon as possible."

"Aye." Alfred inclined his head, then muttered something about the importance of getting a good night's sleep. Ned caught the word *Derbyshire* and suddenly remembered.

He was going to be taking his very first railway journey the next day.

"Why yes, of course! Your visid to the Peak Districd!" Mr. Harewood began to rub his hands together. "I musd say, I'm looking forward to your findings, Mr. Bunce. If you can discover the secreds of your spear, we shall all be a *deal* better off . . ."

14

ᗰEETING ᗰOTHER ᗰAY

Ned sat in a second-class carriage on a train heading for Derbyshire. Wedged between Alfred and a fat man with a cold, he didn't have much of a view out the window. He also felt embarrassed every time he caught the eye of the lady sitting opposite, who would sniff and turn away in a very pointed manner. It was obvious that she regarded him as the sort of person who ought to be traveling in third class.

So he spent most of the journey staring at his boots, thinking about recent events, as the train rocked and swayed and chugged along. Saint Pancras Station had been so huge—so magnificent—that he'd been dazzled. From a ticket office fitted with cathedral windows and acres of polished wood, he had emerged into a train shed so large that he could barely see from one end to the other. Seven locomotives had been lined up like horses in a stable, their carriages arranged neatly behind them. Ned had boarded the very longest of these trains, which was more comfortably furnished than he'd ever imagined it would be; the seats were padded, there was glass in every window, and the luggage racks were made of solid brass.

Even the train's departure had been exciting. The blast of the whistle and the engine's gathering speed had filled Ned with exhilaration. Plunging into dark tunnels had been quite a thrill, at first. The trip itself, however, had proved to be a bit of a disappointment. The carriage was cold but stuffy. The windows quickly steamed up, which limited Ned's view of the outside even more. Passengers would get on or off, but they never did anything of interest and tried not to look at each other. Some slept, some smoked, and some read books or newspapers. When the shabbily dressed clergyman near the window peeled an egg into a paper bag, his movements were furtive, and he kept his head down.

Alfred slept. With his arms folded and his chin on his chest, he dozed through stop after stop as Ned listened to the porter calling out station names. According to Alfred, their destination was a town called Long Eaton. "We'll change trains at Trent," he'd explained before nodding off, "so you must wake me when we reach Leicester."

In the meantime, Ned had nothing to do but reflect on his situation. He still ached a little from the bogling job at Apothecaries' Hall, where he'd bruised some ribs, bumped his head, and singed his eyebrows. Luckily he'd been offered a cab ride afterward; *walking* home would have left him feeling much worse. But he'd been forced to spend the whole trip listening to Mr. Gilfoyle bicker with Mr. Harewood about chimney bogles. Did the existence of chimney bogles disprove the theory that bogles used sewers to get around? Mr. Gilfoyle had insisted that there were different types of bogles, some of which didn't need underground water. Mr. Harewood had argued that the Fleet Sewer ran beneath the very doorstep of Apothecaries' Hall, so there *had* to be a connection.

Alfred had kept his opinion to himself.

He'd remained very quiet and somber, even after arriving back at Orange Court—where Jem had been waiting impatiently, anxious to tell them a wonderful piece of news. After nearly an hour with Mr. Chatterton that morning, both Jem and Birdie had been hired for the Theatre Royal pantomime. "We start rehearsing tomorrow," Jem had grandly announced, "and they'll pay me two shillings for every performance!" Birdie would be earning more, he'd added, because she had been engaged as a soloist. "I'm only in the chorus, but if I dance well enough, they might give me summat special to do. I might even get to dance with Mr. Vokes!"

Remembering the radiant expression on Jem's face, Ned

didn't feel the least bit jealous. A stage career wasn't something he'd ever wanted; in fact, the thought of performing in public made his blood run cold. And he was glad that Birdie had achieved her heart's desire, because she deserved to be famous. She was the bravest, prettiest, noblest person he'd ever met, and her voice was good enough to be admired all over the world. As far as Ned was concerned, Birdie *belonged* in the spotlight.

But with Jem employed elsewhere, the burden of the bogling would now fall on Ned—and he wasn't sure exactly what that would involve. He didn't even know why he'd been invited to Derbyshire. He had a sneaking suspicion, however, that he wasn't there just to carry the luggage.

Alfred had some sort of plan in mind.

When the train finally arrived at Trent Station, some three hours after leaving Saint Pancras, Ned and Alfred found themselves in the middle of nowhere. Though the station was large and handsome, with lavatories and refreshment rooms and glass canopies over both platforms, it was surrounded by fields and woods as far as the eye could see. Once the London express had rolled away and the smoke and steam had cleared, Ned was confronted by a vast expanse of leafless treetops.

"There ain't no town," he murmured, awestruck. He'd never in his life set foot outside London—and the fresh, scented breeze that blew in his face was a revelation.

"Trent Station's nowt but an interchange," a passing guard informed him. "All tha can do here is switch lines."

"'Tis new since I were last in the neighborhood," Alfred confessed. "Where must we go to catch the train to Long Eaton?"

"Ower that way." The guard directed Alfred to a connecting train almost empty of passengers. Alfred and Ned had a whole carriage to themselves. And since there was no one around to overhear them, Ned finally found the courage to ask, "Is this where you was raised, Mr. Bunce?"

Alfred shook his head. "Nay," he said, staring out the window as the engine gathered speed. "I were born in Derby. Daniel Piggin brought me to Long Eaton nobbut two or three times to visit his sister. She worked on a farm just out o' town."

Surprised to hear Alfred so chatty, Ned tried another question. "So where did yer master do his bogling, then?"

"In London, chiefly. I weren't five years old when I moved there. But sometimes we was hired to do jobs up this way, by folk as knew us." All of a sudden Alfred's pensive gaze shifted back to Ned. "Daniel Piggin trained me up to take his place. There was other boys as came and went, but I allus stayed close, even when carting loads to make ends meet." Pausing for a moment, Alfred seemed to expect some kind of comment, but Ned didn't know what to say.

So Alfred continued. "I weren't twenty when Dan passed. A fever took him quick and clean. He left me his pipe and his spear, which I still have." After briefly surveying Ned from top to toe, the bogler finally said, "I bin a-thinking I might give 'em to you, in time."

Ned blinked.

"Jem's found another path for hisself, and I'm glad of it, for he ain't steady," Alfred went on. "He's quick and brave, so he made a good 'prentice. But it takes more'n that to be a bogler. A bogler needs to have a clear head and a firm hand." As Ned shifted uneasily, Alfred finished, "I ain't never had no other 'prentice kill a bogle—and you done it twice, lad. Seems to me you was born to the job."

Still Ned didn't know what to say. He should have been honored; that was clear. Yet his heart sank like a stone at the thought of becoming Alfred's successor.

"Y-you ain't ill, Mr. Bunce?" he stammered.

"Nay, lad. I'm tiring, though. And coming back here don't make me feel no younger." Alfred frowned as his gaze drifted back to the window. "Wait," he said, leaning forward. "What's this? This ain't Long Eaton."

But it was. To Alfred's dismay, a new railway station had been built since his previous visit. What's more, it was in a different part of the town, so when at last he emerged onto the platform, he didn't know where he was. He had to ask one of the guards for directions to Coffee Pot Farm, while Ned stood waiting in a light drizzle, wondering uneasily if they had come all this way for nothing.

If Long Eaton had uprooted its whole railway station, what were the chances that May Piggin still lived at her old address?

"The other station were on Toton Lane, just down the road from Mother May's house," Alfred observed when they finally set off. "Now we must go up Station Street, which used to be Tithe Barn Lane." They were heading east, across a footbridge suspended over the railway tracks, when he stopped suddenly. "Look there," he said, nodding at a cluttered vista of factory chimneys and railway sheds that lay to the west. "Most o' them mills is new since I were a lad. It's changed, right enough."

"It's a big station," Ned observed.

"It is. And less'n ten years old, that guard said."

"Will Mother May be living here still, Mr. Bunce?"

Alfred shrugged. "She weren't one for shifting about," he replied, "and the farm seems to be where I left it."

Though Ned had begun to doubt that May Piggin was even alive, he obediently followed Alfred up Station Street, which had a strangely patchy appearance at first, as if it couldn't make up its mind whether it belonged to the town or the country. Grand new houses had been built alongside brand-new streets, but here and there a chunk of old hedgerow or a tumbledown barn remained. The road was macadam for a while, then degenerated into muddy ruts scattered with puddles.

After about twenty minutes, they were trudging past overgrown paddocks and tilled fields. A horse stood alone behind a stone wall. Alfred kept muttering under his breath ("Where's Grange Farm? This don't look right. The old tithe barn's gone . . .") as water slowly dripped from his nose and hat brim. Ned soon realized that country walking was more difficult than city walking. The road was so uneven and the rain so relentless that he didn't say another word until they came within sight of their destination.

"There," said Alfred, pointing at a row of gritstone houses sitting forlornly on an otherwise deserted stretch of road. "There it is. The one at the end."

Ned was puzzled. "That's the farm?" he queried, wondering where the barns were.

"Nay, the farm's up yonder. This here is where the farmhands live. Or *used* to live." Alfred struck out for the closest cottage, which was two stories high. Ned thought it very grim looking, with its gray walls and tiny windows. The small garden plot in front was full of mud and brown stalks. A leafless vine was growing over the front door, which was set quite low. The smoke oozing from the chimney drifted downward, as if the damp air weighed on it.

Alfred hesitated for a moment before knocking. Ned

thought he was paler than usual, though that might have been because of the cold.

"Hello?" said Alfred. "Mother May?"

The only sounds were the trickle of water and the sighing of the wind. Ned couldn't get over the lack of noise; London was never this quiet, not even at two o'clock in the morning.

"Hello?" Alfred repeated. "Is anyone there?"

Suddenly Ned heard shuffling footsteps, followed by the scrape of a bolt and the creak of hinges. Next thing he knew, he was staring at a little old lady wrapped in a gray shawl. Her hair was gray too, as were her eyes, buried deep in two nests of wrinkles. She wore a rather limp white cap on her silvery hair and carried a wooden cane.

"Who's there?" she cawed, blinking at Ned—who was taller than she was. "Dost ah know thee?"

"Mother May?" said Alfred.

"Aye." All at once she seemed to get her bearings. Turning to Alfred, she croaked, "And th'art?"

"Alfred Bunce. I used to work for yer brother, Daniel." As the old woman peered at him, silent and motionless, Alfred cleared his throat and shifted his weight. "I came here from London, Mother May. There's summat I need to know, and I thought as how you might have the answer."

"Alfred Bunce?" The old woman's face brightened. "T'Derby lad?"

"Aye."

"Well, ah'll be . . ." With a gap-toothed smile, Mother May edged backwards into the gloom of her cottage. "Come in! Come in, tha must be clammed! Ah've some oatcakes for thee, and a drap o' cider . . ."

15

THE BLASTING ROD

Mother May's oatcakes were as dry as dust, but her cider was good. One sip was all it took to warm Ned on the inside. And her fire thawed the rest of him, slowly warming his wet feet, his chilled hands, and his frozen ears.

The fire was built in a brazier, which occupied one corner of the old woman's huge inglenook fireplace. This fireplace was so big that it seemed to take up half her kitchen. The rest of the low, dark, sooty room was crammed with furniture: a table, a dresser, a chest, a barrel, a sink, a bed, several mismatched chairs, and piles of domestic junk.

Looking at the clothes and pots and tools that covered every surface, Ned realized that Mother May was *living* in her kitchen. He guessed that the rest of the house was probably unused, except for storing firewood.

As someone who lived in a tiny London garret with two other people, he found such a waste of space hard to comprehend.

"So tha'rt a bogler," the old woman said to Alfred, in a voice that crackled like the fire. She had lowered herself into a well-worn rocking chair beside the hearth, having placed Ned and Alfred on a rickety settle opposite her. "And this bonny lad—is he yorn?"

"Nay," Alfred rumbled. He sounded almost sheepish, Ned thought, and quite unlike himself. "Ned Roach is me 'prentice."

Mother May clicked her tongue. "Ah thought he must be kin, what with t'big, brown eyes that's on 'im. Hast tha no children, Freddie?"

Alfred shook his head.

"Eh, now, that's a shame," the old woman lamented. "But poor Dan had t'same problem, traveling about as he did. He couldn't settle long enough to find hissen a wife."

"I don't travel much," said Alfred. "I don't need to. There's bogles enough in London to keep me busy."

"All in t'one place?" Mother May kept dipping her oatcake into her cider, and Ned wondered if she did this because she didn't have many teeth. "Well, ah never. What a wicked town it must be!"

"'Tain't the wickedness as draws the bogles, Mother May. 'Tis the number o' children living there." Alfred leaned forward and said quietly, "Yer brother gave me all he had when he died. His pipe, his baccy pouch, his boots . . . and his spear, ma'am. Do you remember his spear?"

The old woman nodded as she masticated her oatcake. "That ah do," she replied, spraying crumbs.

"He told me it were Finn McCool's spear. Did he ever tell *you* that?"

"*Finn McCool's* spear?" She began to cough. "Gerron with thee!"

Alfred frowned.

"'Twas nowt but a blasting rod!" Mother May continued, still coughing. She didn't find her voice again until she'd drained her cup of cider. Then she smiled at Alfred. "Dan was telling thee tales, ah expect, tha being a little laddie. But he cut that spear hissen, and *ah* was t'one that hexed it."

Alfred stiffened, his eyes widening. Ned asked, "What's a blasting rod?"

"Why, 'tis a witch's staff, me duck. Made o' blackthorn and used for cursing, though we piggled away at it till we had a bogling spear. Mam taught me how 'twas done, for she was a cunning woman, like her own mam—"

"Blackthorn, you say?" Alfred interrupted. "That spear is made o' blackthorn?"

"With a head cut by the stonemason down the lane,

from a cross blessed by t'owd priest at Duffield," said Mother May. She looked quite pleased with herself for remembering this. "Ten shillings it cost, but Dan knew 'twould pay for issen."

"So the spear is just a stick o' blackthorn with a consecrated point on it?" Alfred seemed taken aback. "That's all it is?"

"Nay, lad, 'twould be rammel without herbs!" the old woman exclaimed, balancing her empty cup on an overturned bucket. "Tha canna cast a bane without herbs, Freddie, else tha'd like to come a cropper."

"Which herbs did you use?" Ned chimed in. He was genuinely interested — and he sensed that Mother May liked him. But instead of answering his question, she smirked and bridled and said, "Well now, tha may well ask."

Ned was surprised. Why was she being so coy all of a sudden? He glanced at Alfred, who was studying the old woman gravely, an untouched oatcake in one hand and a full cup of cider in the other.

"You're still in business, Mother May?" the bogler queried.

"Ah am that," she replied with a cackle. "For there'll allus be lassies in love and lads with grudges. Not to mention owd men with sore teggies."

Ned still didn't understand. "What's a teggy?" he asked, bewildered.

Mother May grinned and tapped one of the last teeth in her gums with a crooked finger. "This is a teggy," she said, "and tha may be thankful there's a full set of 'em in that fine head o' yorn."

"Mother May, I ain't about to take none o' your potions without paying a fair price," Alfred cut in — and it dawned on Ned that Mother May's business had to be her magic. She was earning money with charms and cures and curses, and although Mr. Harewood had referred to her as a folk healer, she was clearly more than that.

She was a witch.

Ned stared at her in amazement. So *this* was what a witch looked like! He should have known it; there was something about her dim, damp, untidy kitchen that unnerved him.

"The boy and I — we ain't alone in this," Alfred was saying. "We're on a committee, see, as is charged with ridding London of all its bogles —"

"A what?" Mother May looked perplexed. "What's a committee?"

"A kind o' guild," Alfred explained. "Like a boglers' guild."

"Oh, aye." The old woman nodded.

"And this committee . . . well, 'tis a government committee, with government money behind it." Alfred paused as he allowed this to sink in, then took a deep breath. "If you tell us which herbs is on yer brother's spear, Mother May, we'll pay you a fair price for the receipt."

Mother May narrowed her eyes. "How much?" she croaked.

"Five pounds. In yer hand." Before the old woman could respond, Alfred continued, "'Tain't no use asking for ten, on account of our Chairman. He's the feller with the final say, and he said five. I cannot bargain with you."

"Dunna wittle, lad. Ah'll take five pound." Mother May held out her hand as Alfred produced several gold coins from one of his pockets. But to Ned's surprise, he didn't immediately pass the coins to her.

"Shall I put these in yer chamber pot, Mother May?"

"Nay!" She spoke sharply. "Ah dun keep t'money in that no more!"

"Then I'll lay 'em down here." Alfred placed the coins on a low footstool between them. "And when you've told us what's in yer potion, you may take 'em as you like."

"Monkshood," said Mother May. "That's for death-work. Also rue and crampweed, which drives away devils. Hag's taper for protection, peppercorn for attack magic, and henbane mixed with black nightshade for poisoning."

The ingredients came tumbling out as if she couldn't keep them to herself any longer. Ned tried to commit them to memory. *Monks ruing their cramps,* he thought. *Hags and hens, a pinch of peppercorn . . .*

Not for the first time, he wished that he could write.

"Use all of 'em in equal measure," the old woman went on, "mixed to a paste with holy water, if you have it. Then add a dob o' goose fat to make it stick."

"Rue, peppercorn, monkshood, henbane, hag's taper, crampweed, nightshade, holy water, and goose fat," Alfred recited. Then he stood up. "Thank'ee, ma'am."

"Tha'll not be staying a little longer?" Mother May protested as Ned joined Alfred. "Ah can put the kettle on for tea . . ."

"We've a train to catch." The bogler reached for his hat, which he'd hung from a pot hook. "By the by, have you any blackthorn bushes hereabouts?"

"Any blackthorn?" the old woman echoed. "Why, every blessed hedge in this shire is a blackthorn hedge! There's one down the road."

"Then I'll take a little, if there ain't no objection." By this time Alfred had donned his hat and was edging toward the door. "Thanks again, Mother May," he said gruffly. "I'll have the committee send you a letter. Mebbe you can find someone as'll read it to you."

"Thanks for the cake, Mother May. *And* the cider," Ned murmured. He felt bad about leaving so abruptly when she seemed so anxious to have them stay. But with a three-hour train journey ahead of them, they couldn't really linger.

"Art tha bogle bait, lad?" she suddenly asked as she struggled to rise from her chair. On Ned's cautious nod, she turned to Alfred, who was already opening the door. "There's more'n one way to bait a boggart," she announced. "Dust tha know that? They can be raised with herbs, like any spirit."

Alfred paused to look at her, his dark eyes wary under his hat brim.

"Elfwort'll do it. And dogsbane," she continued slyly. "Tell yer master ah can give thee another recipe for another five pound."

Shocked by this unexpected news, Ned glanced at Alfred. But the bogler was still regarding Mother May. At last he said, "Why would yer brother take me on if all he needed were a potion?"

"A bogle summoned is a bogle primed to fight," the old woman retorted. "Lure it with a tender bit o' bait and it willna be ready for thee."

She was right. Ned could see that. But Alfred looked unimpressed.

"I'll ask the Chairman," he growled. "Good day to you."

Then he opened the door, tipped his hat, and departed into the drizzle—with his hand clenched firmly around Ned's arm. They were well away from the cottage before Ned was released, in front of a spiky hedge so overgrown that it was more like a copse. "This here is blackthorn," said Alfred. "I'm sure of it."

"Are we going to make another spear?" asked Ned.

"Aye." Alfred took his tobacco knife from his pocket and began to saw at one leafless, thorny branch. Ned stood in the mud, watching, as the silence dragged on.

Finally he said, "Will you tell Mr. Harewood about the summoning herbs?"

"Aye." It was barely more than a grunt.

"If they work, you'll not need a 'prentice no more."

"*If* they work," Alfred replied. There was so much disdain in his voice that Ned was puzzled.

"Don't you think she told the truth, Mr. Bunce?"

Alfred shrugged. His face was already red from the effort of hacking away at a thick branch with a small knife. "She ain't called a cunning woman for nowt," he spat. "She wants more chink—that's why she spoke at all."

"I thought she were trying to make us stay a little longer." When Alfred didn't comment, Ned observed hesitantly, "She were happy to see *you*, right enough."

"All she cares about is money." Alfred passed his knife to Ned, then began to tug and wrench at the half-cut bough with both hands. "When I were a lad, I heard her say as how 'twould be cheaper to use stray boys and let the bogles eat 'em than to keep feeding a 'prentice."

Ned's jaw dropped. He had to swallow before stammering, "Oh, b-but . . . she weren't serious, Mr. Bunce? She didn't *mean* it?"

"Who knows what she meant? All I know is she cares for nowt but that hoard o' coins in her piss pot." With a mighty yank, Alfred finally managed to detach his chosen bough from the blackthorn bush. "She married a man for his house, gave him no children on account o' the expense, and wouldn't stump up for a train ticket to her own brother's funeral," he finished. "If she's lonely now, she's got none to blame but herself."

Having delivered this verdict, Alfred pocketed his knife, adjusted his hat, and headed back toward the railway station, using his new staff as a walking stick.

16

An Evening Performance

It was early evening before Alfred and Ned arrived at Miss Eames's house, on their way home from Saint Pancras Station. Alfred had told Ned that he wanted to acquaint Miss Eames with his latest discovery, so that she could write to Mr. Harewood.

He didn't expect to find Mr. Harewood already on the premises.

"Why, what a stroke of luck!" the engineer exclaimed, jumping to his feet as Alfred and Ned crossed the threshold of Miss Eames's front parlor. "We were just this moment wishing that you were with us, Mr. Bunce, and here you are!"

Startled, Alfred gazed around the room—which Ned had always admired. Like Mother May's kitchen, it was very cluttered, but this clutter was beautiful. There were gilded chairs, framed pictures, glazed bookshelves, embroidered firescreens, and crystal vases stuffed with hothouse flowers. An inlaid workbox sat on a carved writing desk. A glossy piano was draped with a fringed damask cloth. The walls were papered, the floor was carpeted, and a low table was laid for tea.

Surrounding the table were half a dozen familiar faces. Miss Eames was wielding the teapot, richly clad in a mauve gown with a low neck. Beside her sat her elderly aunt, Mrs. Heppinstall, who owned the house and most of its contents. She wore her usual black silk dress, but to Ned's eyes—fresh from a murky witch's dwelling in Derbyshire—she looked very clean and cheerful, with her neat gray ringlets and starched white cap.

Mr. Gilfoyle was perched on the couch opposite Mrs. Heppinstall. He was decked out in a white tie and black tailcoat. Mr. Harewood, in contrast, was dressed for a day's work and didn't look entirely respectable—perhaps because he still had bruises on his face. Jem and Birdie sat on opposite sides of a plum cake, which was already half eaten. Birdie was as pretty as a china doll in an outfit of embroidered pearl-gray satin that Ned recognized. But Ned *didn't* recognize the sailor suit that Jem was wearing.

"'Tain't mine," Jem said sharply when he saw Ned's raised eyebrows. "Miss Eames borrowed it from a neighbor."

"He couldn't have come to the theater in his own clothes," Miss Eames quickly explained. "Won't you sit down, Mr. Bunce? Ned?"

"We're going to see *Tom Thumb*," Birdie announced. She had already jumped up and was guiding Alfred toward a chair. "Mr. Gilfoyle is taking us. Ain't you, Mr. Gilfoyle?"

"I thought it only proper," Mr. Gilfoyle agreed, coloring. "No lady should have to attend the theater or ballet unaccompanied."

"I want Jem and Birdie to see the show as audience members before they actually perform," Miss Eames continued. She sounded embarrassed, and as she went on, Ned realized why. "Of course you're welcome to accompany us, Mr. Bunce, if you could somehow organize a change of clothes . . . and perhaps a wash . . ."

"Nay." Alfred was wet through and resisted Birdie's efforts to make him sit in an upholstered armchair. Instead he dropped onto the piano stool, still clutching his blackthorn staff. "I'll wait till Birdie's up on stage. *That's* when I'll go."

"And what about you, Ned?" Miss Eames smiled, but Ned wasn't fooled. He could sense from her creased brow and preoccupied gaze that she was wondering where, at this late hour, she could possibly acquire a decent set of clothes for him.

"I'll wait till Birdie's singing," he mumbled. "I'll go when Mr. Bunce goes."

"And I'll go with you," Mr. Harewood broke in. He had seated himself again and was rifling through his coat pockets. "I'm afraid I'm not dressed for the theater at present. In fact, I'm not even here at Miss Eames's invitation." He dragged out a handful of papers and said to Alfred, "I merely called to show her these. And to find out whether she'd heard from you, of course . . ."

"They're telegrams," Birdie piped up. "From all over town."

Miss Eames shot Birdie a reproving glance, but Mr. Harewood proceeded as if he hadn't noticed the interruption. "I was just telling our friends, Mr. Bunce, that the memorandum I circulated among various government departments has had a remarkable response. I've heard from the Customs Commissioners, the London Docks, Saint Bartholomew's Hospital, even from some of the railway companies. Word must have got out, I suppose. There seems to be an enormous demand for your services." He leaned forward, his elbows on his knees. "Which prompts me to ask: Did you have any luck in Derbyshire?"

As Alfred began to describe his trip to Long Eaton, Ned

reached for a jam tart. He was very hungry, having eaten nothing since Mother May's oatcake. Mrs. Heppinstall was the only person who noticed. She poured him a cup of tea while everyone else listened intently to Alfred.

" . . . henbane, crampweed, and black nightshade," he was saying. "She greased the head with it. I brung a piece o' the wood back with me, in case the blackthorn thereabouts is different from London's. I thought as how we could use it to craft a new spear." And he raised his staff, so that his audience could examine it.

There was a brief silence. At last Mr. Gilfoyle observed, "Mother May's concoction doesn't sound very difficult to make. I'm sure I could prepare it myself, *without* the assistance of a trained apothecary."

"We'd need help with the spearhead, though." Mr. Harewood sounded thoughtful. "I know several good stonemasons and could apply to one of them for help. But where are we to find consecrated stone?"

"Oh, I'm sure I could do *that* for you," Mrs. Heppinstall unexpectedly offered. Having passed Ned his tea, she set down the teapot and looked around the table with a placid smile.

Miss Eames explained, "My aunt knows a great many clergymen."

"Why, then we have our plan!" Mr. Harewood exclaimed. "If you can supply the blessing, Mrs. Heppinstall,

I'll arrange to have the stone shaped to a point, and Razzy can provide the final touches." He beamed at Alfred. "You may be testing your new spear very soon, Mr. Bunce!"

"Oh dear," said Miss Eames. "Won't that be dreadfully dangerous for Ned?"

Everyone stared at Ned, whose cheeks were full of jam tart. He flushed.

"It'll be less dangerous with two spears than one," Jem remarked, just as Alfred cleared his throat.

"There's summat else I should tell you," the bogler said. He went on to describe Mother May's offer of a summoning recipe. "She'll need to be paid, and I ain't sure we'll be getting our money's worth. But I thought as how, if the new spear works, we should mebbe go back and buy the other charm. The one as draws bogles."

"My word, yes!" said Mr. Harewood. Meanwhile, Jem and Birdie were exchanging wide-eyed looks. When they turned to Ned, he shrugged, embarrassed by the attention.

"A summoned bogle is more dangerous, on account of it's primed to fight," he muttered. "That's what the old witch told us. Bait is better, she said."

"Yes, but I'm sure *something* could be done!" cried Miss Eames. "Some clever device could be employed, and then there would no longer be any *need* to put children in peril!" She swung around and appealed to the engineer. "Do you not think so, Mr. Harewood?"

"Er . . . well . . . ye . . ."

"Mr. Harewood and I were just discussing Ned," Miss Eames continued, addressing Alfred. "We agreed that he's a very clever boy and wasted as a bogler's apprentice." She turned to Ned. "I'm sure you'd prefer to be doing something else with your life. Wouldn't you, dear?"

Ned swallowed. It was true; he *didn't* like bogling. But he had a duty to Alfred.

"I'm a bogler's boy," he answered at last. "Mr. Bunce needs me."

"Not for much longer," Miss Eames reminded him. Her tone was brisk. "Not if he can replace you with an herbal solution."

"Ain't no herb can replace a good 'prentice!" Alfred snapped. And seeing the bogler leap to his defense, Ned felt even more indebted to him.

"Mr. Bunce needs me," Ned repeated.

Suddenly there was a knock on the parlor door and a maid appeared on the threshold. She had frizzy red hair and wore a white apron over her black dress.

"Begging yer pardon, miss, but yer carriage is here," she announced.

"Oh dear. Is it that late? Thank you, Mary." Miss Eames stood up, prompting everyone else to do the same. "We must go now, Mr. Bunce, but we'll certainly discuss this at a later date," she went on. Before Alfred could reply, she said to Birdie, "Find your mantle, there's a good girl. Have you seen my gloves, aunt?"

"On the piano, dear."

During the bustle that ensued, Ned and Jem managed to polish off five more jam tarts between them. Mr. Gilfoyle offered Alfred a ride to Drury Lane. Mrs. Heppinstall wished the theater party a very pleasant evening, and Alfred said to Mr. Harewood, "Will you be coming with us?"

"I doubt I'd fit. It will be rather cramped in that vehicle with *six* passengers, let alone seven." When a chorus of voices assured Mr. Harewood that room could certainly be found — that children could sit on knees — that a spacious hackney coach had been ordered, rather than a hansom cab — he hastily added, "I'm heading east, in any case. Please don't concern yourselves."

"If you ain't coming with us, sir, may I ask how you fared with the police?" Alfred inquired. "Only I bin a-thinking on it, and wondering what they might have done about finding the feller as struck you."

"Oh." As every eye turned toward him, Mr. Harewood smiled crookedly. "To tell the truth, I've not had much satisfaction on that front," he admitted. "There must be so many footpads around Newgate that my black eye simply doesn't measure up to all the cracked skulls and cut throats that infest the neighborhood. I certainly haven't heard from the police. They seemed quite unimpressed when I spoke to them, as I believe I may have mentioned yesterday."

Alfred frowned. "You went to Smithfield Station House, did you not?"

"I did indeed. On your recommendation, Mr. Bunce."

"You should have talked to Constable Pike," said Birdie.

"Oh, yes." As Jem and Ned nodded in agreement, Mr. Gilfoyle declared, "Constable Pike is the man you want. *He* would have helped."

"Who is Constable Pike?" asked Mr. Harewood.

Alfred explained that Constable Pike was a market constable at Smithfield and that he had helped arrest Sarah Pickles. "He knows all about Salty Jack Gammon," Alfred explained. "*And* he's seen me bogling."

"Then the next time I'm assaulted, I shall certainly appeal to Constable Pike," Mr. Harewood remarked in a bantering tone. "Meanwhile, I must take my leave or you'll be late for the theater. Good evening, Miss Eames. Mrs. Heppinstall. Have fun, old boy." He flipped Mr. Gilfoyle a mocking salute, bowed to the ladies, and said to Alfred, "Let me take your blackthorn staff, Mr. Bunce. I want to see what I can do with it. And I'll look you up tomorrow, shall I? For I've a pocketful of bogles here, and you must decide which of them you should tackle first. Personally I think we should begin with Tothill Fields Prison, since no one there can actually *run away* from an attacking bogle . . ."

Even as he spoke, he was donning his hat. Then he turned on his heel and plunged through the front door, which had been standing open. By the time the others had emerged into the street—fully equipped with hats, gloves, and umbrellas—Mr. Harewood had disappeared into a thick fog.

17

Behind Bars

The entrance to Tothill Fields Prison was a large granite gateway in a massive wall of beige brick. Its double doors were made of iron, set under a raised portcullis. Its door knockers were as big as dinner plates.

As Alfred lifted a knocker and let it drop again, Mr. Harewood remarked, "Did you see the streets we passed on our way here? Pool Place. Pond Court. I've heard that this prison was built on a swamp, and those names seem to confirm it."

Alfred didn't comment. He was watching a little hatch in the right-hand door, which suddenly snapped open.

"State yer business," a deep voice growled.

"My name is Mark Harewood." Consulting the telegram he was clutching, the engineer added, "This is Alfred Bunce and Ned Roach. We are here at the request of Mrs. Spraggs, the Principal Matron."

"One moment, please, sir."

The hatch closed again. Ned heard a murmur of voices and the squeal of bolts being drawn. Suddenly the door opened, revealing a uniformed warder with brass on his collar and keys at his belt. His waxed mustache was so large that it stuck out on either side of his head, eclipsing his ears.

"Kindly step inside," he barked. "Mrs. Spraggs has bin sent for." He ushered his guests into a little office just inside the gateway, which contained a clutch of chairs, a desk, a small fireplace, and a row of cutlasses strung together on a chain. With four people squeezed into it, the room felt very cramped.

"May I inquire as to what yer business is with Mrs. Spraggs, sir?" the warder asked Mr. Harewood, who promptly gave him the matron's telegram. As soon as he'd read it, a great change came over the warder. He lost his stiff, military air and addressed Mr. Harewood in the mildest of tones.

"Are you the bogler?" he asked.

Mr. Harewood shook his head. "Mr. Bunce is."

"Then I'm right glad to meet you, Mr. Bunce. *Right* glad," the warder said, vigorously shaking hands with Alfred.

"It's time we did summat about this here bogle, for we've lost too many girls already."

Ned blinked. "You have *girls* in this prison?" he exclaimed. The telegram had mentioned three missing children — but not that they were girls.

"We take women, girls, and boys under seventeen," the warder replied. "It's the females as work in the laundry, and that's where the bogle is."

Alfred frowned. "Are you sure there's a bogle?"

"That's what I bin told, Mr. Bunce." The warder went on to explain that the missing girls had all been laundry workers and had disappeared in the vicinity of a hot closet. "The first time it happened, 'twas called an escape. The second time, we thought the first lass had set a bad example. But the third time . . ." He shook his head sadly. "The third time, someone heard a scream."

Ned shuddered. It wasn't an unusual story, but it somehow seemed much worse in these grim surroundings, which filled Ned with a deep sense of unease. He hadn't wanted to come to the prison. But after carefully considering Mr. Harewood's pile of telegrams, Alfred had ruled against the job at Saint Bartholomew's Hospital because it was too close to Newgate. Crossness Pumping Station, on the other hand, would be too far out of London. And the job at the docks would be so close to the job at the Custom House that Alfred had felt they ought to be tackled together. As for Blackfriars

Station, or the Thames Tunnel, they both belonged to private companies, and Mr. Harewood wanted the government jobs tackled first.

So Alfred had decided to start at Tothill Fields Prison — despite Ned's misgivings. Because his own father had died in gaol, Ned feared imprisonment more than anything else. And he wasn't the only one. That very morning, Jem had quietly confessed to an abiding dread of the "stone jug," before wishing Ned good luck with heartfelt sympathy — even though *Jem* was the one about to face his first matinee performance. ("I'll stay at the back o' the line till I've got me steps right," he'd declared when asked if he was ready.) Birdie wouldn't be onstage for a few nights yet, because she was still working on her new part. But she was far too busy to help Alfred.

So it was Ned, and Ned alone, who found himself standing next to Alfred inside Tothill Fields House of Correction, hoping desperately that he wouldn't catch sight of someone he knew among the inmates.

"Ah! Here's Mrs. Spraggs," the warder suddenly observed. He stepped out of his office to greet a tall woman in a gray gown, whose brown hair was parted in the middle and drawn back severely under a starched white cap. She had a long face, a square jaw, and small, dark, chilly eyes that seemed to weigh everything they focused on. A set of keys jingled at her waist.

As the warder introduced her to Alfred and Mr. Harewood, Ned's gaze drifted to the huge courtyard framed in the doorway behind her. This green space was divided by straight gravel paths and dotted with drooping ash trees, so that it looked more like a public garden than a prison exercise yard.

"And who's this?" Mrs. Scraggs inquired, peering at Ned, who stiffened.

"That's Ned Roach," Alfred told her. "He works with me."

Mrs. Spraggs nodded slowly. "You must mind what I tell you, Ned Roach," she warned. "Don't stray from the path I set, nor speak to none o' the prisoners. We follow the silent system here, and if they talk, they'll be punished."

Ned swallowed, speechless. Alfred growled, "He's a good lad, ma'am, and may be trusted anywhere."

"I'm sure that Ned may be trusted, Mr. Bunce. But our prisoners, on the whole, cannot," Mrs. Spraggs replied. Her voice was as cold as her eyes. "Happily, we'll be passing through no busy places to reach the laundry, which is well away from our dormitories and workrooms. If you'll follow me, gentlemen, I'll take you there." Without further ado, she swung around and set off, heading in an easterly direction down the path that ringed the octagonal courtyard.

Alfred and Mr. Harewood exchanged doubtful glances as the warder said in a very low voice, "She's a trifle abrupt in her manner, but she knows what she's about. By gad she does! You're in safe hands, gentlemen."

"I can see *that*," Mr. Harewood muttered with a crooked smile. Alfred simply grunted. Then they both followed the matron past a series of doors and windows, with Ned trailing along behind them.

He was acutely conscious of being watched. Nearly a dozen buildings ringed the courtyard, many of them multistoried, and he sensed that the worst of the prison was concealed behind the bland, symmetrical façades. He felt as if hundreds of eyes were fixed on his scurrying figure and was greatly relieved when they finally plunged into a modest single-story structure.

"Can you tell me about the missing girls, Mrs. Spraggs?" Alfred asked, his voice echoing off the stucco walls of a long passage lined with doors. Some doors stood open, revealing rooms stacked from floor to ceiling with box-shaped cubbyholes, each of which contained a bundle of clothes, a pair of shoes, and a bonnet. If the clothes had been identical, Ned would have assumed that they were uniforms. But they were all very different, and he realized that they must be the inmates' own garments, stored until their owners were released.

He shivered as Mrs. Spraggs answered Alfred's question.

"Clara Birks was eight years old. She was serving a three-month sentence for stealing a pair of shoes. Mercy

Radbourne was a year older, sentenced to twelve months for picking pockets. Georgina Dugby was twelve but stunted. She was in for six months—theft of four silk handkerchiefs." Mrs. Spraggs came to an iron gate and unlocked it, talking all the while. "Laundry work is popular, so it's mostly women and older girls in the laundry. But they need young'uns to fetch and fold—and to crawl into the hot closet." After locking the gate behind Ned, she turned to Alfred and said, "The boggart's in the closet flue, Mr. Bunce. There's no doubt o' that. Each girl went in there to pick up fallen garments, and not one of 'em was ever seen again."

Ned didn't ask what a hot closet was; he didn't want to sound stupid. He just followed the others silently into a large, triangular yard bounded by the prison wall on two sides. Tucked into a corner of the yard was a squat building with two wings. One contained the washroom, Mrs. Spraggs explained; the other contained the laundry.

This hardly needed saying, since the yard was full of sheets flapping on laundry lines. A girl in a blue-and-white spotted dress was hanging out rows of flannel drawers.

"Maud!" Mrs. Spraggs addressed the girl sharply. "Come here!"

Maud spun around and curtseyed. She was about sixteen years old, Ned thought, with a pink nose, flaxen hair, and almost invisible eyelashes. As she scuttled over to Mrs.

Spraggs, the matron said, "Maud is a witness. She saw Clara go into the hot closet and heard her scream. Is there anything you wish to ask her, Mr. Bunce?"

"Nay," mumbled Alfred, who couldn't even meet the girl's eye. Mr. Harewood looked just as uncomfortable; his face was red, and he kept adjusting his collar.

"Very well." Mrs. Spraggs dismissed Maud, then ushered her guests into the laundry. It was large and steam filled, with wooden troughs arranged around the walls. A giant wringer in the center of the room was being turned by a woman in a spotted uniform and white calico cap. Other women, identically dressed, were standing on wooden grates, sloshing clothes in troughs or scrubbing flannels against ridged boards. Scattered around their feet were baskets full of wet towels and dry blankets.

Ned noticed a large boiler, a stove for sad irons, and a curious cupboard made up of eight long, thin doors, each bearing a steel handle.

"That is our hot closet," Mrs. Spraggs announced, striding toward the cupboard without appearing to notice the other women. Ned tried to do the same, but the women kept stealing glances at him—and at Alfred—and especially at Mr. Harewood, who looked very large and handsome in that dingy, bedraggled place, despite his black eye.

Ned thought he heard a smothered giggle.

"*Who was that?*" Mrs. Spraggs whirled around, enveloping the room in a ferocious stare. "*I did not give anyone permission to speak!*"

A deathly silence fell. The washerwomen scrubbed away furiously, their eyes on their suds. *Creak-creak-creak* went the wringer.

After a brief, tense pause, Mrs. Spraggs turned back to Alfred. "This is the hot closet," she said with eerie calm, before seizing a handle and dragging one of the skinny doors out of the wall. As she did so, a cloud of steam engulfed her. When the steam cleared, Ned saw that the door was connected to a kind of upright frame, or ladder. The doors were lined up in a small room like books on a shelf. Each could be pulled out separately, and each was laden with damp flannel petticoats.

"You see how the closet is heated." Mrs. Spraggs pointed to a hot-water pipe that coiled around the walls of the little room. "The steam escapes through a flue in the ceiling." Her gaze fell on Ned, who was peering into the closet. "I wouldn't get any closer if I were you," she added drily.

At the same instant, Alfred pulled Ned back out of harm's way — though not before Ned had caught a glimpse of the gaping void above the row of drying frames.

"If a garment falls to the floor, someone must be sent in to retrieve it," said Mrs. Spraggs. "We thought Georgina must have climbed the horse and escaped up the flue, under cover of all that steam—"

"But she didn't," Alfred finished. He was squinting into the closet. "Aye," he muttered, "this feels like a bogle's lair to me."

It didn't feel like one to Ned. He hadn't been over-whelmed by any creeping sense of dread and despair. Then it occurred to him that he'd been so full of dread and despair since his arrival at the prison that he wasn't well placed to judge.

"This ain't going to be easy, Mr. Bunce," he murmured.

"I know it," Alfred replied, his gaze drifting to the sopping-wet floor.

Then, without warning, a pair of newcomers appeared on the laundry threshold. One of them was a warder, jingling a set of keys.

The other was Erasmus Gilfoyle.

18

TESTING

Pardon me, Mrs. Spraggs, but this gentleman was inquiring after the other gentlemen. So Mr. Crimp told me to bring him in here," the warder announced.

Mr. Gilfoyle looked like a startled rabbit. Sweaty and breathless, the naturalist kept darting nervous glances at the silent women laboring away at their troughs. "I'm — I'm so sorry to intrude," he stammered, "but I thought you might need this, Mr. Bunce." And he held up a canvas-wrapped, stick-shaped bundle.

Mr. Harewood exclaimed, "Is that the new spear, Razzy?"

"It is. Yes."

"Bravo!" Catching the matron's eye, Mr. Harewood added, "Oh — er, this is Mrs. Spraggs, the Principal Matron. Mrs. Spraggs, this is Mr. Gilfoyle."

Ned heard a muffled snigger as the matron nodded briskly at Mr. Gilfoyle, who bowed back. If Mrs. Spraggs was aware of the snigger, she didn't show it. Instead she turned to Alfred and said, "Do you want this room cleared, Mr. Bunce?"

Alfred nodded.

The matron raised her formidable voice. "All inmates form a line! On the double! Leave everything where it is!"

Though none of them uttered a word, it was obvious from their disgruntled expressions that the prisoners resented having to leave. As Ned watched them line up, their arms still red and soapy, he could almost hear what they were thinking. *Bloomin' old haybag. Hatchet-faced cow.*

Even after they'd marched out, with Mrs. Spraggs at their head, the steamy air felt thick with suppressed anger.

"Thank heavens," Mr. Harewood remarked, once the last shuffling figure had gone. "Now we may speak freely."

"What a dreadful place!" Mr. Gilfoyle was pale with distress. "Such very young women! I had no idea —"

"Is that spear blessed and greased, Mr. Gilfoyle?" Alfred interrupted curtly. "Can we use it now?"

"I believe so," the naturalist replied. He went on to explain that, at Mr. Harewood's request, he had collected the finished spear from a Board of Works stonemason that very morning. He had then delivered the spear to Miss Eames's house, where Mrs. Heppinstall had been entertaining a helpful clergyman. Once the spearhead had been consecrated, Mr. Gilfoyle had carried it to his own residence. "I had mixed an herbal paste last night, after the show," he revealed, "so it took me no time at all to add the finishing touches today."

"Well done, old boy." Mr. Harewood was rubbing his hands together. "We'll be able to test it here—eh, Mr. Bunce?"

"Aye," Alfred rumbled. He took the spear and examined it while the others clustered around him. Unwrapped, it looked rather disappointing. Its shaft was roughly sanded, its head crudely chiseled. But it was sharp and well balanced and covered in a smelly coat of brown grease that had a very toxic appearance.

"Where's the bogle?" Mr. Gilfoyle murmured. "Does anyone know?"

"In there." Mr. Harewood jerked his chin at the hot closet.

"Dear me," said Mr. Gilfoyle. "How are you going to work inside that?"

"We ain't." Alfred spoke flatly. "We cannot use salt in here—it's too wet. And I'll not put Ned in that closet. 'Twould be like throwing him into the bogle's mouth."

Everyone considered the cluttered space beneath the flue. Mr. Harewood began to nod thoughtfully.

"If we was to take one o' them blankets," Ned finally suggested, thinking aloud, "and lay it flat on the floor out here, and trace a circle on it . . ."

"The damp's in the air, lad. That salt won't stay dry for more'n a minute." Alfred raised his eyes to the beams overhead. "I bin thinking about the roof."

"The *roof?*" Mr. Gilfoyle echoed, aghast.

"The pitch is low enough. And there's chimneys to hide behind." Turning to Ned, Alfred said gravely, "'Tis a dry day, with no wind to speak of. If there's steam, it won't linger. I'm persuaded it'll be safer on the roof than it is in here."

Ned swallowed. He glanced at the ceiling.

"If you balk, lad, I'll not hold it against you," Alfred went on. "But I'll tie us to the roof with ropes. And if the bogle takes its time, we shan't wait about. Not this late in the day—"

"All right." Ned cut him off. "I'll do it."

"Are you sure?" asked Mr. Harewood, frowning. "It seems rather unwise."

"I'll do it," Ned repeated stubbornly. He had a duty to Alfred, who deserved—and required—a brave apprentice. Besides, if Alfred said the roof was safe, then it probably was.

Only after he'd scrambled up onto its slippery slates and felt an Arctic breeze on his cheek did Ned begin to wonder.

"You don't think it'll snow, Mr. Bunce?" he quavered, squinting up at the sky.

"If it does, we'll stop," the bogler answered grimly. "Hush, now, and stand still. For I must tie this rope around yer middle."

The roof had a low pitch, as Alfred had promised, and could be reached by the ladder Mrs. Spraggs had provided. The chimney stack was large enough for Alfred to crouch behind and sturdy enough to tie a rope to. Thanks to the encroaching walls of the prison, there was only one stretch of gutter to fall from. As a final touch, a row of laundry baskets had been placed beneath this gutter, to ensure a soft landing if something went wrong.

But with the gray walls looming and the dark sky pressing down on him, Ned felt a bit queasy. *Mebbe it's the bogle,* he thought as he edged carefully along the roof toward Alfred's ring of salt. The ring had been laid near the washroom chimney stack, instead of the one built above the laundry—and Alfred had also tied Ned's rope to a washroom chimney pot.

Not that Ned was expected to jump off the roof. If something went wrong, Alfred wanted Ned to stand and fight.

"I'll be testing this'un," Alfred had explained, holding up the new spear. "If it don't work, you've nowt to fear, lad—for you'll have Mother May's blasting rod. You must hold fast and defend yerself, as you did in Water Lane. I know you can do it. I *seen* you do it. But I'm hoping you'll not have to."

Ned wasn't so sure. He didn't entirely trust the new spear. And he didn't know how well he would use the old one either, with his chilled fingers and unsteady foothold. As he positioned himself inside the magic circle (which was keeping its shape quite nicely, despite the slant of the roof), he couldn't help wishing that he were Jem. For someone as spry as Jem, the roof would have presented no problems.

All Ned could do was take off his shoes and hope.

Turning his back on Alfred, he clasped Mother May's spear to his chest and braced himself. Reflected in his mirror, smoke and steam mingled above the chimney pots. The prison wall lay beyond and drew Ned's eye northward toward a distant wedge of exercise yard. Trapped by a high-wire fence, dozens of hunched figures were circling the flagstones, round and round, their heads down and their feet dragging. They looked bone tired, freezing cold, and utterly miserable. Yet Ned would gladly have changed places with any of them as he cleared his throat, took a deep breath, and launched into a nursery rhyme.

> *"Simple Simon met a pieman*
> *Going to the fair.*
> *Says Simple Simon to the pieman,*
> *'Let me taste yer ware.'"*

His voice was whisked away by a fitful breeze. Somewhere beneath him, inside the laundry, Mr. Harewood and Mr. Gilfoyle were anxiously waiting. Apart from the prisoners trudging around the exercise yard, there wasn't another soul to be seen.

Ned felt very lonely—and very exposed. His coat wasn't thick enough to keep him warm. As he chanted away, his breath emerged in filmy white clouds.

"Says the pieman to Simple Simon,
'Show me first yer penny.'
Says Simple Simon to the pieman,
'Indeed I have not any.'"

All at once Ned spotted in his mirror a gush of steam issuing from a flue behind him—and knew instantly that the bogle was on its way. The steam grew thicker; it seemed to bubble out of the flue and roll across the slates like foam. And it was followed by something that briefly plugged the mouth of the flue, something big but not black.

To Ned's amazement, this bogle was the color of salt, bleached and stringy and hairless. Though it seemed to have no eyes at all, its mouth was huge—and its long snout twitched like a pig's as it tested the air. Ned was grateful that the wind was blowing from the east so that the bogle would not smell Alfred.

"Simple Simon went a-fishing
For to catch a whale.
All the water he had got
Were in his mother's pail."

Ned watched the bogle haul itself out of the flue behind a veil of steam. One arm popped out, then another, then another. They lashed about as boneless as whips before attaching themselves to the roof with suckers. Then the bogle slithered down the chimney and began to slide across the slates toward Ned—who suddenly spied Alfred in his mirror. The bogler was sneaking into view, a dark shape at the very edge of the frame. He braced himself, aimed his spear, and flashed a warning glance at Ned.

"Simple Simon went to look
If plums grew on a thistle—"

"Now!" yelled Alfred.

Ned hurled himself toward the washroom chimney. There was a sharp hiss and then an ear-ringing pop as he lost his balance.

"Help!" Ned flailed about frantically, but his feet kept sliding toward the edge of the roof. "Mr. Bunce!"

He caught a brief glimpse of the bogle, which was collapsing like a blister. Gray steam spurted from the wound that Alfred's new spear had made. The writhing arms were shriveling. The long snout was caving in.

Alfred himself was already scrambling past his handiwork, thrusting an outstretched hand toward Ned.

"Hold fast, lad!" the bogler roared. He was too late. Ned was falling.

Luckily he didn't hit the ground. His rope wasn't long enough. Instead he swung off the gutter like a fish on a hook, his bare toes brushing the fluffy pile of sheets packed into the basket below him. Alerted by his cries, Mr. Harewood and Mr. Gilfoyle burst out of the laundry. Within seconds the engineer was supporting Ned as the naturalist frantically picked at the knot in the rope.

"Mr. Bunce!" Ned croaked. "Is Mr. Bunce all right?"

"Mr. Bunce!" shouted Mr. Harewood. *"Are you hurt?"*

"Nay." Alfred's head suddenly appeared above them. "How's the lad?"

"He's well," said Mr. Harewood. "And the bogle?"

"Dead."

"You mean it was killed by our new spear?" Mr. Gilfoyle demanded.

"Aye."

The naturalist beamed. "Then our experiment worked! Mark—do you hear? It was a success!"

"For which we should be profoundly grateful, in light

of what just happened to the other spear," Mr. Harewood replied.

And he jerked his head at Mother May's blasting rod, which lay on the ground, broken, where Ned had dropped it.

19

"MURDER!"

I'm so sorry, Mr. Bunce," Ned repeated for perhaps the hundredth time. "I can't even remember dropping it . . ."

"Don't fret yerself, lad." Alfred coughed, then spat on the floor. "A split shaft is easily mended. Look at that one now — as good as new."

Ned glanced toward the blasting rod on Alfred's table, its shaft wound around with string. "What if it don't work no more?" he croaked.

"Why would it not?" Alfred sounded impatient. He had dragged on his nightshirt and wrapped himself in his old green coat. Now he sat on his rickety bed, puffing away at his last pipe of the day. "A spear's head is what kills, not its shaft.

And that shaft is still sturdy enough, for the split weren't nobbut a small one." Seeing Ned's crestfallen face, the bogler added gruffly, "I'll not have you dwelling on summat as weren't your fault."

"But what if a flaw in the wood spoils the magic?"

"Then it *still* don't signify, for we've another spear to replace it. And will be making a good many more, if Mr. Gilfoyle has his way." Alfred gave a snort. "You heard him. He'll be opening a factory soon, I'll be bound."

Ned smiled feebly. It was true; the naturalist already had plans to reproduce Alfred's spear in vast quantities. He had talked of nothing else during the cab ride from Tothill Fields Prison. Mr. Harewood had tried to calm him down, pointing out that even a thousand spears wouldn't improve the life of the average bogler's apprentice. On the contrary, it would mean a thousand more apprentices. But Mr. Gilfoyle had remained optimistic. "If Mother May's potion worked, then her other recipes may also be effective," he'd declared. "And if we're *very* lucky, we may find that her summoning herbs render all boglers' boys unnecessary."

Pondering this remark, Ned wished that he could be as excited as Mr. Gilfoyle. He knew that the naturalist was probably right, but his feelings were mixed when it came to the prospect of boglers' boys becoming obsolete.

"He-e-elp! Murder!"

"That's Jem!" the bogler exclaimed.

"Murder! Help me!"

The shout was coming from outside. Ned and Alfred lunged for the window, which Ned shoved open with a *bang.*

"He-e-e-elp!"

Shutters were slamming. People were yelling. As he leaned out over the windowsill, Ned caught sight of candles flickering in at least a dozen windows overlooking the alley, which wasn't well lit. No gas lamps had been erected in Orange Court. No lanterns hung above doorways. But thanks to a full moon, a clear sky, and the golden glow of the candles, Ned was able to spot Jem.

"There!" Ned cried, pointing at a dark shape hanging off a downpipe on a neighboring house. Jem was two floors above the ground and still moving up the pipe.

Below him a door swung open, casting a square of light onto the cobbles.

"'Ere!" A girl appeared on the threshold. "What's all the bloody fuss about?"

"He tried to kill me!" Jem wailed. "He's got a knife!"

"Who does?" It was Alfred speaking, loudly and roughly. He jostled Ned aside, craning his neck to catch a glimpse of Jem. "Who tried to kill you?"

"I — I dunno." Jem turned his head gingerly to peer down into the dark alley. "He ain't there no more."

"I'm coming down," Alfred declared.

"No! Don't you come down! I'll come up!"

"But—"

"He may be hiding! He may come back!" Before Alfred could argue, Jem swarmed up the pipe until he reached a washing line. By following the line from shutter hook to shutter hook—hand over hand, feet swinging—he made it to the window two floors beneath Alfred's garret. By this time Ned was almost falling out the garret window in his struggle to see what was going on. As far as he could tell, Jem was quite right; Orange Court looked deserted. No one was skulking among the costers' carts or sidling back into Drury Lane.

Two floors below, however, a pair of thin white arms reached for Jem as a sickly neighbor begged him to crawl into her room. "You'll fall to yer death!" she screeched over the fretful whimpering of her child. "You'll dash yer brains out!"

But Jem kept climbing. Perhaps he didn't trust the neighbor. Perhaps he didn't have faith in the strength of her arms.

It was Alfred who finally pulled Jem inside the garret, with a heave that sent them both sprawling. For a moment they lay on the floor, stunned. Then Ned sprang forward to help Alfred while Jem staggered to his feet.

"What happened to yer coat?" was the first thing Alfred said, once he'd recovered.

Jem glanced down at himself. Even in the leaping yellow firelight he looked pale. His hair was ruffled, his knuckles were grazed, and there was a rip in the knee of his trousers.

"I — I lost me coat," he admitted.

"You *lost* it?"

"'Tweren't down to me, Mr. Bunce." Jem's voice cracked. But he cleared his throat, took a deep breath, and continued. "That cove out there — he tried to nobble me. I only got away by slipping out o' me coat." He glanced at the window. "It might still be in the street," he faltered. "He might've left it where it fell."

"Did you see him?" asked Ned. "D'you know who done it?"

Jem wiped his eyes, which were bloodshot. His grubby hands were shaking. "It's dark as a chimney out there," he said. "But he were big. I could see *that*. And he didn't have no hair."

Ned blinked as Alfred sucked air through his teeth.

"No hair?" the bogler repeated sharply.

"I seen his bonce gleaming like glass," Jem insisted.

"Did he have a scar on his brow?" Ned demanded. He clearly recalled Mr. Harewood's description of the footpad who had attacked him in the court off Newgate Street.

"I told you, I couldn't see much." Jem turned to address Alfred. "He followed me, Mr. Bunce. I'm sure of it. I were coming home from the theater, and when I turned into Orange Court he grabbed me from behind."

"Aye," said Alfred, retrieving his pipe from the bed. "I'm a-thinking he were one o' Jack Gammon's cronies. Same cove as struck Mr. Harewood, I'll wager."

"But how did they find us?" Ned couldn't understand it. "We bin so careful! How did they track us here?"

"I'll tell you how," said Jem. His tone was flat, his expression grim. "They bin reading playbills. Like half o' London."

"Playbills?" Alfred echoed.

"They was posted yesterday. New'uns. With Birdie's name on 'em." Glancing from face to face, Jem added hoarsely, "That there bald cove must have bin watching the Theatre Royal. I expect he wanted to follow Birdie, in case she met up with me —"

"But he didn't have to," Ned interrupted.

Jem gave a curt nod. He was still very pale. In the pause that followed, Alfred squatted down and reached under his bed.

"Playbills," Ned muttered at last. "I never thought o' that."

Jem shrugged. "Why should you? None of us can read. I only found out about them bills from Birdie."

"Birdie?" Ned was struck by the sudden, horrible

thought that she might also be in danger. "Don't tell me you saw *Birdie* there tonight?"

Jem quickly assured Ned that Birdie had left the theater much earlier that day after rehearsing with some of the cast. She wouldn't be making her debut until Saturday, he said, because Saturday night pulled in the biggest crowds. "Mr. Chatterton decided to wait a few days, so as word would get about," Jem went on. "He's bin posting bills and advertising in newspapers. 'Birdie the Bogler's Girl,' 'Child Prodigy Astounds Theatrical Profession,' 'London's Latest Marvel' — that kind o' thing. He thinks she'll boost the takings."

"So no one followed her home?" asked Ned.

"I doubt it." Jem's attention shifted to Alfred, who had picked up Mother May's blasting rod. "W-what are you doing, Mr. Bunce?" he stammered. "You don't think that feller'll be coming up *here?*"

"I ain't taking no chances," Alfred replied coolly.

Ned and Jem exchanged a frightened look. Jem croaked, "Mebbe we should leave."

"And go where? To Miss Eames's house?" Ned frowned at him. "We can't have no lurking nobbler follow us to Bloomsbury. Mrs. Heppinstall would die o' fright!"

"We ain't going nowhere. Not while it's dark." Alfred was heading for the door, his stool in one hand, his spear in the other. "Shut that window, Ned, and bolt it. I don't expect no one'll come over the roof, but it's best to be careful."

As Ned rushed to the window, Alfred stationed himself by the door. It was obvious from the way he settled down, with his back to the wall and his spear across his knees, that the bogler intended to stay there all night.

"Are you taking the first shift, Mr. Bunce?" asked Jem.

"Nay, lad, I'll be here till morning." Before anyone could protest, Alfred continued, "Did you leave tonight's pay in yer coat pocket, by the by?"

"No, sir." Jem plunged a hand into the pocket of his trousers and pulled out a modest collection of coins. "I didn't lose me wages."

"Good." With his teeth clenched around the stem of his pipe, Alfred remarked, "You can keep half o' that, if you think you earned it."

"I earned it right enough. I didn't put a foot wrong tonight, though I did mistime one exit." Jem hesitated, then asked, "How did you fare at the gaol?"

Ned shrugged. It was Alfred who said, through a puff of smoke, "The new spear worked."

"It *did?*"

"And the old one split up the shaft, on account o' me," Ned mumbled. "I only hope *it* still works . . ."

"It'll work," Alfred said impatiently. "The bogle seemed uncommon. White as snow. Stunted. And so much of it left behind, the warders talked o' shoveling it into a boiler." As Jem's eyes widened, Alfred added, "Aye. Summat's wrong.

There's strange things afoot. But we'll not fret on it to-night—we've enough to worry us. You boys go to bed now. I've bolted the door. If anyone tries to break it down, I'll gut him like a fish."

There was an edge to Alfred's tone that made the boys flinch. Finally Jem asked, "But what'll we do tomorrow, Mr. Bunce? If that feller's still sneaking about . . ."

"Tomorrow we'll speak to Constable Pike," said Alfred. "He knows all the streets around Newgate, *and* those as live in 'em. I'm persuaded he'll have a notion of who that bald villain might be and how we might lay our hands on him." As the two boys absorbed this plan, Alfred concluded, "Constable Pike will listen. He'll not turn us away with an empty promise."

"But I'm due at the theater for a matinee tomorrow," Jem pointed out.

"Aye. And I'll take you there meself, once we've talked to Constable Pike."

Jem appeared satisfied with this assurance, but to Ned it seemed that Alfred had left a lot of questions unanswered. Constable Pike was stationed at Smithfield, just a stone's throw from Jack Gammon's shop. How were they going to smuggle Jem into the neighborhood without putting him in danger? Would they hire a cab? And what if the bald man was waiting for them as they left their room the next morning? What if he was *just outside the door?*

Ned decided to be ready for anything: a midnight raid, a morning ambush—even a fire, if someone decided to burn the house down. So before going to bed, he quietly moved the water bucket, tucked a kitchen knife under his paillasse, and made sure his boots were standing, loosely tied, where he could easily find them.

Despite these precautions, he took a long, long time to fall asleep.

POLICE BUSINESS

Y ou're in luck, Mr. Bunce," Constable Pike announced.

He was standing with his hands behind his back, straight and stocky and trimly dressed in a dark blue uniform. Behind him, flames danced in a modest fireplace under a portrait of the queen.

"It so happens we've a gentleman in our custody who matches the description you've just given me," he continued. "Tobias Fitch is his name, and he was arrested early this morning on a charge of unlawfully uttering counterfeit coin." The policeman's keen gaze shifted from Alfred to Ned to Jem, taking in every detail: the knife handle protruding from Ned's pocket, the torn flannel shirt that Jem wore instead of a coat, the bags under Alfred's eyes.

Constable Pike's own eyes were large and gray, ringed by thick black lashes. With his curly hair, full cheeks, and red lips he looked almost cherubic — though his rigid posture and toneless drawl undermined this impression. "Fitch is an associate o' John Harold Gammon, butcher, and is well known to us here at Smithfield Station House," he continued. "We were about to send him off to the police court, with our regular delivery o' felons. But you got here just in time, Mr. Bunce. He's still here for your lad to identify."

Ned grimaced. He didn't envy Jem. Looking Tobias Fitch in the eye wouldn't be easy.

"Mebbe we should fetch Mr. Harewood," Alfred murmured. "*He* saw the feller in broad daylight."

"The more the merrier," said Constable Pike. "Our only witness to the counterfeit charge lives in White Hart Street, which is a deal too close to Gammon's shop for my liking." Spotting another policeman across the room, he stiffened. "I must have a word with my sergeant. If you'll wait here, Mr. Bunce, I'll be back directly. It won't take long."

He strode off briskly, leaving the others marooned like driftwood on a mudflat. The station house was an unfriendly place, lined with hard benches and studded with barred windows. The policeman who stood behind a high desk at one end of the room never raised his eyes from the ledger that occupied him. Distant wails and moans issued from one dark doorway; another was protected by a locked gate. Everywhere he looked, Ned saw chains and keys and bolts and batons.

"We needn't have hired a cab to get us here after all," Jem muttered at last. "Not with Fitch banged up in a police cell."

"You still don't know if Fitch is the one," Ned pointed out.

But Jem snorted. "He must be. How many big bald men could be working for Jack Gammon?"

"Shh! Hold yer tongues!" Alfred snapped. Constable Pike was on his way back, jingling a set of keys.

"We'll go downstairs now," the policeman said, "and if Fitch don't prove to be your man, I'll send him off to Clerkenwell with the rest of 'em." He led Alfred's party along a short passage lined with metal doors as the sound of moaning grew louder. "It's a stroke o' luck you're here, Mr. Bunce," he went on, "for I've bin hard at work trying to break Fitch. Now that he's lagged, I thought he might open up a little on the subject o' Salty Jack. I promised him no end o' trouble if he didn't. But he refused to cooperate." Constable Pike paused at the end of the passage, where a stone staircase plunged into the bowels of the station house.

"Seems to me he's less scared o' the *gallows* than he is o' Jack Gammon — but, then, most people are, hereabouts. That's why I can't find one solid witness against the worst villain this side o' the Thames. But your boy's appearance might shake Fitch, especially if I threaten the fellow with two counts o' felonious assault. That's a hanging crime. He'll not be doing six months' hard labor for *that*."

"'Tain't Fitch as wants Jem dead," growled Alfred.

"Exactly. It's Gammon. And I'll remind Fitch it's Gammon who should swing for it, not him." Having made this promise, Constable Pike continued down two flights of narrow stairs and into a cellar almost as foul as the slaughterhouse beneath Newgate Market. After years scavenging along the banks of the Thames, Ned was familiar with foul stenches. But the air in the lockup nearly choked him, smelling as it did of sweat and vomit and worse things.

Jem began to cough as Alfred covered his nose.

"We've had ten drunkards come in overnight," Constable Pike said cheerfully, without flinching, "and won't be able to clean up till they leave. But Fitch is in his own cell." Suddenly he raised his voice above the sound of moans coming from behind one of the numbered doors that lined a dim, dank passage. *"Be quiet now, Mr. Bates! You'll be out o' here in a minute!"*

The moaning stopped. Bustling down the passage, Constable Pike finally stopped at another door—iron studded, double bolted, and fitted with a small metal grate. He then turned to Jem, indicating the door with a jerk of his chin.

Jem hesitated. But after Alfred had given him a prod, he shuffled forward and stood on tiptoe to peer through the grate into the cell.

He immediately ducked down again.

"Well?" said Constable Pike.

Ned could tell that Jem was loath to pass judgment. But Constable Pike wasn't about to let Jem express any doubts—not within earshot of Tobias Fitch.

"He's the one, is he? I thought as much." The policeman raised his voice. "You're in trouble, Fitch. D'you hear me? I've a boy here who was attacked on his way home last night, and he's identified you as the culprit." There was no reply. Ned couldn't even hear the prisoner breathing. So Constable Pike continued, "You also punched a gentleman in Angel Court on Tuesday—a respectable gentleman who'll have no qualms about testifying against you and who'll cut a fine figure in the witness box." The policeman turned to Alfred. "What was the gentleman's name, Mr. Bunce?"

Alfred gave a start. "Er . . . ah . . . Mark Harewood," he mumbled.

"D'you hear that, Fitch? You're facing two counts of felonious assault. Even one conviction'll send you to the gallows."

Still Tobias Fitch didn't speak. It was another prisoner somewhere down the passage who suddenly erupted into a stream of abuse.

"*Shut your mouth, O'Flaherty, or I'll shut it for you!*" Constable Pike barked before once again directing his comments through the grate in the door. "We know you were hired, Fitch, and we know why. Jack Gammon don't like witnesses. Not living ones at any rate. But Jack's a fool. If he'd let the boy alone, we wouldn't be here now. There'd be no cause for the lad to peach — he'd have too much to lose. What's he got to lose now, though? He's dead if he talks and he's dead if he don't. So he might as well talk."

Ned saw the color drain from Jem's face.

"I want you to think about it," the policeman continued. "I want you to think about what you owe Jack Gammon, who's happy to let you swing for his own misdeeds. It was Gammon who sent you after Jem Barbary. It was Gammon who set you to watch over that newsboy, with orders to nobble anyone who might pursue him. Why — for all I know it was Gammon who paid you with counterfeit coin!"

Again Constable Pike paused, peering into Fitch's cell. But as the seconds ticked by and no one answered, Pike caught Alfred's eye and gave a rueful shrug. "You've ten minutes before I send you off to King's Cross Road, Fitch, with two more names on your charge sheet," he finished. "And if I do that, you're done for. You'll be hoisted in

Newgate yard before the month's out. Think on that, for it's worth pondering."

The policeman then sniffed, sighed, and motioned to the others. As he was walking away, a voice like a creaking millstone suddenly said, "'Ere! You! Peeler!"

Constable Pike halted and glanced back at the cell. "What?" he asked.

"I got summat for you."

Ned could see that Tobias Fitch was now right behind his cell door. A wedge of cheek, heavily scarred and bristling with a two-day growth, was visible through the grate.

Constable Pike hesitated and seemed to be weighing his options. At last he approached Fitch's door again.

"What is it?" he asked.

A gob of spit landed on his collar.

Ned gasped. Even Alfred winced. But the policeman simply turned on his heel and marched off.

He was dabbing at his collar with a starched white handkerchief by the time he reached the bottom of the staircase. "I've had worse," he told Alfred, who was just behind him. "Policing can be a dirty business."

"Shall we send for Mr. Harewood to identify Fitch?" Alfred said gruffly. He seemed rattled, Ned thought.

"By all means." The policeman began to head upstairs. "I'm not convinced we'll get any more out o' Fitch, though. It's my belief he's more scared o' Gammon than he is of anything else. And I daresay he thinks Gammon'll spring him from gaol by getting rid o' witnesses. It's happened before."

Ned swallowed. As he trudged after Constable Pike, he glanced back at Jem, who was bringing up the rear.

Poor Jem looked as scared as Ned felt.

"I'll be the talk o' the division, now that you've paid me a visit," Constable Pike was saying. "By the by, have you bin hunting down bogles in any station houses lately? The newspaper said you've bin hired to exterminate all the bogles on government premises — and there's a good many police stations with drains under 'em."

Alfred stopped in his tracks halfway up the stairs. He looked shocked. "What newspaper are you talking about?" he demanded.

"Why, today's *London Times*," the policeman said. "Didn't you read it?"

Alfred opened his mouth, then shut it again. Ned wondered if the bogler was too embarrassed to admit that he couldn't read. Breaking into the sudden silence, Jem piped up, "Mr. Bunce?"

"Wait." Alfred set off again, with Ned close at his heels. Upon reaching the top of the stairs, Alfred asked Constable Pike, "What did that newspaper say about me?"

"It said you were employed by the Sewers Office," the constable replied. Fixing Alfred with a quizzical look, he added, "The tone of it wasn't too friendly, sir, if you get my meaning. Questions were asked about wasting public funds on fairy tales. But you'll be accustomed to that, I expect—folk who don't believe in bogles."

"Aye," Alfred growled. "There's plenty as don't."

"Mr. Bunce?" By this time Jem had reached the top of the stairs and had jostled Ned aside.

"What is it?" Alfred glared at Jem but didn't manage to quell him.

Jem grabbed Alfred's sleeve and hissed, "There's one thing as might scare Tobias Fitch more'n the butcher—and that's a *bogle*, Mr. Bunce." Seeing Alfred's blank expression, Jem continued in a low voice, "What if we threaten Fitch with a bogle?"

Ned's jaw dropped. He couldn't believe his ears. As Constable Pike gave a snort of laughter, Alfred said, "Don't be a fool, boy. We can't do that!"

"Believe me, lad—if there was a bogle in this here station house, I'd know about it," the policeman drawled.

Jem ignored him. "It wouldn't be a *real* bogle, Mr. Bunce! We'd just pretend it was." As Jem glanced uneasily down the staircase, Ned wondered if he was serious. He certainly *looked* serious, with his white face and furrowed brow. "We'd have to find a good cellar with a sufficiency o' places to hide," Jem continued. "There's a man at the Theatre Royal can make a puff of smoke appear wherever you want it. And if Constable Pike could hold on to Fitch just a *little* longer, I know someone we could ask to play a bogle." Seeing Alfred narrow his eyes, Jem's tone became more urgent. "He's at the penny gaff on Whitechapel Road, Mr. Bunce. *You* know where I mean. The cove I'm a-thinking of—why, he plays bogles for a living! And all we'd need to do is make it worth his while."

21

A Bogle for Hire

Josiah Lubbock was the manager of a penny gaff on Whitechapel Road, where he mounted shows featuring dwarves, snakes, clockwork heads, stuffed freaks of nature, and anything else that people might pay to see. Ned had met Mr. Lubbock several times: once at Alfred's place, once on Giltspur Street, and once outside the derelict house where Salty Jack had tried to feed Jem to a bogle. But never had Ned visited Mr. Lubbock's establishment in the East End.

He'd heard a lot about it, though. And he was relieved to find that Mr. Lubbock was still staging his show at the same address—a small, two-story building tucked between a pastry shop and a public house. Standing with Alfred in a bitter wind, with snowflakes drifting and whirling like ash, Ned studied the shop front with keen interest.

There were playbills all over its windows, and its front door was firmly shut.

"Too early in the day for a show," Alfred speculated.

"Does anyone *live* there?" asked Ned.

Alfred shrugged. His hands were buried deep in his pockets. His voice was muffled by the thick scarf wound around the bottom half of his face. "I wish there was some way o' doing this without alerting Lubbock," he said morosely, "but I don't expect there is. Whatever money's on offer, he'll get his cut of it I've no doubt."

"He might not reckanise me," Ned observed. "Mebbe *I* should knock on the door. What's the name o' the feller we want?"

"Eduardo." Alfred heaved a sigh that turned to steam when it hit the air. "Nay," he said, "I ain't no sneaking speeler as juggles with the truth. Not like Josiah Lubbock. I'll walk up and speak out, like an honest man."

Alfred boldly stepped off the pavement into the dirty, slushy street. Ned followed. Whitechapel Road wasn't as busy as usual, perhaps because the weather was so bad. It was the kind of weather that made Ned offer up a silent prayer of gratitude. As a mudlark, on a day like this, he would have had to choose between starving or freezing. But thanks to Alfred, he now had to endure nothing more taxing than a walk from the nearest omnibus stop.

They had taken an omnibus from Smithfield instead of a cab. It was Jem who had been sent to the Sewers Office in the safety of his very own hired vehicle, with orders to inform Mr. Harewood that he was needed at Smithfield Station House. "See if Mr. Harewood will give you a ride to Drury Lane for yer matinee," Alfred had urged Jem. "And be sure he sets you down on the theater's very doorstep, lad. Tell him you ain't safe on yer own. Tell him Tobias Fitch may not be Salty Jack's only nobbler."

As Alfred banged on the door of the penny gaff, Ned wondered uneasily if Salty Jack *would* send someone else to kill Jem — and what could possibly be done to prevent it. Even if he moved lodgings, Jem would still be working at the Theatre Royal. Unless he gave up his job there, he would be easy enough to find.

The only real solution was to get rid of Jack Gammon. And the only way to do *that* was to get him locked up in gaol . . .

"Who's there?" a shrill voice demanded from behind the door.

Alfred cleared his throat and spat on the ground. "It's Alfred Bunce," he rasped. "I'm looking for Eduardo."

"For whom?"

"*Eduardo.*" After a moment's hesitation, Alfred admitted, "I don't know his other name."

There was a pause, then a scraping of bolts. At last the door swung open to reveal a short, plump girl with dirty blond hair and a pasty face. There were dark circles under her eyes, and traces of makeup above them. She wore an untidy collection of garments, topped off by a mangy fur stole. Ned judged her to be about sixteen.

"I remember you," she said accusingly. "You're the Go-Devil Man." Before Alfred could confirm this, she suddenly cried, "I ain't played Birdie McAdam in weeks! Birdie's name is off our boards now! I'm Delia the Dragonslayer—can't you read? We don't *have* a Birdie in the show! Not since you was here last."

"I don't—"

"If you've come to complain, you needn't talk to me. It's Mr. Lubbock you want, and he's out." The girl was closing the door when Alfred wedged his foot in the doorway.

"Wait," he said. "I ain't here to fret you, miss. I know you don't use Birdie's name no more."

"We want to talk to Eduardo," Ned interrupted. "We want to hire him."

The girl blinked. "*Hire* him?"

"To play a bogle."

For a moment the girl stood motionless, wide-eyed and open-mouthed. Then her expression brightened. "A job, is it?" she asked Alfred, who nodded.

"Aye."

"Well, come in, then!" She pulled open the door. "I'll fetch Eduardo—he's backstage at present. *I'm* Bedelia Moss. I don't recollect if we was formally introduced last time we met." Bedelia peered at Ned as she bolted the door behind them. "What happened to the other lad? The one with black hair? Did he get ate by a bogle?"

"No!" snapped Alfred.

"Jem's a dancer now," Ned mumbled. "I'm Ned Roach."

"A dancer, is he? So am I. I can dance *and* sing. But I ain't engaged at the Theatre Royal." There was a waspish edge to Bedelia's tone—and Ned suddenly realized that she must have seen one of Mr. Chatterton's playbills. Upon following her into a dim, dusty vestibule that contained an empty ticket booth and three large display cabinets full of stuffed and pickled creatures, Ned could see why Bedelia might be jealous of Birdie. Mr. Lubbock's penny gaff was a far cry from the Theatre Royal on Drury Lane.

"Eddie! You got visitors!" the girl bellowed, pushing aside a plush curtain to reveal a very large room with a raised platform at one end. From the rows of wooden benches facing the platform, Ned deduced that he had entered the actual theater—which smelled of stale sweat and sawdust. A

door to the left of the platform stood open. Beyond it were a rack of clothes and a chest piled high with props.

"Whatta you want?" a deep voice roared. "I'm a-very busy!"

"Job for you, Eddie!" Bedelia turned to Alfred. "Is it regular work?"

"No," Alfred had to confess. "We'll not be needing him more'n once."

"When?" asked Bedelia.

"Tomorrow morning. Early."

"Well, *that's* all right. We don't do morning shows." Bedelia suddenly turned to address a hulking figure framed in the doorway. "D'you remember Mr. Bunce, Ed? He came here last month, with Birdie McAdam."

Ned stared in astonishment at Eduardo, who was immensely tall, with a massive, square-jawed head, the shoulders of an ox, and legs like tree trunks. His black hair was shaved very short on his head but was thick and luxuriant on his arms and hands and chest—all of which were clearly visible because he wore an open shirt with rolled-up sleeves over a loose pair of canvas trousers.

"What job?" he said, his eyes flicking from Bedelia to Alfred and back again.

Alfred cleared his throat. "Last time we came here, Mr. ...er..."

"Miniotto," Bedelia supplied.

"Last time we came here, Mr. Miniotto, you was playing a bogle onstage."

"He still is," Bedelia interjected.

Alfred stared at her for a moment from beneath his bushy eyebrows. Then he turned back to Eduardo and said, "We need a bogle. For an hour or two tomorrow morning, around six o'clock, at the Clerkenwell Station House on King's Cross Road."

Eduardo frowned. He looked puzzled.

"They don't want a *real* bogle, Eddie, they want you," Bedelia explained. "Ain't that right, Mr. Bunce?"

"Aye."

"And we want his costume, too," Ned added quickly. "He'll need to wear that."

"Of course!" Bedelia exclaimed. "He can't be a bogle without a pelt!" Smirking, she put her hands on her hips and announced, "It'll cost you ten shillings."

"Ten shillings!" squeaked Ned. It was a monstrous sum.

"Five," said Alfred.

"Come now, Mr. Bunce, you can do better than that," Bedelia protested. "I read about you in the newspaper this morning. You've a fancy new position with the Sewers Office." Seeing Alfred scowl, she reduced the fee. "Eight shillings."

"Five," Alfred repeated. "That's me final offer."

"His position ain't *that* fancy," Ned murmured, just as Eduardo stepped forward with his hand outstretched.

"Five-a shilling issa good," he announced.

Bedelia squealed, "But, *Eddie*—"

Eduardo cut her off. "I put on a suit, stamp and roar, make-a good money. For a fee I do this." He shook hands with Alfred, then asked for an advance.

Alfred gave him half a crown. "Clerkenwell Station House, six o'clock in the morning," he repeated.

"Why do you need a bogle in a police station?" Bedelia seemed genuinely curious.

Alfred changed the subject. "If you'd keep this to yerselves, I'd be grateful. Once Josiah Lubbock finds out, he'll want a cut o' the fee. And he'll make a nuisance of hisself besides."

Bedelia and Eduardo exchanged a quick glance. Bedelia replied airily, "Don't you worry about Josiah. We know how to get around *him*."

Alfred gave a satisfied nod, then tipped his hat and turned to go. Before heading back into the vestibule, he paused and addressed Eduardo.

"Bogles seldom roar," he growled. "They hiss. You'd best remember that."

With a final nod he took his leave out into the snow again. Ned followed him. As they trudged down Whitechapel

Road, weaving their way between scurrying pedestrians and rattling carts, Ned's gaze drifted longingly back toward the pastry shop.

He could smell hot pies.

"Where shall we go now, Mr. Bunce?" he asked, hoping that Alfred, too, might be hungry. But before the bogler could respond, someone else answered Ned's question in a roundabout kind of way.

"Mr. Bunce! Ahoy!"

Startled, Ned spun around. Mark Harewood was leaning out of a hackney carriage just across the road.

Alfred had stopped in his tracks. "Mr. Harewood?"

"Come quickly!" The engineer beckoned. "You're wanted!"

The bogler obediently struck out for Mr. Harewood's vehicle, with Ned at his heels. They dodged a coster's cart, splashed through a puddle of slush, and ended up at the door of the carriage, which Mr. Harewood was holding open for them.

"Mr. Daw has called an emergency committee meeting," he said, reaching down to grab Ned's arm.

"Mr. Daw?" Ned was stumped until he remembered that Mr. Daw was the Principal Clerk at the City of London Sewers Office.

"I've been sending messages all over London." Mr. Harewood moved aside for Ned, then shut the door behind

Alfred. "I thought I'd *never* find you. But when Jem arrived, he told me where you'd gone."

"We ain't neither of us bin back to Smithfield yet," remarked Jem, who was sitting in one corner of the carriage. Ned offered him a weak smile.

Alfred didn't seem to notice Jem at all. "What's this about?" he demanded, peering at Mr. Harewood.

The engineer shrugged. "I'm not sure, but I've a notion it may have something to do with today's newspaper article." He thumped on the roof with his stick and cried, "Guildhall, please! Quick as you can!" As the carriage gave a lurch, he added, "This is my fault. Someone must have passed my memorandum to the press. But what else could I have done? After all, we can't investigate bogles unless we know where to find them. And how can we possibly find them without the public's help?"

22

MR. DAW'S DISPLEASURE

Mr. Joseph Daw's office at Guildhall was handsome enough to be a chapel. It had stained-glass windows, a coffered ceiling, velvet curtains, and dark, heavy furniture. Mr. Daw himself was dressed in priestly black. His waistcoat was silk and his spectacles were gold-rimmed. Despite his slight build and sickly complexion, he somehow managed to fill the room with an atmosphere of chilly disapproval, like a schoolmaster confronting eight disobedient children.

"I assume that you have all read this piece," he said, pushing a newspaper clipping across the desk in front of him.

Mr. Harewood nodded. So did Mr. Wardle. Mr. Gilfoyle

murmured, "I'm afraid so" as Miss Eames leaned forward to get a better look.

"Oh dear," she remarked. "Yes. I did see that."

Ned and Jem glanced at each other. From the moment of their arrival, they had been treated by Mr. Daw as if they didn't exist. Perhaps it had something to do with Jem's missing coat or Ned's muddy shoes. Whatever the reason, Ned knew that anything they said would be roundly ignored. So, like Jem, he remained silent.

It was Birdie who spoke up. Because she was so nicely dressed, in chestnut cashmere trimmed with silk braid, she had received a guarded nod from Mr. Daw as she entered his office. Now she sat up straight and defiantly announced, "Not everyone here can read, Mr. Daw."

"Aye, but I know what's in the newspaper," Alfred hastened to assure her. "Mr. Harewood told me the gist of it."

"I see." Mr. Daw's stern gaze traveled from Alfred to Birdie, then from Birdie to Miss Eames. After skipping over Jem, Ned, and Mr. Wardle, it finally came to rest on Mr. Gilfoyle, who was standing shoulder to shoulder with Mr. Harewood because there weren't enough chairs. "Did I or did I not convey to you from the very start that this committee was convened *unofficially?*" said Mr. Daw. "Did I not make it clear that the Chief Engineer was anxious not to arouse too much interest among the public? Perhaps the wisdom of this request has become apparent to you, now that the Sewers Office is a laughingstock. May I ask, Mr. Harewood, how this came about?"

Mr. Harewood shifted uncomfortably. He was looking a little ink stained, and his black eye was turning mauve and green and yellow. "I'm not sure how the news spread," he confessed, "but it might have had something to do with my memorandum."

He then explained, as Mr. Daw's expression became more and more sour. When the engineer proposed that some government clerk must have leaked the memorandum to a journalist, Mr. Daw produced from one of his desk drawers a wad of crumpled paper. Some of the sheets were telegrams; some were letters; some appeared to be jottings on ledger leaves.

"Since the article was published, I have received more than two dozen requests for help," he said tightly. "Some of these messages concern missing children. Others relate to sightings in sewers. One is about a blocked drain." He shot a withering look at the engineer. "This is not what I had in mind when the committee was formed, Mr. Harewood."

"No, sir. I quite see that." The engineer fished a handful of papers from his own pocket. "As a matter of fact, I've also received further communications this morning. From a military barracks and from the Treasury Department—"

"Clearly the problem is widespread." Mr. Daw cut him

off—quite rudely, Ned thought. "Could we somehow have unleashed a plague, Mr. Harewood?"

"I doubt that very much." It was the naturalist who answered. "In my view, this is a phenomenon frequently seen in the modern world, where a newspaper will alarm its readers about something to which they have previously paid very little heed. It is quite likely that many of your correspondents did not accept the reality of bogles until their existence was confirmed in print. Now, of course, there is a full-scale panic."

"Quite," Mr. Daw said drily. "Which leads me to ask this committee: Are you in a position to allay the public's fears?"

There was a pause as everyone looked at each other. Finally Mr. Gilfoyle said, "As a matter of fact, there *has* been a breakthrough. We've discovered how to reproduce Mr. Bunce's spear. And with more spears we can hire more boglers."

"Ahem." Mr. Daw raised his hand suddenly. "The Sewers Office does not hire boglers. The Town Clerk has already made a statement to this effect."

Ned caught his breath. Even Mr. Gilfoyle looked startled.

"The Committee for the Regulation of Subterranean Anomalies has undertaken to hire Mr. Bunce," Mr. Daw continued, "but the Sewers Office itself knew *nothing about it.*" Leaning back in his chair, he steepled his fingers and let his chilly gaze sweep over the people arrayed before him. "Henceforth, the Sewers Office will not be informed of any discoveries you might make. You were not here today and will not make any visits in the future. Do you understand me?"

Mr. Harewood nodded as he stuffed his telegrams back into his pocket. Ned caught Birdie's eye and grimaced. He knew exactly what was going on. Mr. Daw didn't want any more newspapers accusing his department of wasting rate money. So he was distancing himself from the committee to ensure that he wasn't blamed for anything that went wrong.

"From now on your invoices and reports will be submitted to Mr. Edward Rider Cook, a member of the Metropolitan Board of Works who has undertaken to fund the committee as a . . . ahem . . . *private* patron," Mr. Daw continued. "He is a soap manufacturer with a high regard for all forms of scientific research, though he has a special interest in chemistry." Rising, Mr. Daw executed a stiff little bow and said to the group, "May I wish you the very best of luck in your future endeavors? If you have any further questions, you should direct them to Mr. Cook."

The others exchanged stunned glances. Birdie was scowling. Mr. Wardle had turned pale. Alfred didn't look at all impressed.

Mr. Harewood asked, with an edge to his voice, "May we hold our next meeting at the Sewers Office, Mr. Daw? Or is it closed to us now?"

"As I said, Mr. Harewood, you should apply to Mr. Cook for an answer. He is, after all, on the Board of Works. If you'll excuse me, I'm very busy. I had to postpone several meetings to make time for this one. You know your way out, I think? It's left, then left again . . ."

Two minutes later, the entire committee was standing in a Guildhall corridor. Ned felt as if he'd been cut adrift like a castaway.

"Well," Mr. Harewood said at last, "I suppose I should have foreseen *that*. Clerkish fellows always scuttle for cover when a storm threatens."

"But what is expected of us, Harewood?" Mr. Wardle spoke plaintively, his plump face creased into anxious lines. "Is the committee part of my job anymore?"

Mr. Harewood shrugged.

"I'm persuaded that Mr. Daw wants us to continue as before but doesn't want to know anything about it." Miss Eames turned to the naturalist. "Did you receive that impression, Mr. Gilfoyle?"

"I did," Mr. Gilfoyle replied crisply. "And I believe that he will come to regret his lack of confidence when we have managed to exterminate all the bogles in London."

"I say! Steady on, old fellow." There was a note of re-proof in Mr. Harewood's voice. "We've not triumphed *quite* yet."

"No, but we are well on our way." The naturalist began to explain to Miss Eames that he had already passed the recipe for Mother May's potion on to Mr. Warington, of Apothecaries' Hall, who had promised to supply him with a large quantity of the finished product. Mr. Gilfoyle was also expecting, from Mr. Harewood's friend the stonemason, two dozen more spearheads to be delivered within the week. And then there was the matter of the blackthorn shafts. "I have been contemplating a trip to Derbyshire, where I intend to collect a load of blackthorn gathered from the hedge near Mother May's house," the naturalist explained. "And while visiting Derbyshire I shall, of course, make further inquiries about those so-called summoning herbs."

"Yes, indeed," Miss Eames interrupted. "For there can be no benefit to more spears if they simply result in the need for more bait. That *would* be a step backwards."

"Aye, but I ain't so sure about no summoning herbs," Alfred remarked. He looked very uncomfortable. His gaze kept darting up and down the gloomy passage, as if he was expecting some kind of ambush. "These witch's tricks don't sit well with me. Chanting and potions and such—'tain't what I were trained for."

"And besides," Birdie added, "who's going to find more

boglers? You can't hire just any old mumper off the street. It takes more'n two good eyes and a strong arm to kill a bogle!"

"That's true," said Jem — and Ned nodded vigorously. All the salt and spears and summoning herbs in the world wouldn't do any good unless they were wielded by properly trained experts.

Then something occurred to Ned. What if they *didn't* need an army of boglers? What if half a dozen would do?

"Mr. Wardle?" he piped up. Everyone turned to stare at him. "You was telling me at the Board o' Works that every sewer in north London empties into the Abbey Mills pumping station, up beyond the River Lea. Ain't that so?"

"It is," Mr. Wardle agreed. "Save for when storm water causes an overflow into the Thames. The high- and middle-level intercepting sewers join together to form the northern outfall sewer, which then intersects with the low-level intercepting sewer before it reaches the pumping station."

Ned was thinking hard. "So if there were some way o' luring all the north London sewer bogles out o' their lairs, you could do it from Abbey Mills?" he asked.

"I suppose so. Theoretically." Mr. Wardle frowned. "But would a few herbs be strong enough to influence bogles eight and a half miles away? I can't see how."

"Perhaps we needn't be quite so ambitious," Mr. Harewood broke in. "What about using the penstock chamber at Old Ford? You could drop a few penstocks, then tackle whatever gets caught at the Old Ford junction—which is big enough to accommodate any number of bogles. Why, it must be thirty feet high and at *least* a hundred long!"

"A hundred and forty," Mr. Wardle conceded.

"Well, then! What could be better?" the engineer exclaimed.

"But what is a penstock?" asked Miss Eames. "Is it a weapon?"

"No, indeed. It is a gate that controls water flow—usually very large and round and watertight. No bogle could get past one, if it were closed." Mr. Harewood was starting to sound excited. "Once we isolate all the bogles in Hackney, we can lure them out of the high-level sewer, one or two at a time, and meet them with a ring of spears!"

"Which is all very fine in theory," Miss Eames interposed, "but how are they to be lured? Not with a child, I hope."

"Of course not!" Mr. Harewood seemed quite shocked at the suggestion. "One child in a chamber full of bogles? You must think me a brute, Miss Eames."

"And I doubt even Birdie could sing loud enough to haul in a load o' bogles from halfway across Hackney," Jem pointed out.

"I never said Birdie had to do it!" Ned was appalled

that he should have been so misunderstood. "I were think-ing there might be other ways. Like if you was to burn a good load o' Mother May's summoning herbs — the smoke might spread through the sewers for half a mile or so."

"Perhaps," said Mr. Gilfoyle. "We'd have to test that theory first, though. Meanwhile, I suppose you could make inquiries about the penstock chamber at Old Ford, Mr. War-dle? There must be procedures for sealing it up."

"Oh. Yes. I suppose so," Mr. Wardle reluctantly agreed.

"And I shall pay a visit to Mr. Edward Cook, just as soon as I've identified that Fitch blackguard," Mr. Harewood an-nounced. "What about you, Mr. Bunce? I assume you'll keep responding to every legitimate appeal for help in the meantime?"

"Aye. I'll do that," Alfred mumbled.

"As I said earlier, I've received several more." Mr. Hare-wood produced a handful of rustling telegrams from his coat pocket. "Apparently there are bogles at Saint George's Bar-racks and at the Treasury and the Monument—"

"I'll get to 'em." Catching Ned's eye, Alfred added, "First I've some business to attend to back in Drury Lane."

Ned knew what *that* must be. Having secured Eduardo's services, Alfred now wanted to hire one of the gas men at the Theatre Royal. According to Jem, this stagehand could produce a cloud of smoke at the drop of a hat.

"You won't forget about tomorrow night, Mr. Bunce?" Birdie reached out to tug at Alfred's sleeve. "You'll come and hear me sing? You and Ned?"

"We'd not miss it for nowt," Alfred replied solemnly. "Would we, lad?"

"No." Ned racked his brain for a pretty way of assuring Birdie that he would sooner miss tea with the Queen. Before he could think of the right words, however, Mr. Harewood forestalled him.

"I believe we'll *all* be there. Isn't that so, Wardle?"

"Oh . . . er . . ."

"The research subcommittee will certainly be attending," Miss Eames interjected. "Mr. Gilfoyle has kindly offered to escort me."

Ned saw Mr. Harewood shoot a sideways look at the naturalist, who coughed and rubbed his nose. Then Alfred said, "Mebbe you can tell us about Mr. Cook tomorrow night, Mr. Harewood."

"Yes, indeed," the engineer drawled. "We can have a committee meeting in the theater's crush bar, like civilized people." He spoke in a sardonic tone that Ned found puzzling. It wasn't until later, when Mr. Harewood and Mr. Gilfoyle were being terribly polite to each other about sharing a cab, that Ned suddenly understood.

Mr. Harewood was jealous.

23

IN THE LOCKUP

Clerkenwell Police Court stood next to Clerkenwell Station House. They were separated by a large iron gate, which opened onto a cobbled yard behind the two buildings. Peering through, Ned could just make out that the yard was enclosed by a string of smaller structures: a stable block, a carriage house, and a row of prison cells, small and mean and dismal in the murky dawn light.

"Gives you the jitters, don't it?" said Humphrey Cundle, the gas man from the Theatre Royal. He was wizened and middle-aged, with a mouth so full of big, yellow teeth that he couldn't seem to shut it properly. His scalp gleamed through his close-cropped gray hair, and his sallow skin was spotted with burns, scars, and splotches.

On his back he carried an enormous basket, tied across his shoulders with a pair of leather straps.

Ned could only assume that the basket contained Humphrey's apparatus — a smoke pot, perhaps, or a flash box. The previous afternoon, Humphrey had shown Alfred and Ned a huge collection of stage equipment, starting with a tiny jar of magnesium and ending with a large pair of bellows mounted on a brazier. The tour had been accompanied by a running commentary as the gas man tried to explain the function of every pipe, flap, wire, and screen. "A flash box is full o' lycopodium powder. If you blow the powder through a flame, you get a nice, bright flare . . . Or I can make you a smoke pot out o' sugar and saltpeter. You'll get more smoke from a smoke pot, though it ain't so easy to manage . . . A bit o' salt will turn a flame yellow . . . Colored smoke's best done with lights and gauze . . ."

In the end, Alfred had told Humphrey to bring along whatever he thought suitable — and had grudgingly agreed to pay an extra twopence for sulphur. "It'll give you a lovely brimstone stench, as if yer bogle's come straight from the fires of hell," Humphrey had promised, on pocketing Alfred's twopenny bit.

Now, as they stood outside the station house waiting for Eduardo, the gas man was talking again — excited, perhaps, to have a captive audience after so many years spent working in the wings. He entertained Alfred and Ned with grisly tales of all the backstage accidents he'd witnessed, until a policeman suddenly hailed them from the door of the station house.

"Hi! You there! Would you be the bogling party by any chance?"

The policeman was young and slim, with shiny black hair and thick black eyebrows. There was a five o'clock shadow on his chin, despite the early hour.

"Aye," said Alfred. "I'm Bunce the bogler."

"And I'm Constable Evans." The policeman darted forward to shake Alfred's hand. "Pleased to make your acquaintance, Mr. Bunce—I read about you in the newspaper. Seems you've made quite a name for yourself."

"Oh, aye?" Alfred didn't look very pleased.

"Len Pike told me what you wanted, and I think I've found it. But you'd best hurry in, for your felon will arrive with the next delivery, and I'm expecting *that* within the hour."

"We're a-waiting for one more—" Alfred began, but Ned interrupted him.

"There he is." Ned pointed. "There's Mr. Miniotto."

An enormous figure was lumbering toward them down King's Cross Road, which was practically deserted and swathed in a damp gray mist. The showman looked even bigger than usual thanks to his tall hat, his bulky dread-nought coat, and the overstuffed burlap bag on his shoulder.

Constable Evans blinked at the sight of him.

"Well, now," said the policeman, "I hope *that* one'll fit in the basement."

"You're taking us down to the basement?" Alfred asked, frowning. "But I saw a dozen cells off the yard back there."

"You'll not find what you want in those court cells. They're whitewashed boxes, and noisy besides. But this station house is brand new, built straight over the old cellars, and down below there's a lot left unfinished. It's where you'll find any number of boltholes, ideal for your purposes." The policeman's blue eyes glinted as a smile tugged at the corner of his mouth. "I'll tell your friend Fitch that we've run out of room in the cells, so we must confine him downstairs instead."

Eduardo was quickly introduced to Humphrey and Constable Evans, both of whom regarded him warily, as if he were an exotic animal. "He ain't no Englishman, that's clear enough," mumbled the gas man. And the constable declared in a dry voice, "Len Pike has vouched for you, Mr. Bunce, and I know you're well respected in your profession. But I tell you now, if this gentleman here makes one misstep, he'll end up in the same cell as Toby Fitch."

Ned wasn't sure if Eduardo fully understood; the performer had a puzzled expression on his big, square, unshaven face. It was Alfred who scowled at Constable Evans and rumbled, "You've no call to insult Mr. Miniotto. He's a working man like me. And there's nowt in that bag but his bogle pelt."

"If you say so, Mr. Bunce." The policeman shrugged, then turned on his heel and plunged back into the station house. It was a looming box four stories high, made of brick and stone and dull gray slate. After a moment's pause, everyone followed him. They passed through the front entrance into a lofty hallway lined with closed doors. The air smelled of soap, sweat, and fresh paint. The scarred walls were hung with signs that Ned couldn't read.

It was so early that the gas lamps were still lit.

Constable Evans turned right when he reached a stairwell near the end of the hallway. He led his visitors down two flights of stairs and across a small room cluttered with stacks of loose timber and old paint pots. Dust was everywhere — mostly brick and plaster dust. But the air felt damp all the same.

The policeman pushed open a door made of raw unpainted wood. "There's no gas laid on down here. No steam pipes either. And no facilities, of course . . ."

Ned peered through the open doorway into the dim space beyond it, which looked half finished. There wasn't, in fact, much of anything. Old stone walls jostled new brick ones oozing clots of dried mortar. Rusty iron-barred grates alternated with neat sets of shelves made from fresh-cut wood. A brand-new boiler stood beside a blocked-up fireplace.

"See that gate?" Constable Evans pointed. "There's a key in the lock. Beyond it lies a disused storeroom." He stepped aside, allowing the others to shuffle past. "You'll find it well supplied with nooks and crannies," he continued, "though they'll be hard to see in this light. I'll fetch a lamp so you may judge what suits you best. Watch where you put your feet in the meantime."

He disappeared, leaving his guests huddled near the door to the stairwell. Alfred finally made a move. He let his bag slide off his shoulder before crouching down to rake through its contents. Ned could only assume that he was searching for his dark lantern.

"This place smells bad," Ned muttered, unnerved by the darkness and the moldy, swampy odor.

"It does," Alfred grimly agreed. A match in his hand fizzed and flared. Then he lit his lantern, straightened up, and tossed away the spent match. Ned followed as Alfred picked his way carefully through the shadows toward the gate, which swung open on creaky hinges when the bogler touched it.

In the soft gleam of the lantern, Ned could just make out a series of cupboard doors set into the wall opposite. Some stood open, revealing dark holes framed by fluttering cobwebs. When Ned saw the slatted shelves and the rusty oven around which they were clustered, he realized that he was looking at an old fumigation cupboard, where lice-ridden clothes had once been stacked before they were engulfed in clouds of sulphur-laden smoke.

"What do you think, Mr. Bunce?" Humphrey asked from the stairwell. "Is there room enough for the big lad?"

"Aye."

"Then give us a little space, if you please."

Obediently Alfred stepped aside to let Humphrey and Eduardo pass him. The gas man then took charge. Eyeing the array of cupboards in the storeroom, he directed Eduardo's attention to the largest. Ned was amazed when Eduardo managed to squeeze into it *and* pull the door shut behind him. ("You fold up small for a big'un, don't you?" Humphrey said admiringly. "Just like a carpenter's rule.") Soon the gas man was busy knocking a tiny hole in one wall of the same cupboard, while Eduardo climbed out and hastily donned his bogle pelt, which was covered in fur and crowned with horns.

"I'll be leaving a double-chamber flash box with Mr. Miniotto," Humphrey continued, hacking away. "He'll not need to touch it, though, for I'll light it meself through this here hole—after he's jumped out, of course. We don't want to singe his fur."

"You mean you're going to hide in *that* cupboard?" Ned

asked, frowning. He pointed at the cramped cabinet adjoining Eduardo's roomier one.

"It won't bother me none. I've spent a whole first act inside a sea chest," the gas man replied cheerfully. He then went on to explain that a "very pleasing effect" would be achieved if Eduardo were to burst out of his hiding place an instant before the flash box was ignited. "For he'll look black against the bright flare behind him, and then he'll be swallowed up by smoke."

"What's in the flash box?" Ned inquired.

"Oh, a little o' this and a little o' that." Humphrey turned to Alfred. "We use red for villains, normally, so I've added a dash o' strontionite. And brimstone, as promised. And chlorate powder, for a bit of a bang—it's what's used on percussion caps." Chuckling, the gas man concluded, "It'll frighten the life out o' the cove, no matter how hard he thinks hisself."

"You're sure o' this?" asked Alfred. "I'd no notion you'd be *locked up* with such a rogue."

"Aye, but this great big feller here is to be locked up with me, Mr. Bunce," Humphrey nodded at Eduardo. "We could bring down the devil between us, it seems to me."

All at once a muffled voice was raised in surprise or anger above them. Ned heard footsteps, followed by a loud *thump*. More footsteps followed, moving closer and closer.

Constable Evans soon clattered into view, carrying an oil lamp.

"Mr. Bunce?" the policeman exclaimed. "Your man's arrived. He came with the rest. Are you ready for him?"

Alfred glanced at Humphrey, who said, "Not yet."

"Well, you'd best make haste. We cannot hold Fitch for more'n a few minutes up there. We need him under lock and key."

"Then give us what minutes you have," Alfred rejoined before addressing the gas man. "Would you put yer back into it, Mr. Cundle?"

"That I shall, Mr. Bunce."

As Constable Evans clumped back upstairs, Humphrey worked frantically to finish his hole. When it was done, he pushed his flash box into Eduardo's cupboard, scrambled into the adjoining one, and shut himself behind its worm-eaten door.

Eduardo took longer to position himself. With his costume on, he was bigger than ever; Alfred had to give him a shove or two before his cupboard door would shut properly.

"When I want you out, I'll knock on the floor with me spear. Three times—like this." Alfred demonstrated. *Bang bang bang.* "Can you hear that?" he asked loudly. "Knock once for yes."

Eduardo gave a thump that Ned felt through the soles of

his feet. Then a deep, hoarse voice came rumbling down the stairs.

"What's all this, then? This ain't right! I don't belong in no basement . . ."

Ned had heard the voice before, at Smithfield Police Station.

"This basement is *just* where you belong, Fitch, make no mistake." Constable Evans was coming down the stairs, accompanied by someone with a heavy, lumbering tread. Hearing all the grunts and curses, Alfred hustled Ned out of the storeroom just as three figures staggered into view. With Constable Evans was another policeman, small and stocky and silver haired. Caught between them was a big, bald man dressed in corduroy trousers, a red neckerchief, and a frock coat that looked much too tight for his bulging muscles.

Though the scar on his eyebrow wasn't visible in the poor light, there was no mistaking Tobias Fitch.

₿OGLE ₿AITING

T here weren't but six other coves in that van!" Fitch growled as the two policemen shoved him toward the store-room. "How can the cells be full? You've a round dozen of 'em at least, and I *know* how tight you pack 'em . . ."

"You weren't our first delivery, Fitch. Besides, we had Clerkenwell lags here already." Constable Evans wasn't half Fitch's weight, but he somehow wrestled his prisoner through the storeroom's open gate, which he managed to shut and lock between them before Fitch had even turned around. It was only then that the prisoner noticed Ned and Alfred lurking in the shadows of the outer room.

"What the devil?" Fitch spluttered. His face looked like a gargoyle's, all glaring eyes and gap-toothed snarl. "Who's that? What's yer caper? I ain't no mad cove in Bedlam, to be gawked at like a monkey in a cage!"

"This here is Mr. Alfred Bunce," Constable Evans replied flatly. "We hired him on account of our bogle problem. Which is *your* problem too, Fitch. We have a bogle, see. And it's in that cell with you."

The prisoner snorted. "I dunno what you're prating on about," he said, without so much as a glance over his shoulder. Ned wondered with a sudden chill if Tobias Fitch might be immune to the threat of bogles. Sarah Pickles had spent months feeding babies to a bogle that lived in her chimney and had never once come to any harm. Maybe Fitch knew that. Maybe he understood that bogles didn't normally attack adults.

"D'you hear me, Fitch?" Constable Evans continued. "There's a bogle in that cell with you, and unless you tell us the truth about Salty Jack, we'll not let you out."

"I ain't never heard o' no Salty Jack," Fitch retorted. It was such an outrageous claim that both Constable Evans and the other policeman smirked.

"We know you work for Gammon, Fitch," Constable Evans said patiently. "I don't believe there's a soul living between Saint Paul's and Chancery Lane who *doesn't* know it.

But we want to hear it from your own lips, in front of witnesses. We want to hear how Jack Gammon told you to kill Mr. Bunce's apprentice."

Fitch's blank stare swung toward Ned, who flinched.

"I don't know Mr. Bunce," the prisoner growled. "*Nor* his 'prentice."

"Well, that's hard to believe, since Mr. Bunce is by way of being a famous man." Constable Evans spoke in a light drawl, his head cocked and his arms folded. He didn't hold himself stiffly, like many other policemen of Ned's acquaintance, and his voice was as flexible as his carriage. "Come now, Fitch. This is your last chance. Tell us why Salty Jack wants this boy dead — or I swear, Mr. Bunce'll bring down the wrath of hell upon you."

"'Tain't *me* was attacked!" Ned blurted out. But Alfred hushed him, and Tobias Fitch spat on the floor.

"You must think I'm glocky," the prisoner scoffed. "This here is a racket, and you're all flamming. There ain't no bogle. And I ain't no fool."

Constable Evans glanced at Alfred, who jerked his chin at Ned. It was the signal. Ned cleared his throat, took a deep breath, and began to chant the first song that sprang to mind.

"This is the house that Jack built.
This is the malt as lay in the house that Jack built.

This is the rat as ate the malt
As lay in the house that Jack built."

"You calling me a rat?" Fitch cut in, hoarse with fury.
"Is that yer game? Well, I ain't bringing down Jack's house
no matter *what* yer malt is, for I don't know nothing and
I'll not say nothing!" He launched into a string of curses,
then suddenly stopped to peer at the wall of cupboards behind him.

Straining to hear, Ned detected a faint scraping sound,
followed by a dull knock. Ned wondered who it was —
Eduardo or Humphrey.

"Hah!" the prisoner exclaimed. "So you've put a dog in
here to scare me, have you? Well, I'm more'n a match for the
best ratter in London and will tear the throat out of any dog
as tries to sink its teeth into *this* carcass!"

He lunged at the cupboards, much to Ned's alarm. But
as Alfred raised his spear, a creak of hinges stopped Fitch in
his tracks.

The oven door had swung open.

Ned could just make out a dark, squirming shape in its
depths.

"M-mister Bunce?" he stammered.

A long, gray, triple-jointed arm flopped out of the oven,
slowly unfurling onto the floor. The end of this arm was
forked, crowned by two curved talons that buried themselves

between the flagstones. Each talon was iron gray, six inches long, and barbed like a fishhook.

Alfred hissed. Someone gasped. Ned felt a sudden pang of hopeless dismay that announced, as clearly as any fanfare, that he was in the presence of a genuine bogle.

Tobias Fitch must have felt something similar, because he whirled around, clutched the bars of the gate, and squawked, "Lemme out! You can't keep me in here! *Lemme out!*"

"Mr. Bunce . . . ?" Constable Evans spoke hoarsely. He was gazing at Alfred, his face deathly white in the gloom.

Beside him, his colleague looked even more disturbed. "This ain't right," the silver-haired policeman croaked. "No one ever reported nothing strange in this basement."

"Mebbe it ain't bin here long," Alfred muttered, before turning to Ned with a curt "Keep singing."

Ned swallowed. Although he knew that bogles didn't usually attack adults, he was appalled that Alfred hadn't chosen to unlock the gate. There were three people sharing the storeroom with a bogle. Surely they couldn't be left in there?

"But the bogle—" he began.

"Keep singing."

So Ned obeyed.

*"This is the cat as killed the rat
As ate the malt as lay in the house that Jack built.*

This is the dog as worried the cat as killed the rat
As ate the malt as lay in the house that Jack built."

Another long, gray arm joined the first, followed by another and another. Reaching across the flagstones, they groped about in a slow, sinister way, fanning out like antennae.

The gate began to rattle furiously. "Lemme go! Now!" Fitch screamed.

Constable Evans cleared his throat. "Not until you tell the truth," he said, his gaze riveted on the bogle. "Who told you to nobble Jem Barbary?"

"Please! Lemme go! I'm begging you!" Fitch's voice was a high-pitched squeal. He was reaching through the bars, his eyes bulging with fear. Behind him, the bogle was halfway out of the oven, drawn to Ned's voice like a fish on a line. Ned caught glimpses of a flabby gray mass puddling on the floor. He couldn't see much because of the bars, the dim light, and Fitch's large frame—but it looked as if the bogle wasn't very well. It moved sluggishly, its eyes dull. It didn't seem aware of all the adults around it.

Feeling Alfred nudge him, Ned launched into the next verse.

"This is the cow with the crumpled horn
As tossed the dog as worried the cat

As killed the rat as ate the malt
As lay in the house that Jack built."

"Jack Gammon did it!" the prisoner wailed. "He hired me! He said to kill the kid before he — gawd help us! Lemme go, *please!*"

"Before he what?" Constable Evans took a step forward. "Before he *what*, Fitch?"

"Before the kid peached on him and got him nibbed!"

"Will you swear to that in court?" the constable asked roughly.

"Yes! *Yes!*"

"Mr. Bunce." Ned couldn't stand it anymore — the fear, the screeching, the darkness, the groping claws and growing stench. He gazed beseechingly at Alfred just as Constable Evans threw a harassed look in the same direction.

"Time we killed that bogle," said Alfred. Then he and Constable Evans both converged on the gate.

Tobias Fitch, meanwhile, was throwing himself against the iron bars in a frenzy. *Bang! Bang! Bang!* And the bogle was slowly spreading across the floor like a gray tide with teeth . . .

Crash! A cupboard door burst open. Eduardo lurched out. Huge and hairy, he began to wave his arms and waggle his horns. Ned barely had time to wonder if he'd mistaken Fitch's banging for Alfred's signal when there was a loud *crack* and an explosion of red flame so bright that Ned had to turn away. As he did so, he saw the bogle flinch and retreat back into the oven.

"Graaugh!" roared Eduardo through a billowing cloud of smoke.

Fitch screamed. He fell through the gate as it slammed open, then collided with Constable Evans, who lost his balance. The other policeman quickly jumped on Fitch, and in the ensuing scuffle the criminal ended up flat on the floor, with both constables piled on top of him.

By that time the smoke was so thick, Ned couldn't see whether the bogle had fully retreated into the oven.

"Don't you — try anything — you'll regret —" Constable Evans breathlessly warned the prisoner, who was bleating, "Shut the gate! Shut the gate, you half-wits!"

"Here." Alfred tossed a bag of salt at Ned. "Lay down salt for yerself. *Now.*"

"Graaugh!" Eduardo was still playing his part, lumbering around in the smoke, his arms outstretched. *"Graaugh!"*

"Get outta there, you daft beggar!" Constable Evans exclaimed, coughing, just as Alfred said loudly, "Mr. Cundle! Mr. Miniotto! You'd best get back upstairs!"

Ned tried not to panic. He carefully traced a circle of salt on the floor around him while Eduardo blundered about and the two policemen steered Tobias Fitch toward the stairwell. *How can Mr. Bunce say I'm a born bogler,* Ned thought anxiously, *when I didn't feel a thing?* He hadn't sensed the presence of a bogle—not the way he usually did—and his own failure frightened him. He couldn't stay safe if he wasn't skilled enough. What if he let Alfred down? What if he put them *both* in danger?

"Close that circle," Alfred warned Ned, stepping into the storeroom just as Humphrey Cundle stepped out of it.

"What's amiss?" the gas man inquired, coughing. "Did the trick fail?"

"There's a bogle in the oven," Alfred replied gruffly. "A real one."

"A *what?*" Humphrey peered through the thinning cloud of smoke. "Where? I can't see it."

"You'd best leave now, Mr. Cundle. 'Tain't safe down here."

The gas man seemed reluctant to go, but Alfred's grim expression and brooding gaze soon drove him upstairs.

Only when he was out of sight did Alfred finally approach the gaping oven. Tentatively he raised his lantern and lowered his spear. The smoke had cleared a little; from where he was standing, ringed by salt, Ned could just make out the dim shape of the bogle, stuffed into the oven like a bag of coal.

"The noise scared it. The noise and the light," Ned whispered, hoping that his voice wouldn't lure it back out again.

"That ain't no surprise," Alfred muttered. "If you ask me, I'd say it were poorly. Which might account for why I didn't feel nowt. Mebbe it had no strength left with which to poison the air." He leaned forward, prodding the motionless bogle cautiously with the tip of his spear. "It's dead," he announced.

Ned gasped. "But you ain't barely touched it!"

"I don't claim I'm the one as caused it to die. Best to be on the safe side, though." Alfred lifted his spear and drove it into the bogle — which didn't so much as twitch in response. Then he set down his lantern, yanked the spear free, and wiped it with the handkerchief that he'd removed from his pocket.

Ned stared at the bogle in amazement. It hadn't shrunk. It hadn't exploded. It hadn't evaporated. It had died like a sick rat, leaving a sizeable corpse.

"What's happening, Mr. Bunce?" he croaked.

"That I can't tell you," said Alfred.

"You don't think it died o' fright?"

"I don't know. I don't know if it starved or were poisoned or died of old age. This is summat I ain't never seen nor heard of."

"If it died o' fright, mebbe the flash box killed it. For the flash box scared it right enough." Ned's mind began to race. "Mebbe *that's* what we need," he continued, with mounting enthusiasm. "A dozen flash boxes, scattered round the sewers, to drive all the bogles into the penstock chamber at Old Ford."

Alfred was noncommittal. "Mebbe."

"That's if they don't die o' fright afore they reach the chamber," Ned added. "We should tell Mr. Harewood, don't you think?"

"Aye," said Alfred. "And from what he said last night, I'm persuaded he should be arriving here shortly. To testify against Fitch in court."

"We should tell him about the flash box." Ned was thinking aloud. "We should have him talk to Mr. Cundle." Ned could picture it all: the network of sewers; the flash boxes placed at strategic points; the coordinated ignition; the surge of terrified bogles. "If this works, Mr. Bunce, all our troubles will be over."

"That's as may be," Alfred rumbled, and Ned was suddenly reminded that without bogles there would be no more need for boglers.

"But even if it does work, there's still the southern sewers to clear," Ned pointed out quickly. "Not to mention all o' them bogles as don't live in the sewers — and those from outside London —"

"One step at a time," Alfred said shortly. He had already packed away his spear and was hoisting his sack onto his shoulder. "Come along. We've a lot to do. And I want it all done afore Birdie's show this evening."

Ned gave a start. *The show! Of course!* He had forgotten all about it.

I should be ashamed o' meself, he thought as he followed Alfred back upstairs.

25

ᛏHE ᚻIDDEᚾ ᛚABORATORᚤ

Mark Harewood arrived at the Clerkenwell Police Court with Jem Barbary, who had shared his hansom cab. They were both scheduled to testify against Tobias Fitch, so Mr. Harewood had arranged to pick Jem up from Orange Court. They were delighted to hear that Fitch had informed on Jack Gammon.

"So your ploy worked?" asked Mr. Harewood.

"Not quite," said Constable Evans. He glanced at Alfred, who stood nearby with Ned and Jem. They were gathered in the cobbled yard between the courthouse and the police station, surrounded by ragged, unhappy people, most of whom were related to the prisoners in the cells.

"It were the real bogle as scared Fitch, not the false one," Ned explained.

"The *real* bogle?" Mr. Harewood echoed.

Jem's jaw dropped.

"There was a slight hitch," Constable Evans confessed. "But it is of no consequence. We got our confession. I'll be sending word straight to Len Pike, so as Salty Jack may be nibbed. You'll not have to fret about Gammon no more. Nor Tobias Fitch neither, for we'll be laying charges of assault and attempted murder on him, in addition to the counterfeit coin charge."

"Well, *that's* a relief," said Mr. Harewood. And Alfred remarked, "So Jem will be safe on the streets again?"

"As long as he gives a good account of himself in court." Constable Evans eyed poor Jem like a butcher eyeing a pig. "You must stand up straight when you're in the box, and speak clearly," he instructed. "And remember to address the magistrate as 'Your Honor.'"

Jem flushed and mumbled. Ned knew that he had appeared in court before, on thieving charges, and didn't like to be reminded of it. But the policeman seemed satisfied; after bidding farewell to Alfred and Mr. Harewood, he hurried back into the station house.

"What's all this about a real bogle?" Jem demanded.

Before Alfred could answer, Ned jumped in. "We scared it with the flash powder. It tried to run away." Turning to the engineer, he added, "*That's* how we could clear the sewers, Mr. Harewood. We could put a flash box in every main line and block off the smaller pipes. Mr. Cundle could fix us a score o' flash boxes. What do you think, sir?" Ned was so excited that he addressed the engineer without a trace of his usual awkwardness. "We'll be needing to divert a good portion of Hackney's sewage system. Is Mr. Wardle likely to balk at that?"

"I'm sure the entire Sewers Office will balk at it," Mr. Harewood replied. "But I'll see what I can do. Perhaps we could test the theory with a smaller section."

"Mr. Harewood, sir?" Jem tugged at the engineer's sleeve. "I think they're a-calling for us."

Sure enough, the bailiff was shouting across the cobbled yard, summoning them into court. Mr. Harewood glanced at his fob watch.

"We must go," he said. "But as soon as we're finished here, I shall consult Wardle. Where are you going now, Mr. Bunce?"

"I've a crop o' jobs to do. You gave me a list yesterday," Alfred reminded him. "The Monument and the Custom House and the London Docks—"

"Yes, of course. But I'll see you this evening? At the theater?"

"We'd not miss it."

"Very well, then. I'll be interested to hear how you fare."

Clerkenwell was a long way from the City, so Alfred

decided that he and Ned would catch a green omnibus from Gray's Inn Road. Then he navigated toward the Monument from Fleet Street, through a district of rotting warehouses, dilapidated churches, and sooty, dismal little churchyards. Ned spotted a few handsome structures here and there — including two that might have been guild or company halls, judging from the coats of arms set over their front doors — but for the most part the streets were lined with ugly office buildings or dank, ancient half-timbered inns converted into shops or cheap lodging houses.

To Ned, the whole district looked like a bogle's den.

"Once we've done our work at the Monument, we should have time for the Custom House, which is close by," Alfred said as he trudged down Pudding Lane. He looked soiled and shabby, even against the dreary shop fronts that he was shuffling past. "But I'll not attempt no job at the London Docks. Not today. We've not time enough after wasting so much of it at Clerkenwell."

Ned didn't reply. He was wondering how he could broach the subject of his own incompetence. Alfred was relying on him; Ned knew that. But was he really all that reliable?

"I don't think I have a nose for bogles, Mr. Bunce," he said at last, his feet dragging, his gaze on the ground. "You said I were born to the job, but that ain't so. I didn't feel the bogle at Clerkenwell. I fainted when I speared the one on Water Lane—"

"That weren't no faint," Alfred interrupted. "You was knocked out."

"Which *you* never was while killing a bogle."

"Lad, I'm nearly twice yer size at present. Though I don't expect I shall be for much longer, the way you're growing." In the pause that followed, Ned shot a quick glance at Alfred—who was studying him intently, with narrowed eyes, from beneath the sagging brim of his hat. "You expect too much o' yerself," Alfred said at last. "You'll make a fine bogler. I'd swear to it, if that's what's troubling you."

Ned didn't answer. How could he tell Alfred that he didn't *want* to make a fine bogler?

"I never felt that bogle at Clerkenwell neither," Alfred went on. "Not till it showed itself. I told you—it had no strength left with which to poison the air."

Alfred fell silent as he turned left into a narrow alley that widened into a spacious square. The square was ringed by fine, big, ornate buildings, and at its center was the Monument, like a giant gray candle with a gold flame on top. The towering stone column stood at least two hundred feet high, on a square plinth as big as a watch house. Ned was aware that it had been built by someone named Christopher Wren, to commemorate something called the Great Fire of

London, because Mr. Harewood had told him so. But he knew nothing else about it and had never actually been close to it before — though he had caught glimpses of its fiery crest rearing above the rooftops.

"Mr. Harewood told me to speak to the guard," said Alfred, peering across the cobbled expanse that surrounded the Monument. Sure enough, there was a door at the base of the column's pedestal, and a man sat there smoking a pipe. As Ned drew closer, he saw that the man had brass buttons on his fraying blue coat and wore a stiff cap rather like a telegraph boy's — beneath which his warty, weathered face was set in lines of blank boredom and resentment.

"It's threepence a body to get in," the man drawled before Alfred had even opened his mouth.

"Not for me it ain't," Alfred replied. "I'm here on a job. Bunce is the name. Alfred Bunce. You sent for me."

"*I* did?"

"You got a bogle," said Alfred, causing the guard to straighten so abruptly that he nearly fell off his chair.

"Oh — ah — yes!" Recovering, the guard jumped to his feet, his face reddening. "So you're the bogler, then?"

"I am." Alfred produced a crumpled sheet of paper from his pocket. "You sent this telegram to the Sewers Office, asking for help. Well, I'm yer help."

Watching the guard take the telegram and stare at it dumbly, Ned began to doubt that it *had* been sent by such a seedy-looking fellow. His suspicions were confirmed when the guard said, "This telegram weren't down to me, though it were me as told Clarkson about the bogle. I expect he sent you this."

"Clarkson?" Alfred echoed, frowning.

"At the Guildhall. He's the one as banks the fees." Squinting up at the mighty edifice that loomed over them, the guard added, "I can't let you in just yet. There's a lady and a gentleman still up at the top, and we cannot have *them* eaten by a bogle."

"Bogles don't eat ladies and gentlemen." Alfred eyed the guard in a speculative manner. Ned wondered fleetingly if it were still true that bogles didn't eat adults. The city's bogles had been behaving so oddly that he wouldn't have been surprised to learn that the bogle in the Monument had started attacking every human being in sight.

"How do you know it's there?" Alfred inquired of the guard. "This bogle. Did you have a child go in and never come out?"

"I seen it," the guard replied. "It's in the cellar."

Suddenly Ned remembered something else that Mr. Harewood had told him. There was a basement laboratory under the Monument—and this, Ned assumed, must be where the bogle was hiding.

"I don't normally go down the cellar, save to fetch a mop or a bucket," the guard continued, his gaze skipping around the square as if in search of potential sightseers. "But the other day I heard a strange growling noise, and when I lifted the grate I spotted the bogle."

Alfred regarded him intently for a moment. "You're sure it were a bogle?"

"Ain't no mistaking a bogle, Mr. Bunce." The guard began to wave his pipe around, his voice rising dramatically. "It had huge great claws and great big teeth, and it roared like a lion!"

Ned caught Alfred's eye. It was unlikely that the bogle had roared. Ned had already decided that the guard was either imagining things or embroidering the facts. Alfred must have thought the same thing, because he remarked drily, "'Tis strange behavior for a bogle, Mr. . . . uh . . ."

"Copperthwaite," the guard supplied. Then the click of a latch made him turn his head. "Ah! Here's the other visitors come down again."

The Monument door swung open and two people emerged. One was a man with luxuriant dark whiskers; he wore a tall hat and carried a cane. The other was a lady dressed in the very latest fashion, with a huge bustle and lots of feathers in her bonnet. Both were damp and red and puffing like bellows.

"I must sit down!" the lady whined, leaning on her companion's arm.

"I'll take you to a tea shop," the gentleman promised before fixing his angry gaze on Copperthwaite. "Those stairs are a deal too much for a well-bred young woman!"

"Three hundred and eleven of 'em, sir" was the guard's jovial response. "I told you they'd be a challenge." As the couple moved away, he said to Alfred in a sly undertone, "It's worth twice the money to stop down here, but folk will never be warned. Oh no!"

"You'd best show us the basement," said Alfred, "afore someone else comes along."

"You can't miss it. You get to it through a grate in the middle of the floor." Copperthwaite abruptly sat down again. "I'll stay and guard the entrance. You'll not need *me* in there."

Ned decided that Copperthwaite must be telling the truth after all; why else would he be so scared to step inside? Alfred sniffed, jerked his chin at Ned, and advanced toward the Monument's shadowy little door, which looked so much like the door to a tomb that Ned found it quite unnerving.

But he summoned up the courage to follow Alfred into the darkness, only to discover that the Monument's interior wasn't so dark after all. The endless shaft above them was lit by a series of windows set into deep alcoves, placed at regular intervals up the circular staircase. This staircase was made of black limestone and was coiled around a gap that reached from the ground floor all the way to the column's highest point—which Ned couldn't even see from where he was standing.

He remembered Mr. Harewood's words: *By opening a trapdoor in the gilded orb at the top of the tower, you can watch the night sky from a laboratory in the basement.* This gap, then, was obviously part of the "giant zenith telescope" that Mr. Harewood had mentioned. And if the trapdoor in the orb was directly above Ned, then the entrance to the basement had to be . . .

"Down there," said Alfred. "Under yer feet." As Ned quickly stepped aside, Alfred let his sack drop to the stone floor. Only after he had retrieved his spear did the bogler stoop to shift the circular manhole cover. "Stand back now," he warned his apprentice. "We don't know what's down there."

Ned swallowed. He couldn't actually *feel* the presence of a bogle, but he knew quite well that this meant nothing—not anymore. Edging back toward the doorway, he kept his eyes fixed on Alfred, who was dragging the heavy iron cover aside.

Clan-ng-g! The cover hit the floor, exposing a round black hole just big enough for a man to squeeze through. Ned was craning his neck to peer into it when the Monument door swung shut behind him.

"Tell Copperthwaite to open that up again, will you?" Alfred was squatting by the hole, studying it intently. "Tell him we need an escape route."

The words were hardly out of his mouth when Ned heard the clink of a key turning in a lock. *"Mr. Copperthwaite?"* he cried. *"We need that door open, sir!"*

But no one answered. And as Ned spun around to hammer on the iron-studded door, he was nearly deafened by a huge explosion.

Bo-o-om!

Someone had fired a shot inside the Monument.

26

THE VIEW FROM THE TOP

*N*ed! Run!" yelled Alfred.

The bogler had fallen back onto the floor and was groping for the spear he'd just dropped. Someone large and dirty had reared up through the open hole — someone with a shining bald head, bushy black side-whiskers, and a huge mustache.

When Ned saw the smoking pepperbox revolver clasped in this stranger's hand, he screamed, *"Open the door! Please! Mr. Copperthwaite!"*

The door didn't open. But Ned's shout distracted the hulking intruder, whose pale eyes swung toward him. Alfred's fingers closed around the shaft of his spear. And as the intruder aimed his revolver at Ned — who stood frozen with shock—Alfred lunged forward, thrusting his spear into the gunman's arm.

The man roared. He fired wide and his pistol ball ricocheted off one wall, spraying tiny chips of stone. Ned ducked and ran. There was nowhere to go but up, so he made for the circular staircase, screaming for help. Then another shot rang out.

Boom!

"Mr. Bunce!" Ned cried, glancing over his shoulder. But Alfred, he saw, was already behind him, still clutching the bloody spear.

"Run! RUN!" Alfred shouted.

Ned pounded up the stairs, frantic with terror, expecting a ball in his back at any instant. He could hear Alfred gasping for breath.

"Ain't no way out!" a cracked voice called after them. *"And I got one more shot in this here pepperbox!"*

"Keep going," Alfred wheezed to Ned. "Don't stop."

Ned had no intention of stopping. As he passed one of the alcoves, he briefly wondered if it would provide any cover, then decided it wouldn't.

Would there be any cover where they were going?

"I'll shoot you first, Bunce!" the man bellowed. *"And then I'll throw that boy off the top o' the tower!"*

Ned couldn't suppress a frightened moan. He heard Alfred pause a few steps behind him.

"You can't do that, Gammon!" the bogler rejoined, panting heavily. "Ain't *no one* can jump off the gallery no more—not since they shut it up in a cage!"

Ned froze. This terrifying man was Salty Jack Gammon!

"Then I'll just have to chop him into pieces and throw the pieces through the bars!" Jack Gammon bawled. Ned could hear him mounting the stairs at an uneven canter and wondered how badly hurt the man was. Would he collapse and bleed to death before he could reach the top? Suddenly Ned caught a glimpse of Gammon's dark shadow, bobbing into view against the curving wall opposite, and saw that the butcher would soon have a clear shot at Alfred since there was no stone core in the middle of the winding staircase.

"Go, boy—*run!*" Alfred groaned. And Ned ran as Gammon laughed.

"You can't escape! Ain't nowhere to go!" the butcher taunted. *"You're trapped in here like rats in a barrel!"*

"You got the . . . wrong boy . . . Gammon." Alfred's lungs were laboring so hard that he could barely speak as he staggered after Ned. "This here . . . ain't Jem Barbary. Didn't you see? You'll do . . . yerself no good . . . killing *him*."

"'Tain't the boy I want, it's *you*. You've crossed me once too often." Before Alfred could reply, Gammon continued doggedly, in a harsh tone, "Oh, I devised all this to catch the boy. *That* I'll own to. I put a friend o' mine down here to cut yer throats and sent the telegram meself to summon you.

For Copperthwaite is an old mate—the Monument being so close to the Butcher's Hall—and he's bin useful when I've had things worth concealing. No one ever thinks to look under the Monument."

I didn't see the Butcher's Hall! Ned thought in despair as he heaved himself up the staircase.

" . . . but I had to change me plans," Jack Gammon was saying. He sounded breathless, and his footsteps were slowing down. "I heard what you done to Fitch this morning." As Alfred choked on an indrawn breath, the butcher snarled, "Oh yes. You think I ain't got spies at Smithfield Station House? I skipped out o' Cock Lane just ahead o' them coppers as came to nib me."

By this time Alfred was lagging so far behind that Ned had to run back and tug at the bogler's sleeve. "Come *on,* Mr. Bunce!" he whispered. "I got an idea, but you have to hurry!"

"Ain't no one else knows I'm here, save Copperthwaite, and he ain't going to blab. So I can't be letting *you* out to peach on me, can I?" The butcher seemed almost to be thinking aloud as he stamped up the stairs. "I'll hide you both in the basement, then go out tonight and arrange a berth on one o' them eel boats. Eelers is no strangers to smuggling—I know *that* well enough. And they'll not balk at dropping human remains overboard, providing the remains is a manageable size."

"Ssst! Mr. Bunce!" hissed Ned, who had finally reached the open door that led to the caged viewing gallery outside. It was a solid door with a hefty lock, but Ned didn't have a key. And there was no way of bolting it from the other side.

If we lean against it to keep it closed, he'll just shoot straight through it, Ned decided. Then he glanced down at Alfred, who was still catching up. The bogler was bent double, pouring sweat and coughing like a consumptive.

Catching his eye, Ned pointed at the ladder set into the wall some distance above them both. The ladder started where the stairs within the column stopped, and Ned knew exactly where it led: straight to the trapdoor in the golden orb at the very top.

Alfred nodded as Ned closed the gallery door with a *bang,* hoping Gammon would assume they'd fled outside to the viewing platform.

"Ain't no good shutting that door, Bunce! It won't keep me out!" Jack Gammon yelled from below. *"I got a filleting knife in me pocket and one shot left in this here revolver! If you had any sense, you'd let me put a ball through yer head, nice and clean—for if I wing you, you'll not like what follows!"*

By this time Alfred had heaved his apprentice up onto the ladder. Ned quickly climbed through the narrow shaft that led to the tip of the Monument, pursued by the sound of Jack Gammon shouting, *"Think you hurt me, Bunce? Think again! I've had worse wounds cutting sides o' pork in the shop!"*

Suddenly Ned's hand struck something metallic. It was the lid of the flaming orb. Relieved that it wasn't locked or bolted down, he gave it a mighty shove, then pulled himself through the hole.

Ned was hit by a blast of wind that almost took his breath away. For an instant he froze, dizzy and terrified; beyond the golden spikes that ringed him like a crown of thorns, he could see nothing but gray clouds and wheeling pigeons. But then he felt something nudging his feet and quickly swung them away until he was crouched amid the gilded flames, which were made of twisted strips of metal, too thick to be razor sharp.

Grabbing the spear that Alfred passed up through the trapdoor, Ned set it aside carefully where it wouldn't fall. Then he reached down and grabbed Alfred's arm, helping the bogler scramble up into the whistling wind.

One glimpse of the cloud-capped steeples surrounding them made Alfred's face turn white as he edged away from the hole, allowing Ned to close it again. The gilded flames gave them both something to cling to and provided excellent footholds, but Ned's instinct was to freeze like a cat stuck in a tree. He had to fight that when he craned his neck for a better look at the structure below.

The gilded orb sat above the metal cage that encased the larger viewing gallery—and Ned saw at once that the cage was much farther away than he had expected. Even farther away was the ground below. The people down there looked like ants, and the buildings like toys.

Ned's original plan had been to climb silently down from the orb and onto the cage, then spear Jack Gammon through the bars just as the butcher emerged through the wooden door and onto the viewing platform. But Ned had miscalculated. Even Jem would have found it impossible to descend the Monument's crest without a rope; though the golden urn beneath the orb was furnished with many footholds, the gray dome beneath *that* was just a smooth, stone curve, damp and slippery. There was no way Ned would be able to reach the top of the cage without falling to his death.

Ned wondered if anyone on the ground would hear his voice if he shouted for help. *Probably not,* he thought. Not with the wind blowing so hard.

Then he caught sight of Jack Gammon's shiny scalp, moving counterclockwise around the viewing platform, and jerked his own head back. He hadn't even realized Gammon had come through the door at the top of the stairs. Any moment now the butcher was going to work out where Ned and Alfred were hiding and would mount the ladder.

"Sit on that!" Ned mouthed at Alfred, pointing at the trapdoor. Only their weight would block Gammon from joining them. But Alfred shook his head. He retrieved his spear and carefully shifted position, his face taut, his eyes bulging.

Soon he was poised to strike at whatever came erupting out of the orb.

Ned could only pray that Alfred's spear would hit the butcher before the butcher had a chance to fire.

Bang! Clang! Thump! Ned felt the orb vibrating beneath him. Gammon must have gone back inside and spotted the ladder. But the ladder would be difficult to climb one handed, and the butcher had a wounded arm. He would have to clamp his pistol between his teeth or stick it in his belt.

Perhaps Alfred should try to spear him *before* he reached the top?

Clang! Thud! There was definitely someone in the shaft just beneath them. Ned motioned to Alfred — a flipping motion, followed by a jabbing one. "Now!" he was trying to say. "Do it now!" But he couldn't speak because he was afraid the butcher would hear him.

Alfred licked his lips. He'd lost his hat somewhere, and his thick, graying hair was whipping about furiously in the cold wind. His coat was flapping like a flag on a ship's mast. His dark eyes in his white face looked like finger holes in snow.

Ned had never seen Alfred frightened before, but the bogler was clearly frightened now — so frightened that he didn't appear to have grasped the message Ned was trying to convey: namely that the broad-shouldered butcher would be at a disadvantage in such a narrow shaft, with his revolver clenched between his teeth and his eyes briefly dazzled by the light as he emerged. Ned was trying to explain all this with hand movements when he suddenly heard a muffled scream.

"A-a-a-agh . . . !"

The orb stopped shaking. There was silence from below. Even the wind dropped for a moment as Ned and Alfred stared at each other. They waited.

Finally Alfred croaked, "Did he fall?"

"I dunno." As Alfred stretched his hand toward the lid, Ned added, "It might be a trick. He might be *pretending* he fell."

Alfred froze and seemed to think before he came to a decision. Then he adjusted his grip on his spear and indicated, with a complicated gesture, that Ned should remove the lid at top speed. Ned saw at once what Alfred was planning. If Gammon was lurking just below, Alfred would catch him by surprise, throwing the spear into the shaft before the butcher could fire his gun.

It was their only option now.

Alfred held up three fingers. "On the count o' three," he mouthed. "One. Two. *Three!*"

Ned flung back the lid. Alfred hurled his spear. But no explosion of gunpowder followed. There wasn't even a roar of pain. All Ned could hear was the sound of the spear clink-ing against hard surfaces as it tumbled down the vast height of the Monument.

It was several seconds before Ned and Alfred slowly, reluctantly, peered down the shaft. One corner of the iron ladder had pulled away from the wall. The coil of stairs receded into the distance, forming a perfect spiral pattern. Below, in the very center of this spiral, was a black dot.

And in the center of the dot Ned saw a spread-eagled shape, pale against the dark limestone.

27

BIRDIE'S DEBUT

I say!" Mr. Harewood exclaimed. "Where have you *been?* The overture's just begun — we shan't be allowed to go in if we don't hurry!"

He was standing in the Theatre Royal's vestibule, which was almost deserted. Dazzled by all the gilt-framed mirrors and polished marble, Ned hadn't spotted him at first.

"I've your tickets with me," the engineer continued, eyeing Alfred's stained and shabby clothes. Mr. Harewood himself looked resplendent in a black tailcoat, white tie, and white gloves. His hair was slicked back, and his bruises were barely visible in the flattering glow of the chandeliers. "You should have joined us in Bloomsbury before coming here,

Mr. Bunce," he said, hustling Ned and Alfred into yet another vestibule, two stories high, with a domed roof. "Gilfoyle brought his spare evening clothes for you to wear. And Miss Eames was very anxious when you didn't arrive . . ."

"We was delayed." Alfred spoke gruffly. After hours and hours spent in the station house on Bishopsgate, he and Ned had been allowed to leave only after the police officers there had communicated with their colleagues at Smithfield. Thanks to Constable Pike's efforts, the Bishopsgate police had at last been persuaded that Alfred's story was true — that he *hadn't* murdered Jack Gammon. But still the bogler and his apprentice had been kept in a small room until long after sunset, making sworn statements and answering questions.

Upon finally being released, Ned and Alfred had found themselves with only an hour to spare. So they had rushed back to Orange Court, dropped off Alfred's bogling sack, washed their faces at breakneck speed, and hurried to the Theatre Royal without exchanging more than a few rushed comments about practical things like cab fares.

As a result, Ned didn't really know how Alfred was feeling. He himself was at the end of his tether. He would never forget the horror of shouting for help and banging on the Monument door, with Jack Gammon's shattered body lying in a pool of blood at his feet. Though a passerby had finally heard Ned's pleas and had gone to fetch a policeman, there had been a delay of at least an hour between the moment

Ned had reached the bottom of the spiral staircase and the moment when the policeman, after searching in vain for Mr. Copperthwaite, had finally broken down the door.

And there had been other horrors. The horror of being accused of murder, for instance. The horror of seeing that Alfred's spear had been irreparably destroyed. The horror of knowing, as he sat in the station house, that he — Ned Roach, one of Birdie McAdam's best friends — was probably going to miss her debut performance.

But he *hadn't* missed Birdie's performance. He and Alfred had made it just in time. And as they followed Mr. Harewood up the stairs to the Grand Circle, Ned tried to ignore the fact that he looked completely out of place in these luxurious surroundings, with his damp, dirty jacket and scuffed boots. He tried to forget the bloody scene inside the Monument. He refused to think about Alfred's smashed spear or what it would mean.

This was Birdie's evening, and he wasn't about to spoil it for her. Neither was Alfred. "We'll tell no one about this. Not tonight," he'd informed Ned on their way to Drury Lane. "Tomorrow we'll pass on the news, but I ain't about to discuss Jack Gammon in a box at the theater."

"We'll be sitting in a box?" Ned had asked dully.

"Aye. Miss Eames arranged it so. Ten shillings and sixpence, she paid. And wouldn't take nowt from me."

It was the lowest box on the right-hand side of the stage.

When Ned followed Mr. Harewood over the threshold, he found himself in something rather like a jewelry box that was encased in gilt and lined with velvet. Glittering in the center of all the plush and gold fringe was Miss Eames, who turned sharply at Mr. Harewood's entrance. She was wearing a gown of glossy gray satin trimmed with crystal beads. There were feathers in her hair and diamonds in her ears.

She looked magnificent.

"Mr. Bunce!" she hissed, glaring at the bogler. "Where on earth have you *been?*"

"I'm sorry, miss," Alfred mumbled. "We was delayed."

"Hush, Edith dear — don't make a scene," Mrs. Heppinstall said. She sat next to her niece, wrapped in a dark fur. On Miss Eames's other side was Mr. Gilfoyle, beautifully groomed in his black-and-white evening clothes. Mr. Wardle was nowhere to be seen, but since there were only three vacant seats left, Ned assumed that the Inspector of Sewers had decided not to come after all.

The overture concluded in a burst of applause, the curtain rose — and Ned was transported into fairyland.

He had never been to a theater. He'd never even been to a penny gaff show. So he was completely unprepared for the dazzling world that unfolded before him: the bright landscapes, the billowing seas, the gleaming battlements and colored lights, the music, the trumpets, the clouds, the animals. He forgot all about flash boxes and smoke pots; he barely remembered that King Arthur was Frederick Vokes or that Jem was dancing in the ballet corps, small and nimble in a page's costume. Instead, swept up in the action, Ned let all thoughts of the *real* Theatre Royal vanish from his mind—along with everything that had happened to him that day.

When a giant's head appeared over the castle wall, Ned gasped. When the giant ate Tom Thumb, Ned squeaked. He clapped when Tom Thumb jumped out of the giant's mouth, then cheered when a huge bird seized Tom in its mighty talons. Like everyone else in the audience, Ned marveled at Rosina's dancing. He laughed at the antics of a pantomime horse—the same horse he'd once seen shuffling along a backstage corridor. He applauded the singing of one young actor who, according to Mr. Harewood, had an operatic background.

But when Birdie sang, Ned couldn't help crying. Perhaps his terrible day had left him feeling vulnerable. Perhaps he cried because at least two of the songs she sang were sad ones, all about motherless children and cold winter snows. Or perhaps he was moved because she looked so beautiful, standing there in a cloud of white gauze, with her hair gleaming and her eyes flashing and her astonishing voice ringing out like church bells.

Hearing the storm of applause that greeted every one of her songs, Ned thought, *She'll be going to places where I can't follow. There'll be no more bogling for Birdie.*

During the interval, he stayed in his seat, ashamed of his red eyes and shabby clothes. Alfred also remained seated. It was Mr. Harewood who went to fetch ice cream, and Mr. Gilfoyle who briefly escorted the ladies out to "take the air." For several minutes Alfred and Ned were left alone together. But Alfred would talk only of Birdie, and Ned decided to follow his lead.

When the others returned, the lights were already dimming again. Mr. Gilfoyle, however, managed to ask about the job at the Monument.

Alfred took a deep breath, avoiding Ned's eye. "We didn't find no bogle at the Monument," he muttered.

"And the Custom House?" Mr. Gilfoyle inquired.

"We didn't have time for that."

Mr. Gilfoyle turned to Ned. "Harewood told me about your clever notion regarding the flash powder. I think it *very* canny. Mr. Wardle has undertaken to make inquiries about closing a portion of the sewers up near Hackney for a few hours. Once we have arranged that, we'll have a better idea of how many flash boxes we'll need. At which point Mr. Bunce will be able to order them from his friend the gas man."

"He ain't no friend o' mine," Alfred remarked. "I hardly know the feller." But that was all he said, because the curtain was rising.

Although the second half of the pantomime was even more magnificent than the first, Ned was distracted by troublesome thoughts. He couldn't seem to concentrate on Tom Thumb's adventures. It was only toward the end of the performance that he once again found himself caught up in the spectacle, as showers of sparkling fairy dust descended on King Arthur's court. Birdie sang her last song during the grand finale; as a fairy princess, she bestowed her blessings on the whole cast with a wand that jingled like bells whenever its starry tip touched anything. The scene ended with a rousing chorus, two booming silver cannons that disgorged more fairy dust, and a lot of well-timed acrobatics from the ballet corps. Jem did several backflips across the stage. Frederick Vokes kicked his legs straight up over his head. Rosina floated through the air on a wire, as if she were thistledown.

Then, as the cast members were taking their bows, Frederick made an unexpected announcement.

As the king of England, he declared, he felt justified in saluting the newest member of their troupe: Birdie McAdam the Go-Devil Girl. "The voice that once lured monsters from their lairs is now luring the public into our noble auditorium!" he exclaimed. "And I can take the credit for that, ladies and gentlemen! For when I first saw Birdie confronting a bogle, I thought to myself: This child deserves a far bigger audience than a monster in a basement! And now she has one, does she not? She has an audience that truly *appreciates* her extraordinary talent!"

His voice was drowned out by an enthusiastic roar as

the costumed performers around Birdie began to clap and grin. Up in her box, Miss Eames cried, *"Bravo!"*—and soon others were following her example. Glancing sideways, Ned saw that Alfred was wiping his nose on his sleeve, his face hidden from view.

When the applause finally died down, Birdie began to speak. She had been smiling and blushing while executing graceful little curtsies. But now her smile vanished. With her head held high, she declared in a clear voice, "Thank you, yer majesty. I am so very grateful to you and yer court!" There was another burst of clapping and cheering as Birdie waved her wand at the cast gathered behind her. "However, we all of us owe an even *bigger* debt of gratitude to someone else. To someone who's bin working away, killing the monsters as lurk beneath this city, for little reward and even less recognition." In the sudden hush that fell over the theater, Birdie's silvery tones became slightly strained. "The truth is, I never faced down no bogles," she finished, a little unsteadily. "The man who did *that* was Mr. Alfred Bunce. And I want to thank him for everything—for everything he's done."

Her voice cracked on a sob, and Frederick Vokes took over. "Yes, indeed, ladies and gentlemen!" he cried. "You must all have read about Mr. Alfred Bunce, the famous bogler, whose name has adorned many of our most respected newspapers in recent days! Well, last Monday, Mr. Bunce destroyed a bogle in the bowels of this very theater! And what's more, he is *in the audience tonight!*" As a wild cheer erupted, the actor swiveled to face Miss Eames's box. "Stand up, Mr. Bunce—do! Allow the people of London to express their heartfelt gratitude for the work you've done in saving so many precious young lives!"

Ned began to clap furiously. Miss Eames and Mr. Gilfoyle had already turned in their seats; they, too, were clapping. So were Mr. Harewood and Mrs. Heppinstall and the entire cast of *Tom Thumb*. It dawned on Ned, as Alfred rose to his feet, that the bogler really *was* famous now. Everyone in the theater seemed to know who he was. Why, everyone in *London* seemed to know who he was! And more than that—they seemed to appreciate him.

As Alfred turned a stunned face to the crowd, Ned wondered if fame would change things for either of them . . .

28

THE PENSTOCK CHAMBER

The light was already beginning to fade at Old Ford railway station, but it was still bright enough to see the two men in oilskin coats waiting on the western platform. One had broad shoulders, grizzled hair, and hands that appeared hacked from chunks of old hardwood. His eyes were a dazzling blue in a face as brown and seamed as a peach pit.

The other man was younger and smaller, with thin, sandy hair. There were heavy pouches under his oyster-colored eyes, and his bushy mustache looked as if it had been pasted on. The fantailed hat he was clutching marked him as a sewer flusher.

"Mr. Wardle?" he said, stepping forward to address

Mark Harewood. His voice was unexpectedly rich and sonorous, as if produced by a pipe organ.

"I'm afraid not. My name is Harewood." The engineer glanced back to where Mr. Wardle was clumsily descending from the train. "*That* is Mr. Wardle. And this is Mr. Bunce, and Mr. Gilfoyle, and this is Ned Roach, apprentice to Mr. Bunce."

"Tom Spiddle, sir. I'm foreman of the penstock gang. And this here is Danny Donkin, from Abbey Mills pumping station. I brought him on account of he knows the northern intercepting sewers better'n anyone else alive."

There was a flurry of handshakes, followed by an exchange of pleasantries. Ned didn't join in. He stamped his feet in the frosty air, exhaling clouds of steam. Already he could tell that it was colder on the outskirts of London than it was in the city center. As he followed the others out of the station and onto Lefevre Road, he was pummeled by an icy wind sweeping down from the north.

Squinting into it, he saw a large expanse of bleak marshland, crisscrossed by muddy paths and dotted with run-down cottages and brand-new factory chimneys.

"It's a dirty walk, but not a quarter-mile long," Tom Spiddle said apologetically. "There's no paved road to Penstock House."

"That's quite all right." Mr. Harewood had assumed the role of spokesman, since Mr. Wardle seemed preoccupied and Alfred was in one of his morose moods. Ned knew that the bogler had exchanged a few sharp words with Miss Eames that morning. Even after all the careful work they'd put into their preparations over several busy days, she still didn't want Ned to become involved in their scheme for scaring bogles out of the sewers with flash powder.

"Surely Ned won't be required today if you're using flash powder," she had protested. "He'll not be needed as bait, so why on earth would you even *think* of taking him on such a dangerous excursion?"

"On account of he's killed a bogle, miss—unlike most other folk in London," Alfred had replied. He had then gone on to point out that Ned would be filling the role of bogler—not bait.

But Miss Eames had remained unimpressed. They had parted on bad terms, and Alfred had been resorting to his brandy flask ever since.

"It was thought as how this affair should be attempted at night, when there's less of a flow," Tom Spiddle remarked as they trudged past a frostbitten market garden. "What we've arranged for, gentlemen, is the closing of the northern outfall penstocks, as well as the high-level intercepting sewer. The only way into the penstock chamber will be through the middle-level interceptor, which we'll block with a flushing gate farther up the line. That'll mean diverting waste into the Limekiln Dock sewer for a spell."

Ned knew all about the flushing gate in the Limekiln Dock sewer. One of the gas men they'd hired had been posted there.

"I'd take you through the field, if your boots were fit for it," Tom Spiddle continued. "As it is, we'll have to go by the Homerton footpath." He stopped suddenly, pointing toward a distant grassy embankment visible across some raw-looking wasteland to their right. "That's the northern outfall sewer, heading for Abbey Mills. And that"—his finger shifted slightly, moving west—"that there is Penstock House."

Penstock House was a modest brick single-story building marooned in a field halfway between the North London Railway and Duckett's Canal. It had a roof lantern, several chimney pots, and arched windows that glowed like molten gold in the dusky light. As they approached it, various pieces of equipment caught Ned's eye: a set of gears, a spool of chain, a four-wheeled trolley, a metal cylinder.

"We've clothes for you all inside," Tom Spiddle announced, then added after a moment's hesitation, "excepting the lad. There's nothing small enough for *him*, on account of we don't hire boys on our gangs. But if he don't mind a pair o' boots three sizes too big—"

"He'll not want those," Alfred interrupted. Ned winced at the thought of trying to outrun a bogle in oversize boots.

"I'll wear me own," he said. Seeing Tom frown, he

explained, "I were a mudlark once. Muck don't worry me none."

Though he looked unconvinced, Tom shrugged and let the matter drop. So while the rest of the bogling party donned oilskins and fantailed hats, Ned sat patiently inside the entrance hall of Penstock House, trying not to look as nervous as he felt. So much depended on the placement of the flash boxes. Had every possible escape route been covered? Ned had spent hours poring over drainage charts and road maps, identifying likely bogle hideouts along the middle-level interceptor. Schools had been an obvious choice: the William Street Infant School, the Wesleyan Chapel School, Mrs. Coborn's Charity School. So had the ropeworks, where boys tended machines, and Bryant and May's Fairfield Works, where young girls made matches.

But there were hundreds of other drains and privies feeding into the trunk sewer, and for all Ned knew, a bogle might be hiding in every one of them. With only two dozen gas men strung out along a mile of main line with their flash boxes, would there be enough flash powder to scare every bogle into the penstock chamber?

"Though we couldn't close as many drains as you requested, we *did* seal every manhole between here and Globe Road," Tom remarked as the bogling party lined up in an array of borrowed coats and hats. Mr. Harewood looked quite convincing, Ned thought, with his broad shoulders and sturdy build. But Mr. Gilfoyle's pale face and willowy figure didn't suit the heavy oilskin, and Mr. Wardle was already sweating like a cheese. "I'm told the first flash box will be ignited at eight o'clock," Tom Spiddle continued. "And then the others will follow in quick succession. Is that correct, Mr. Harewood?"

"It is," the engineer replied.

Handing out Davy lamps, Tom added, "Could you tell me, Mr. Bunce, just how big these bogles might be? Or how small, rather."

Alfred shot him an inquiring glance. "A bogle can squeeze through a six-inch drain, if that's what you're asking," he said. "Though I've seen 'em ten foot tall."

Tom frowned. "In that case, you'll need someone in the lower chamber. You'll see why, presently."

He ushered everyone through a heavy door and into a large, narrow space under the roof lantern. Peering over the railings of a metal walkway, Ned saw the gleam of water some twenty feet below him. Then Danny Donkin nudged his arm.

"Get along," Danny growled, jerking his chin at a ladder that plunged through a hole in the walkway. "I'll take yer sack for yeh."

"Mind that," Ned warned. There were several spears in the sack, all brand new and freshly sharpened. "There's weapons in it."

"I'll treat 'em dainty," the flusher promised. With the sack clasped firmly beneath one arm, he followed Ned down the ladder, which ended about a foot above floor level. In the gleam of the lamps, Ned saw two circular iron penstocks off to his left, each at least eight feet high and firmly closed. To his right lay an enormous, brick-lined passage, as black as soot, with an arched ceiling.

When his boots hit the ground, it felt sludgy underfoot. Dark water lapped at his ankles.

"Those are the northern outfall channels," Tom explained. He had preceded them all down and was now gesturing with his lamp at the giant penstocks. "They lead to Abbey Mills. And over here"—he swiveled around—"that's the end o' the middle-level interceptor."

"It's big," Alfred said grimly. "Bigger'n I thought it would be."

"It gets smaller." Tom pointed out two false walls rearing up inside the passage, just a foot or two from its outer walls. The false walls were weirs, he said. When the water level became too high, they would overflow, flooding the lower chamber. "From there, the discharge pours into the River Lea," he finished, "though we keep those channels closed, for the most part."

"So there's a route to the lower chamber down the outside o' those weirs?" asked Ned, who was drawing a mental diagram.

"There is," Tom Spiddle confirmed. "But you'll find no other way out o' the lower chamber. For its penstock is closed—just like the penstock on the high-level interceptor—and the staircase at the far end has a manhole at the top of it, which we can bolt down."

Alfred studied the tunnel in front of him. Finally he said, "Show us the lower chamber."

Obediently Tom led them back up the ladder, out of Penstock House, and around the corner of the building to a manhole set in the ground. It was already much darker outside; they had to use their Davy lamps to see where they were going.

When Danny uncovered the shaft in the ground, it looked impenetrably black.

"You're sure you ain't heard no peculiar noises hereabouts?" Alfred said, gazing suspiciously down the hole. "Nor seen nowt as might have troubled you?"

Tom and Danny glanced at each other. Tom shook his head.

"Not that springs to mind," he said. "We've had no boys go missing, on account of we don't hire 'em, as I told you."

"I've heard tell o' strange things in the sewers," Danny interposed. "There's some flushers as swear they've seen bogles and the like. But I never gave 'em no credit till I heard the Board o' Works were charged with exterminating such creatures." He spat on the ground. "I know well enough that the Board wouldn't concern itself with ought but common beasties, commonly found. So I bin telling all the gangs, 'Bear up! These things ain't devils, or we'd have clergymen troubling us, not the Board o' Works.'"

"It's been a great relief to some," Tom agreed, "knowing that bogles are plain vermin instead o' magical monsters. There's a deal o' flushers going down the sewers with good courage now, on account o' they're not afeared they might strike something infernal and unholy."

Ned was surprised to hear this. He opened his mouth, then closed it again when Alfred flashed him a warning look.

"Let's set to," rasped Alfred. "For we ain't got all night."

The shaft was damp and noisome, the ladder slippery. But it wasn't a very long ladder, and Ned was soon standing at the top of a flight of stone stairs, gazing down a long brick tunnel. Though the stairs were dry, the floor of the tunnel had water pooling at its base; Ned could see it glinting in the light from the Davy lamps.

"This way," said Tom. He led the party along the tunnel until it opened into a labyrinth of brick arches and vaulted ceilings. Black doorways gaped in every direction. Sludge lay inches thick on the floor.

With a sinking heart, Ned identified at least half a dozen shadowy corners where a bogle could hide.

"These piers are holding up the interceptors," Tom explained, his voice echoing. "The storm-relief channels are at the other end of the chamber — but they're blocked off, as I said before."

"Where are the weirs?" Mr. Gilfoyle demanded through the handkerchief that he was holding to his nose.

"There's one to your right and one to your left." Tom gestured off into the darkness. "Do you want to see the spillways?"

"No." Alfred spoke before the naturalist could reply. "I seen enough."

"So have I," said Mr. Harewood. "And I don't like it. A fellow could spend hours chasing bogles in here. It's too big."

"That's why we'll not be chasing 'em," Alfred rejoined. "After the flash boxes go off and they're smoked out, we'll wait for 'em to come to us." He went on to explain that he and Mr. Wardle would station themselves upstairs, on either side of the middle-level interceptor. As the bogles emerged into the penstock chamber, the two men would spear as many as possible. "We'll not let 'em through," Alfred declared. "Not if I can help it. But there's no knowing how many there'll be. That's why we'll be needing more'n a single bogler. So even if one of 'em does escape us, Mr. Gilfoyle will be posted by the ladder with a spear, to guard that. And if anything slips past *him*, over the weir" — he whirled around to point at the tunnel behind them — "well, I'm thinking it'll head straight for the manhole."

"Which will be bolted down," said Mr. Harewood.

"Aye." Alfred nodded. "So it'll turn around and come back again. And when it does that—"

"I'll be waiting by the tunnel mouth to kill it!" the engineer finished, with obvious relish. Unlike Mr. Gilfoyle and Mr. Wardle—both of whom were looking very nervous—Mr. Harewood was full of enthusiasm.

But Ned wasn't quite as keen on Alfred's plan. He could see a flaw in it. "What if more'n one bogle comes over the weir?" he asked. "What if Mr. Harewood is facing down the first and has his back to the next one as comes along?"

"Then you must help him," Alfred replied. "That's the job I'm a-giving you, lad—to guard Mr. Harewood. For if there *is* a second bogle, you've skill enough to take it on."

"And if there's a third?" Mr. Gilfoyle inquired anxiously.

Alfred frowned. Then he looked Ned straight in the eye and said, "If there's a third, you get out of here. Quick smart. For the floor's too damp to lay down salt—and you'll be the number one target of every bogle in this place, no matter how scared they might be."

29

TOO MANY BOGLES

I t's eight o'clock," Mr. Harewood whispered.

He was standing a few feet away from the tunnel's mouth, his Davy lamp in one hand and his fob watch in the other. His spear was leaning against the wall beside him. Slipping the watch back into his waistcoat pocket, he retrieved the spear and said quietly, "Did you hear anything?"

"No." Ned was skulking on the other side of the tunnel, clutching his own spear and Davy lamp. "Did you?"

"No. I doubt we shall, though the others might. How far away is the ropeworks? About five hundred feet?"

"Yes."

"*That* might be audible—at least from upstairs."

Ned grunted. He knew that the flash box in the rope-works was supposed to ignite exactly fifteen minutes after Humphrey Cundle's detonation at the Limekiln Dock flushing gate. Between those first and the last ignitions, some two dozen more were scheduled to take place at intervals of half a minute, along a full mile of middle-level interceptor.

But there was no telling when the bogles would arrive — if, indeed, they arrived at all.

Mr. Bunce will warn us, Ned told himself as he strained to hear. *He'll shout when the bogles come.* Tom Spiddle had already confirmed that a raised voice in the upper chamber could be heard in the lower one, trickling down like water over the weir. But the noises were always muffled, he'd said, so direct commands were out of the question.

"You're a little too close to the tunnel, Ned," Mr. Harewood remarked. "You should move back a little, I think. Over there, by that pier."

Ned retreated a few steps, his feet sinking into the sludge on the floor. It was several inches thick and smelled almost as bad as the Thames mud banks. But it wasn't the smell that troubled Ned; it was the stickiness of the stuff. Running wasn't going to be easy on such a slick surface.

"In a stench like this, we'll not smell the bogles coming," he muttered. "But we should feel 'em well enough. Like a black cloud. I hope."

"Hush!" said the engineer. "What's that?"

Mr. Harewood swung his lamp back and forth, peering into the dimness as shadows danced around him. Ned wondered how many bogles were heading down the main line at that very moment. Five? Ten? Twenty? The prospect of twenty bogles made him shudder. He thought about Danny Donkin, waiting outside the manhole in case someone needed to escape through it. Would *he* feel the bogles? Or was he too far away? And what of Tom Spiddle, guarding the door upstairs? Or the gas men strung out along the middle-level interceptor? Would they be safe from the black despair generated by an entire hoard of bogles?

"Ten minutes past eight," said Mr. Harewood, checking his watch again.

Ned thought fleetingly of Birdie, who was probably onstage at that very moment, singing her heart out. He was glad that she wasn't with them, in this dismal, stinking sewer. He was grateful that she'd been rescued from her life as a bogler's girl.

"There!" Mr. Harewood stiffened. "Did you hear that?"

"No," Ned mumbled.

"I could have sworn I heard a bang . . ."

Ned reminded himself that his fear and discomfort were all for a good cause. If their plan worked, then they would be well on their way to complete victory, since they would be able to use the same method to clean out other sewers.

And that, of course, would be a wonderful thing—though Ned had mixed feelings. On the one hand, success would mean never having to face another bogle. He'd be able to walk away from his job with a good conscience, because Alfred couldn't possibly blame him for abandoning work that didn't exist anymore.

On the other hand, no more bogles would mean that Alfred might be reduced to killing rats or making flypaper—and Ned would have to find work as a mudlark or a coster's boy again. He was glumly contemplating these two possible futures when he suddenly realized that his spirits were sinking. Fast.

Too fast.

"They're on their way," he blurted out.

"What?" said Mr. Harewood.

"They're coming. I can feel 'em. Can you not feel 'em, Mr. Harewood?"

Before the engineer had a chance to reply, they heard a shout from upstairs. Ned recognized Alfred's voice. And though it was impossible to distinguish the bogler's words, his warning tone was unmistakable.

"There! I told you." Ned's grip tightened around the shaft of his spear as he took a few deep, calming breaths. He was worried about Alfred, who had to cope with a brand-new weapon. Would it work as well as the old one? Would it have the same heft and balance?

"By Jove! I can feel them now!" said Mr. Harewood.
"How extraordinary—"

"Shh!"

There was no mistaking the faint, muffled *crack* of flash powder going off. But there were no other sounds: no yelling, no hissing, no scratching. A sense of profound dread began to leak through Ned's veins like ice water.

"Stand fast!" croaked Mr. Harewood.

Then the shouting started.

Alfred's cry came first, followed by Mr. Wardle's, then Mr. Gilfoyle's. They were rough, sharp, urgent cries full of alarm and outrage. His breath quickening, Ned glanced at the vaults above him. He couldn't tell what was going on.

"Stand fast!" warned Mr. Harewood. "They're not screaming—"

He's right, thought Ned. *They're fighting, not running.* One repeated command sounded like "There! There! Over there!" Ned could even hear splashes, as well as the frantic scuffling of feet.

"You watch the right-hand weir," Mr. Harewood instructed breathlessly. "I'll watch the left." Suddenly he gasped. "Oh my Lord!"

A scrabbling noise was followed by a *splat* as something big and black escaped from the upper chamber. Ned spied a tangle of large, spiky, triple-jointed limbs writhing about on the floor, as if a giant cockroach were lying on its back in the sludge. Then another joined the first—only this slimy, featureless blob slithered down the outer wall like a gob of spit and remained motionless when it hit the ground.

Plop! Plop! Plop-plop-plop! Ned's gaze darted from left to right as more and more bogles spilled over the weirs and into the narrow space between the outer walls and the arches. Some lay where they'd fallen, like shadowy heaps of waste. Others began to writhe about or to crawl up walls or to spread across the muck in a creeping, bubbling tide, their eyes burning red or yellow, their tongues or tentacles uncoiling.

Ned began to shake, overwhelmed by the stink and the misery.

"Run!" cried Mr. Harewood. He gestured down the tunnel. "Get out! Now!"

Ned stared at him, shocked. "But—"

"Donkin's at the manhole! I'll guard your back! There are too many!"

Mr. Harewood was right. There *were* too many. Still, Ned hesitated. Alfred had given him a special job: to watch the engineer. It wasn't supposed to be the other way around.

Mr. Bunce! Ned thought, his stomach clenching. *What's happened to Mr. Bunce?*

"For heaven's sake, *go!*" Mr. Harewood yelled. He had stepped forward to intercept a bogle—a black, bristling form so covered with muck that its features were hard to distinguish. Only its blood-red fangs were clearly visible as it gnashed them at the engineer, moving sluggishly but with dogged purpose.

A bogle on the ceiling dropped to the floor. *Splat!* It thrashed around, churning up goo with its horns and its claws, hissing like a kettle.

Then Ned spied movement beneath the slush near his feet. He snapped out of his numb, hopeless daze and bolted for the tunnel, vaguely conscious of distant bellowing. At the tunnel's mouth he paused.

"Go!" barked Mr. Harewood. "I'll follow you!"

So Ned ducked past him, heading for the end of the long brick tube ahead. *"Mr. Donkin!"* he screeched. *"Open up!"* Glancing over his shoulder, Ned saw that the engineer was just a few steps behind him, backing down the tunnel with his lamp raised, spearhead lashing from side to side. The nearest bogle was several yards away; Ned saw it framed in the tunnel's mouth. Suddenly it collapsed into the slime.

Mr. Harewood whirled around. "Run!" he bawled.

At that instant Ned was jerked off his feet. Even as he hit the ground, he was dragged backwards; something had snaked beneath the surface of the sludge before wrapping itself around his ankle.

"No-o-o!" cried Ned. He kicked off the tentacle and jumped to his feet, still clutching his lamp and spear. Then he hurled himself after Mr. Harewood, who was sliding along through the silt and sewage, his muddy fingers clawing for purchase as he was yanked back into the lower chamber.

Suddenly the engineer was flung aside, through the air, as lightly as the dregs in a teacup. And Ned found himself face to face with a huge, red, gaping maw.

"Ha-a-ah!" He thrust his spear straight at one saucer-size nostril, which was breathing gouts of steam. The impact of the blow jarred his whole body. Then — *whomp!* The bogle blew apart. It exploded like a gigantic pimple.

"Ned!" Mr. Harewood's voice was just a breathless creak. He'd landed at the foot of a brick pier; as he tried to stand up, one knee buckled. Beneath a mask of filth, his expression was groggy. "Look out!" he bleated.

Ned turned, wrenching his spear free. He saw another bogle about four feet away, heaving and wriggling toward him. It had a body like an enormous pancake, from which dozens of glutinous limbs were erupting. Threadlike fingers waved at him feebly as a stubby snout nosed the air.

Ned drove his spear into the snout, which deflated with a soft sigh. The creature's arms collapsed. Its body shriveled. Suddenly Mr. Harewood lunged past him, spearing another bogle nearby. This one wore a shiny black carapace, like some monstrous insect. But the armor cracked and crumbled as the bogle inside it imploded.

Panting, Ned cast around for his next target. His lamp

flashed over a dozen or so black mounds on the floor, each the size of a small cow or a large pig. Some were twitching and quivering. Two were crawling away into the shadows.

Suddenly he realized what was going on.

"They're dying," he wheezed. "They're ill."

"What?" Mr. Harewood began to cough as he reeled against one of the brick piers, clumsily wielding his muddy weapon. He'd dropped his lamp somewhere.

"Look. Can't you see? They're not moving." Ned prodded one motionless blob with his spearhead, piercing its rubbery hide. "It's dead. So is that one. And that one over there."

"Are you sure?" Mr. Harewood's gaze flitted nervously around the chamber. "It might be a trick. They might be waiting for us to turn our backs on 'em."

"No. Look. This one's already drying up."

"But what happened? Did Mr. Bunce injure them?"

Ned shrugged. Then a memory of the Clerkenwell bogle flashed into his head. *That* monster had been ailing. *That* monster had died. "Mebbe this weren't down to Mr. Bunce," he said. "Mebbe it's on some other account . . ."

"We'd best leave all the same," said Mr. Harewood, just as a distant call came echoing down the tunnel.

"*Ned? I'm a-coming, lad!*"

Turning, Ned spotted a flickering light at the tunnel's

end and cried, "We're all right, Mr. Bunce! We ain't bin eaten!"

"Have them bogles started dying?" Alfred yelled.

"They're dead!" Mr. Harewood replied. Sure enough, when Ned glanced around, he saw very little movement; just a twitch here and a shudder there. "Is it the same upstairs, Mr. Bunce?" the engineer continued. "Did you wound them?"

"Nay." Alfred was splashing along the tunnel, his shadow lurching crazily in the light of his Davy lamp. "We speared a few, but the rest lay down and died like old horses."

"What happened?" asked Ned.

"That I don't know. But whatever did happen, I'm grateful for it." Emerging from the tunnel, Alfred grabbed Ned's arm. "You ain't touched?" the bogler demanded breathlessly. "Not so much as a scrape?"

"No." Ned was about to ask about Mr. Gilfoyle and Mr. Wardle when Alfred forestalled him.

"The others is fine. Not a scratch on 'em, save where Mr. Wardle bumped hisself."

"I never expected to see so many bogles," Mr. Harewood murmured. "What an infestation!"

"Aye. The plan worked right enough. It worked too well." Alfred was gasping and coughing, his voice rough as he gulped down the foul-smelling air. "Ned's not to blame, though. Ned flushed 'em out. It's me as should have brought in more boglers. If any one o' you had perished, it would have bin down to me."

"But you wasn't to know!" Ned protested. "How could you? I bet you ain't seen so many bogles in ten whole years o' bogling!"

"That's true," Alfred conceded, "but 'tain't no excuse. I failed you, lad. You did yer own part—you brought 'em in—and I failed in mine." Then he relaxed his vicelike grip on Ned and did something he'd never done before.

He ruffled his apprentice's hair.

30

CONCLUSIONS

T here have been reports from all over London," said Mr. Harewood. "Shadwell. Limehouse. Millbank. Even in Southwark, across the river. People are finding dead bogles everywhere." He plucked a sheet of paper from the table in front of him. "Why, I've just received this request to remove a dead bogle from the Charing Cross Hotel! I can't imagine how the manager discovered my name. No doubt he's acquainted with someone at the Board of Works."

He gazed at the company assembled in Mrs. Heppinstall's dining room. To his right sat Miss Eames, wearing a sober expression and charcoal-colored clothes. Beside her, Birdie looked a little paler than usual. The chair next to

Birdie was occupied by Mr. Wardle, and across from him sat Jem Barbary, yawning and sighing and rubbing his eyes. Jem had been dragged out of bed at noon, having performed late the night before, but still wasn't properly awake, in Ned's opinion.

Mr. Gilfoyle had positioned himself opposite Mr. Harewood. The naturalist had just finished reading aloud the minutes of the previous meeting. Now he sat with his brow furrowed, the very picture of concentration—though his gaze did keep slipping toward Miss Eames, Ned noticed.

Ned was seated beside Alfred. The bogler was in a morose mood; he'd spent most of the day hunched by the fire in his garret, sipping brandy. When Mr. Harewood had arrived on his doorstep, with the news that a committee meeting had been scheduled for that very evening, Alfred had declared himself "not fit for the company o' ladies."

"I've seen worse," the engineer had retorted, evaluating Alfred's condition with a practiced eye. "A little coffee and some fresh air will do wonders."

But Alfred had shaken his head. "You don't need *me* no more. I ain't got nowt to contribute."

"Why, of course you do." Mr. Harewood had refused to be put off. "You were there, Mr. Bunce! You killed fifty-two bogles last night!"

"I did not. I killed seven. And know nowt o' what befell the rest."

"Don't you *want* to know? Gilfoyle might have the answer by now. I'm sure he didn't sleep all night, thinking about it." Upon receiving no response from Alfred, Mr. Harewood had declared, "As an officer of the Committee for the Regulation of Subterranean Anomalies, you have a duty to attend every meeting, unless some sort of infirmity prevents it. And if *I* am able to attend, with a torn ligament in my knee, then you really have no excuse, sir."

So Alfred had allowed himself to be ferried to Mrs. Heppinstall's house, where he'd joined the discussion about the mystery of London's dying bogles. A crew of mudlarks had found one under the dock at Billingsgate, stone dead. A Custom House officer had killed a sick one with a poker in the Queen's Warehouse. After Mr. Harewood had passed around the letter from the Charing Cross Hotel, describing the manager's discovery of a dead bogle in a dumbwaiter, Mr. Gilfoyle remarked thoughtfully, "These deaths seem to be occurring all over the city. There doesn't seem to be a concentration in any particular spot. And they obviously haven't been caused by flash powder, which was a theory we once entertained."

"There's plenty o' poisons dumped in the sewers by tanners and fullers and the like," Ned observed. "And new poisons must be devised every day, what with all the factories opening up across London."

"Aye," said Alfred. "That's true."

"But I don't know how one load o' poison could sicken the bogles all over London, both in and out o' the sewers." Ned was thinking hard. "Unless the poison is in the river and the bogles come from there?"

"If there was poison in the sewers, we'd be seeing dead rats as well," Mr. Wardle volunteered. "And *that* hasn't happened."

"Could someone else be killing the bogles?" asked Miss Eames. "You said that a bogle was destroyed by a Custom House officer, Mr. Gilfoyle. Perhaps other people are doing the same thing and leaving the corpses."

The naturalist didn't reply. It was Mr. Harewood who said, "Even so, that doesn't tell us why these creatures are suddenly so vulnerable. Once, they were impervious to everything but Mr. Bunce's spear. Unless I'm mistaken, Mr. Bunce?"

"No," growled Alfred. "You're right."

"If it ain't poison, it might be magic," Ned suddenly remarked. "Mebbe it's a curse, or a spell." He shot a doubtful glance at Alfred. "That Morton feller's still in gaol, ain't he?"

It had occurred to Ned that someone, somewhere, might be using magic against London's bogle population. And there could be no likelier candidate than the wicked Dr. Roswell Morton, who fancied himself a necromancer and who had once fed several young boys to a bogle in order to gain power over it. But why would he want to destroy the city's bogles?

"Aye, Morton's still in gaol," said Alfred. "He ain't going nowhere."

"So he couldn't be laying spells, then." Ned sighed, then frowned. "You don't suppose it might be Mother May?"

Alfred simply snorted. During the brief silence that followed, Jem yawned and Mr. Wardle shifted in his seat. Then Birdie remarked, "Mebbe dead bogles were always lying about but people ignored 'em. Mebbe everyone knows what to look for now, on account o' the newspapers."

Miss Eames gave a start. "Why, yes!" she exclaimed. "That *could* be the case, could it not? Perhaps nothing has changed except the public's understanding."

"But Mr. Bunce were in the newspapers last summer," Jem reminded her, "and no one started seeing dead bogles back *then*."

"On account o' there was none." Alfred spoke sharply. "Whatever's bin happening to the bogles, it started a few days ago. Around the time we was at the Clerkenwell lockup."

"When it all hit the papers," Birdie reminded him. And suddenly Ned was struck by a strange, illogical, but quite brilliant notion.

"Wait," he said. "Wait." He put his hands to his temples, remembering what Danny Donkin had told him the previous night. *These things ain't devils, or we'd have clergy-men troubling us, not the Board o' Works.* Could that be what *everyone* was thinking?

"It ain't on account o' Mr. Bunce being in the newspapers," he announced, with utter conviction. "It's on account of he's bin hired by the Sewers Office and everyone knows it." Glancing around at all the blank faces, Ned took a deep breath and said carefully, "Last summer, Mr. Bunce were just an East End bogler, and folk thought him either a downy cove or a madman. Nowadays they believe he works for the government, like a sewer flusher. So they think bogling is like street cleaning."

Ned paused, but there was no response; just the same puzzled frowns and pursed lips. Seeing this, he tried another tack. "Mebbe Birdie got it right when she said bogles was magic," he went on. "Mebbe bogles *was* magic once, when people believed they was. But that ain't so no more. To most London folk, bogles stopped being magic when the Sewers Office took over their management. For the Sewers Office don't deal in magic. Any more'n the post office would be sending telegraph boys to work on broomsticks."

There was a long silence. Finally Miss Eames began to nod, as Mr. Harewood and Mr. Wardle looked at each other with raised eyebrows. Even Mr. Gilfoyle seemed struck by Ned's reasoning.

"By Jove," he murmured, "that's an interesting theory.

And a logical one too, though . . . well, the whole notion of *magical beasts* doesn't sit well with me."

He trailed off. Ned, meanwhile, had colored at the sight of Birdie's approving smile. "Why, that *must* be the answer!" she exclaimed. "How clever of you, Ned! But I always said you were as sharp as glass."

"It seems as good an explanation as any, for all that it goes against the grain," Mr. Harewood conceded. "What do *you* think, Mr. Bunce?"

"I think, if it's true, it's a mercy. For it means none of us won't never again see owt like what we saw last night." Alfred had been sitting with his arms folded, staring at the tablecloth. Now he raised his head, adding, "If Ned here is right, then I'm glad of it. For I'm getting too old to be a bogler, and the flypaper trade ain't so bad."

"But you *are* a bogler! And you allus will be . . ." Birdie's voice cracked as Alfred's grim face softened.

"Don't let it fret you, lass, for it don't fret me," he said. "Whether them bogles is wiped out by traps laid with flash boxes, or whether they turn up their toes without our aid, 'tis summat I've worked toward all me life. For bogles is vermin and don't have no place where there's children about."

He turned to Ned, his voice growing gruffer. "The one thing as weighs on me," he confessed, "is the promise I made to you, lad. For I said you'd have me spear when I'd done bogling, but now . . ." He sighed. "Now there ain't no spear to have, nor no livelihood with it. I'm sorry, Ned. 'Tis a cruel blow, and not one you deserve. For you're as good a boy as ever I met, with a hard life behind you."

Ned didn't know what to say. Had *this*, then, been the cause of Alfred's gloom? Was he worried about Ned's future rather than his own? The very idea made Ned feel so guilty that he almost choked on the lump in his throat. For the prospect of becoming a bogler had always filled him with something close to despair.

Mr. Harewood coughed and leaned forward. "You've no cause to concern yourself about Ned's prospects," he assured the bogler, with a touch of embarrassment. "Only yesterday I was discussing with Gilfoyle how we might further the boy's education. For I believe he has a very bright future as an engineer if he is properly schooled. Isn't that so, Razzy?"

Mr. Gilfoyle gave a nod, adding, "Christ's Hospital School takes charity boys, as does the Charterhouse School. With our support, I'm sure he'd find a place."

"And I could teach him his letters before he enrolled!" Miss Eames offered. The smile that she bestowed on Mr. Harewood was so warm and admiring that it made him flush. "What an excellent notion, Mr. Harewood! I do *so* approve!"

"Providing the boy agrees, of course." Mr. Harewood turned to Ned. "Would you like to learn mathematics? I'm convinced that you would excel at it—in fact, I'm sure you'd be a better student than I ever was! Eh, Gilfoyle?"

Ned didn't hear Mr. Gilfoyle's answer. There was a buzzing in his ears and a whirling in his head. He kept opening and shutting his mouth, too stunned to speak. Such generosity hardly seemed possible. Why, Mr. Harewood hardly knew him! And the others—what claim did he have on them, that they should care about his future?

Jem was grinning; he winked as he caught Ned's eye. *Better you than me* his expression seemed to say. Birdie was clapping her hands as she bounced around in her seat. "Oh, Ned is so clever, he'll learn to read much more quickly than I ever did!" she chirruped, beaming and nodding and blinking back tears.

Alfred was staring at the tabletop. But when Ned looked at him, he lifted his dark gaze and offered Ned one of his rare, gentle, lopsided smiles.

"It'd be a weight off all our minds, lad, if you was set on such a course," he murmured. "For I'd die content, knowing all you children had fine lives ahead o' you." Seeing Ned's bottom lip tremble, he frowned. "What's the matter? Don't you want to be an engineer?"

"Of *course* I do!" Ned blurted out. Then he started to cry, overwhelmed by such unexpected kindness.

Luckily Mr. Harewood seemed to understand. "Good!" the engineer said in a jovial manner. "That's settled, then.

And in light of recent events, we should ask ourselves, Do we need this committee any longer? For if there are to be no more bogles and no more boglers and no more boglers' boys and girls . . ."

"Then there ain't no need for a boglers' guild!" Jem concluded briskly. His hand shot into the air. "All those in favor o' making this our *last-ever* committee meeting, raise yer hand!"

Slowly other hands began to join Jem's, until at last Mr. Harewood said, "The *ayes* have it."

"Just in time for supper," said Jem. And he was out the door, calling for toasted teacakes, before Ned even had a chance to blow his nose.

EPILOGUE

A horse and trap pulled up outside a two-story house with very small windows. The driver was a weathered-looking man whose carter's smock was splashed with mud. Beside him sat a smart woman in a buff-colored traveling coat, whose dark hair was touched with silver beneath her untrimmed bonnet. The boy curled up in her lap was about four years old. On the seat behind her, two older children were perched on either side of a big, broad-shouldered man with unruly blond hair, who jumped down onto the road as soon as the wheels of the trap stopped turning.

"Here we are!" he exclaimed. "Out you get!"

The two older children scrambled to join him. One was

a girl of around nine, the other a boy who looked two or three years younger. Though handsomely dressed, they were grubby and rumpled. The boy began to move toward the gray stone house, which was set back from the road behind a garden full of blossoming sweet peas.

"Oswald!" the woman said sharply. "You must wait for the rest of us!" To the blond man she observed, "You'd best take Peter. He's still asleep."

"Poor old fellow." The man stepped forward to relieve her of the younger boy, who whined and wriggled. "What did we decide, Edith? Two hours?"

"I think so," the woman replied.

She then climbed to the ground, taking care not to soil her gloves, while her companion dropped a few coins into the driver's outstretched hand, saying, "Come back in two hours."

The driver nodded, clicking his tongue and flicking his reins. As the wheels of the trap began to move, Oswald gazed pleadingly at Edith.

"May I knock on the door, Mama?" he inquired.

"You may," said his mother.

"But it's *my* turn to knock!" the girl protested. "Oswald knocked last time!"

"Only because you gave Mr. Bunce his tobacco," the boy pointed out.

Edith sighed. "Alice — you may go and knock. Oswald,

your father will give you Mr. Bunce's tobacco, if you can be persuaded to stand still for *one minute* . . ."

The blond man laughed. "It's been a long journey," he remarked, fishing around in his coat pocket. At last he produced a small parcel, which he surrendered to Oswald. Meanwhile, Alice was knocking on the front door of the house. Her bushy hair was untamed by her bonnet, and the lace on one of her boots had unraveled.

"Look, Papa!" she cried, pointing at an upstairs window. "Someone fixed the broken pane!"

"Yes, Mr. Roach told me that he paid for a glazier. It was good of him." Seeing the door suddenly swing open, her father doffed his hat. "Good morning, Mr. Bunce!" he exclaimed. "Or should I say good afternoon? One becomes quite muddled about the time when one sets off at the crack of dawn . . ."

The old man on the threshold was thin and bent and silver haired. He smiled at the family gathered on his doorstep.

"You've chosen a fine day for it," he muttered, his voice low and rough. "Come in, Mr. Harewood. Come in, all o' you. I've oatcakes for yer tea."

Sure enough, there were soft Derbyshire oatcakes waiting on a table by the kitchen fire, along with cheese, milk, and butter. A kettle was boiling on the hob. Oswald tucked in just as soon as he'd thrust his gift of tobacco into Alfred's hands. Alice soon followed her brother's example as Mark deposited his youngest child onto a high stool. Edith was the last to sit down; before joining the others, she made a quick tour of the room, peering into cupboards and sniffing at jars while she untied the strings of her bonnet.

"I don't recognize this," she said, fingering a china slop bowl. "Was this Mother May's?"

"Aye. I found it in the attic, catching drips," Alfred replied.

"But the roof isn't leaking, surely?" Mark looked up from the oatcake that he was buttering. "Why, we just replaced the thatch!"

"Nay, Mr. Harewood, the roof's sound enough now," Alfred assured him.

"That old witch cannot have spent a penny on this place for thirty years." Mark shook his head ruefully. "Generous of her to let it fall apart and then leave it to someone else to repair."

"I ain't complaining" was Alfred's response.

And Edith said impatiently, "Don't be foolish, Mark! Of *course* it was generous of her, though I'd prefer to see Mr. Bunce living closer to London. So would Birdie; she told me as much when I saw her last. I really don't think you should be staying here another winter, Mr. Bunce. Not with your chest. Won't you reconsider?"

Alfred shook his head. "I'm right as I am," he replied. "Derbyshire suits me. I've friends here now."

"Like the thatcher, I suppose. And the glazier. I'm sure they're always delighted to hear from *you*, Mr. Bunce." Seeing his wife's fierce look, Mark hastily added, "Not to say that any of us begrudge a single penny we've spent on this house. Not at all."

"I believe that Ned wants to have new plumbing fitted," Edith began. But she was interrupted by her husband.

"He's determined that you should have a flush-down water closet, Mr. Bunce. That's the truth of it. You know how he loves ball cocks!"

Hearing Oswald snicker, Edith frowned. "Mark, please! Not at the table!"

"Sorry, dear. Force of habit. It comes of spending too much time with rough men on building sites."

"How *is* Ned?" asked Alfred, as if keen to change the subject. "I ain't seen him since he were here last, and that must have bin three weeks ago."

"Why, Mr. Bunce, did you not hear the news?" Edith's whole face brightened. "Ned will soon be building a bridge with Mr. Harewood!"

"Oh, aye?" Alfred turned his slow smile on Mark. "That's a feather in his cap, I daresay."

Before Mark could answer, his wife exclaimed, "It certainly is! Though the bridge will be in Scotland, which is wretched news for poor Birdie, since she must stay in town for the season."

"She went to Paris without Ned last year."

"For six weeks, Mark. Ned will be in Scotland for months and months."

"Then he should put his foot down. She must go with him." Mark spoke in a bantering tone. "After all, that *is* a husband's prerogative."

He winked at Edith as Alfred remarked drily, "Last I heard, him and Birdie ain't married yet."

"And never will be, if Ned doesn't take a stand." Mark poured tea for Alice. "Next thing we know, she'll be off touring America, and where will he find himself then? Pete, old boy, you're dropping crumbs everywhere."

"That don't signify," said Alfred. "I'll sweep 'em up."

"Ned knows what he's about," Edith insisted. "It's Jem who worries me. Have you heard about his most recent business venture, Mr. Bunce? 'Artificial whalebone' of all things!" She shook her head in dismay. "I shudder to think what a disaster *that* will be, after his artificial-hair fiasco."

"You've no need to fret over Jem," her husband argued. "He always lands on his feet. And he might be in the winner's corner at last, what with the cost of baleen increasing, and corsets more popular than ever —"

"*Mr.* Harewood." Edith cleared her throat sternly, ignoring the sidelong smirks of her children. "Must I remind you that there are certain garments we don't mention in polite company?" She went on to describe Birdie's clashes with her leading man and Ned's design for a new kind of steam hammer. There was also a brief discussion of Mr. Gilfoyle's latest book. ("Chapter three is all about bogles," Edith revealed, "but it draws no useful conclusions. Because no one has even *glimpsed* a bogle for years and years, unless you count the Loch Ness Monster, so of course poor Mr. Gilfoyle can only speculate.") Then Edith gave an account of Mr. Wardle's daughter's wedding, which had been "very handsome," before revealing that Birdie's own wedding plans would indeed be postponed, thanks to Ned's job in Scotland. "But she is still insisting that you give her away, Mr. Bunce. And she wants me as her matron of honor, and Alice as her flower girl —"

"Alice will be a matron too, if the pair of them don't hurry up," Mark drawled, whereupon his wife began to speak of Alice's latest accomplishments on the piano. Alfred listened quietly as Edith described her daughter's interest in music, and Oswald's fascination with kites, and Peter's decision to copy down the whole of the Lord's Prayer "without the slightest prompting." Alice was about to recite a poem for Alfred when they heard the sound of a horse and trap rattling down the road outside.

"Oh dear! So soon?" Edith lamented. "It seems no more than a few minutes since we arrived!"

"Time runs away when you're here," Alfred agreed, rising stiffly. "But I know how busy you are. 'Twere good o' you to come."

"If you were to return to London, we'd not have to come so far." Edith couldn't suppress a little shudder as she glanced out the window at a view of dark woods and empty fields. "I'm sure you must miss London. How could you not?"

"I miss some o' the folk in it," Alfred replied. "That's all."

Mark grimaced, like someone pricked with a pin. "Birdie wishes she could visit more often, Mr. Bunce. Ned too. And Jem. It's just that they're so busy—"

"Aye, and making their mark, as they should be. I ain't blaming 'em for it."

"Perhaps you could visit them in London?" Edith suggested. "It's been such a long time—you'd be amazed at the improvements."

"Tell Birdie I'll come for her wedding," promised Alfred.

He followed his visitors outside, then stood watching as they climbed into the hired trap. Mark glanced at his pocket watch almost before the driver had cracked his whip, but the three children kept waving and shouting as the trap rolled away down the road.

"Goodbye, Mr. Bunce!" they bawled. "Goodbye! Goodbye!"

Alfred stayed by his gate, staring pensively off into the

distance for some time after the vehicle disappeared behind a blackthorn hedge. It was the cry of a rook that seemed to rouse him from his trance. With a little shake of his head he turned and went back to the kitchen, where he fetched water from the pump and washed the dirty crockery. Only after he'd finished his chores did he don an old green coat, tuck his pipe into his pocket, slap a wide-brimmed hat onto his head, and set out across the fields.

It took him half an hour to reach the heart of the woods nearby. Here, in a rocky cleft overgrown with ferns, a stream had pooled beneath a small, damp cave. Alfred settled onto a moss-covered slope opposite the cave, with his back against the trunk of an ash tree. He then took out his pipe, stuffed it with tobacco, and lit up.

As the shadows slowly lengthened and the birds began their evening rounds, Alfred sat puffing away. Finally he said, "The Harewoods came from London today. I gave 'em tea. They told me how the young'uns is faring—all well and happy, I hear. They done me proud."

No one answered. But deep in the cave above the pool, something sighed and rustled.

"D'you know what Mrs. Harewood said?" Alfred continued. "She said as how Mr. Gilfoyle mentioned bogles in his new book. So you ain't gone, and you ain't forgotten."

As he paused, the listening silence was broken only by the gurgle of water and the swish of wind-tossed leaves. At last Alfred gave a snort. "You're just old," he murmured. "Old and sick and left ower from times past. But I ain't about to ferret you out. We're both of us too old for that." He cocked his head, watching the mouth of the cave intently. "It seems to me a man shouldn't have no enemies at the end of his life, no more'n he should at the beginning. So if you stay in there and I stay out here, we'll rub along well enough — for all we ain't neither of us too chatty."

Still there was no reply. Yet Alfred stayed where he was, quietly smoking, until the pool was engulfed in shadow.

Only when dusk fell did he finally extinguish his pipe, struggle to his feet, and slowly make his way home.

GLOSSARY

BEAK: a magistrate

BLUNT: money

BOGGART: a bogle

BOGLE: a monster, goblin, bogeyman

BONCE: head

CHAFF: to tease

CHINK: money

CLAMMED: hungry

COCKS O' THE GAME: pickpockets

COME A CROPPER: to fall down

COSTER: a street seller

COVE: a man

CRACKSMAN'S CROW: a housebreaker's lookout

CUT YER STICK: to run

DARKEY: evening

DOWNY: cunning

FLAMMING: lying

FLASH HOUSE: a criminals' rendezvous

FLY: aware

FOGLES: silk handkerchiefs

FOOTPAD: a robber of pedestrians

GAOL: jail

GLOCKY: half-witted

HEAVY WET: port wine

HOIST: to steal or shoplift

HOOK IT: to leave (a place)

HUM: a fabrication or made-up story

KEN: house

KICKSIES: trousers

LAG: a convict

LEG IT: to run

LUSH: to drink

MUDLARK: a child who scavenges on riverbanks

MUMPER: a beggar

NIBBED: arrested

NOBBLE: to assault

NOBBLER: a thug

PEACH: to inform

PEELER: a policeman